BLACKROCK HIGH
INTO THE NIGHT

(PART 1 of 3 IN THE BLACKROCK HIGH TRILOGY)

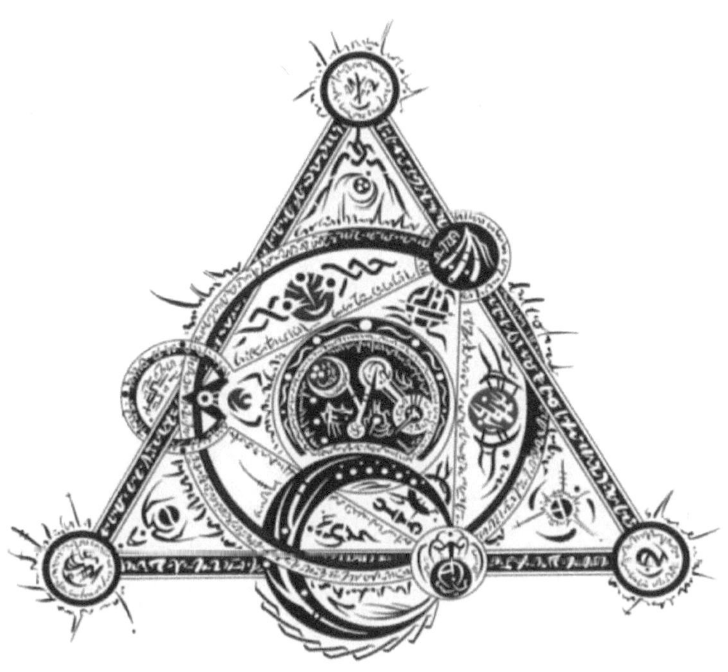

BLACKROCK HIGH
INTO THE NIGHT

(PART 1 of 3 IN THE BLACKROCK HIGH TRILOGY)

Ashe Woodward

EDITINGLE INDIE HOUSE
Mumbai, India
www.editingleindiehouse.com
www.indiebookcafe.com

BLACKROCK HIGH: INTO THE NIGHT
Copyright © 2023 Ashe Woodward
All rights reserved.
ISBN: 978-81-954588-7-5

For more information, please contact:
contact@editingleindiehouse.com
www.editingleindiehouse.com/contact

Editor: In-House

Cover Designer : Portia Ekka Designs
First Edition: March 2023

For Karen, who fought demons.

"Youth is a dream, a form of chemical madness."

-F. Scott Fitzgerald

1

MILA

Mila's focus was fixed on the pages of her book as she lazily shuffled down her new street, making her way to her new school. She stumbled slightly over the unfamiliar terrain several times, but nothing could tear her away from the intrigue of *The Great Gatsby*. She and her mom had watched the movie while packing up the living room at their old house, and she'd been obsessed with F. Scott Fitzgerald ever since. Maybe it was also the Leo Di Caprio of it all—but he was kind of old, so maybe not. She didn't miss a word even as the breeze blew back the page corners. She didn't even notice when the sidewalk ended and where she started walking along the roadside. The flimsy Fitzgerald paperback held her attention completely hostage. She refused to lose focus—refused to face reality. Her deep-down, dark suspicion was that if she acknowledged anything else besides the book—the reality of her new house, a new neighborhood, or her first day at a new school—she might be just fine with being dragged off into traffic.

She commanded her tired eyes to carry on with another page, having spent a large part of the night awake in her new room, wishing there was time to change her face—rearrange it or shave off a few pounds from her round cheeks. She wished there was more time for her to start exercising, get a better sense of style, research how to be popular, or at the very least, how to fade into the background. But it was too late. Her family was here in Blackrock, the small town she'd never heard of, far away from the city where she'd grown up and far away from what her mom called 'the hustle'. Blackrock and Blackrock High were now her future, where she would undoubtedly be the new chubby nerd girl with no friends.

Just before the curb, Mila stopped and let the tattered novel fall closed at her side. Behind her plum-colored frames, her green eyes went dim as she took in the two-story rectangular building. She pushed her glasses farther up her nose and cocked her head to the side, checking the dull, cement-gray high school that nearly disappeared against the equally bleak September sky. The school's name was worn down to thinly embossed letters over the front doorway.

"Black. Rock. High," she read out loud and felt a surprising pang of grief in the pit of her stomach, remembering the puke-yellow brick of her old school that she never thought she would miss. It wasn't as if she loved that place or even the people there, yet a slideshow of old acquaintances whirled through her mind—the jocks that always asked for a pen, the popular girls that shared their shallow thoughts on Hamlet in English class, and the teachers that always looked at her with pitying smiles. A quick, unchecked tear slid down Mila's cheek, but she quickly brushed it away. Thankfully, because she got there early, no one was around to see her.

Looking down at the book in her hand, Mila wished she had more time to read alone somewhere and let this all be a dream. The glamorous flapper woman on the cover had her cheek turned to the side—the one whose hair she had tried to copy that morning and failed. Mila wished so badly to switch places with a woman like that—to be carefree, dancing through life and speakeasies. To be thin, elegant, and not be cursed with her monstrously thick auburn hair that could only be thrown into a messy ponytail. And, of course, not have to go to a new high school.

Mila gathered the nerve to move forward, walking over the lawn past a giant, black boulder with a historical plaque drilled into its middle. She certainly wasn't interested in learning more about the ornamental rock, but as she passed, she did take note of the white bird crap that dried like melted vanilla ice cream against the onyx sides.

She took her time walking up the stone steps. Then, as she slowly pushed at the front doors, the familiar scents of polished floors and a distant cafeteria breakfast wafted up her nose, reminding her it was a school just like any other. But, still, she wrapped her soft arms around herself as her only shield.

Garish red and orange stripes along the hallway walls announced the school colors, leading to an unexpectedly elegant wooden staircase that rose up and opened grandly to the second floor. Following along the railings, her eyes flew to the wood-cased ceiling looming above, which was framed by the black-stained carvings of two oversized rams butting heads over a large, rough slab of the same black rock she saw out front. *Not so ordinary on the inside*, she thought.

She let out a quiet snort as she came upon the typical glass case full of near-ancient awards, trophies, and black-and-white photos that got put in there when people actually cared about stuff like that. She peered in at the photo display of school history: the boys' football team, girls' volleyball, and swimming. She couldn't help but think about how the people in the photos seemed so much older and more enchanting just because they were in black and white. The school dance section featured several photos of girls in poodle skirts and boys in suits and ties with slicked-down hair. At the bottom of the photo, she read *Winter Formal, 1957,* followed by an extensive list of everyone in attendance on that particular night. *Must have been some sort of record,* she thought. But scanning to the end of the list, she read, *Rest in Peace.*

"Geezus," she couldn't help but whisper aloud. She remained still, staring back at the photo.

Suddenly, from behind, someone poked her shoulder and teased, "You new or something?" A boy screeched a high-pitched laugh as he sprung down the empty hallway with two other tall, lanky boys with equally unfriendly faces.

Mila's heart raced from being startled, but she did her best to hide her flushed cheeks from the students that were starting to slowly seep into the hallways. Keeping to the side, she busied herself with finding her schedule and the instructions for getting to her homeroom class. The yellow, school-issued paper was on top of everything in her backpack.

-HOMEROOM MATH. *Good to get it over with.*

-ENGLISH. *Please be reading something I already know.*

-HISTORY. Mila rolled her eyes.

-COMPUTERS. *Time to zone out and read Fitzgerald under my keyboard.*

Then, scanning to the bottom, she strained to read the school's motto in fine print:

SERPENS FIDELIS PROTECTIO FORTIS

Mila jerked the paper farther from view and back in again. She squinted harder at the text, bringing the same letters in and out of focus. But there it was: *'Strong protection by faithful snakes.'* What kind of school was this? It couldn't mean what she thought. She closed her eyes tight, reopened them, and read the line again:

AMICUS FIDELIS PROTECTIO FORTIS

'A faithful friend is a strong defense,' she translated quietly and satisfactorily to herself. She snorted at her mistake and made a mental note to review her old Latin textbooks as soon as possible. How had she gotten it so wrong at first? Mila took a deep breath to relieve her anxieties about the day that was catching up with her. She hid the conspicuous yellow schedule with the school's map inside her bag and headed to her first class with plenty of time to read one more chapter.

Soo

Soo felt like she was dolphin-kicking her behind off, but it still wasn't enough. She was at least two strokes behind Tessa. *Stupid Tessa and her skinny, eel body*. Her last lap would have to be flawless to catch her.

It was morning swim practice, as usual, but every stroke counted. *Breathe. Stroke, stroke, pull, breathe.* Soo took a quick glimpse over at Tessa in her lane—they were dead even. A little more, and she would take her over. She could feel the surge of adrenaline as she pulled ahead. Soo's eyes faced forward—she didn't need to look at Tessa anymore. She knew she had her.

The whistle blew, and Soo pounded her fists on the water in a splash of pride and relief. Tessa was now sending her a scowled expression, and Soo took her time to grin back proudly. Then, ducking under the lane lines, she happily popped out of the pool and, on the deck, stretched her long muscular arms to the roof like a not-so-subtle victory pose. Coach Riley threw her a towel, a little too aggressively, Soo thought, especially since she had just beat the so-called strongest swimmer on the team.

"You used a lot of energy on the last lap, Ms. Kim," she called, approaching Soo and Tessa's staring contest. "Think about your strategy and keep your eyes forward *the whole time*. Now go and get changed."

Soo scurried towards the changing room over the wet tile floor, still beaming with the knowledge that if Coach Riley talked to her like that after the best swim of the morning, the rest of the team would be getting a much worse earful.

In the locker room, Soo got under the warm water of the shower. *Maybe I need to work on my first strokes more to get the advantage earlier. Tessa's entry dives are perfect... I don't know if I can compete with—* she stopped suddenly. The water from the shower was burning up without touching the tap. She jumped back from the stream and carefully reached through the flow to jiggle the chrome handle. Soo tried to turn the tap off, but it continued to stream out boiling water. Just from being near the steam, her hands felt like they were on fire, and her skin was getting red. She jumped back further as the burning water started splashing onto her feet and legs.

Soo quickly grabbed her stuff, shampoo still in her hair and stinging her eyes. She ran to finish rinsing out her jet-black hair in the sink, just in time for Tessa and some of the other girls from the team to see her.

"What, Soo? You too good for the showers like the rest of us?" Tessa jeered.

Soo kept quiet, mostly because she was in an awkward position under the tap, trying to keep shampoo out of her eyes, and also because she knew nothing good would come out of talking back to Tessa after she was sore from losing.

"Oh, you're too good to talk to me too, I guess," Tessa continued.

Soo literally bit down on her tongue to stop herself from saying something she'd regret. After years of sports, she knew once she got into an argument, it wasn't long before she made it physical. She always had poor impulse control, and since high school started, she'd given black eyes to two classmates in gym class field hockey, kicked a basketball at a stand-in referee, and even 'accidentally' pushed her last swim coach into the pool. But, maybe she was maturing because she managed to calm down, reminding herself she just had an excellent swim and didn't need any injuries or suspensions because of Tessa, who was just a bully. Eventually, Tessa got the hint and left her alone. Soo finished up in the sink and dabbed her face dry, wincing slightly as her hands chaffed on the rough towel. She turned her hands over, inspecting them when she saw they were beet red on both sides, with blisters on each of her palms. *Stupid shower. So much for no injuries.*

ROBIN

Robin couldn't hide her black-lipstick smile as the twins hobbled up the steps together. She giggled to herself as Esther strained to open the heavy door of the elementary school and hold it for Enrique. Then, when the twins were safe inside and the door shut, she corrected her overly enthusiastic expression and placed her dark sunglasses back over her eyes.

Once around the corner, the wind blew back her green-tipped black hair, and she took a deep inhale of Raspberry Fusion. She walked through the sweet cloud of exhaled vapor and then stopped to check out some of her old handiwork on a few backyard fence boards. The best was a blue alien giving the middle finger. She smiled, amused. But the next breath was one of frustration as she looked over her hands, which were covered in black and purple paint as usual. The mural she had been working on for the past week was gnawing at her patience. *That outline is killing me*, she thought as she dragged her feet unevenly, wearing out the soles on her heavy black boots. She needed to return to it again that night, risking getting caught by bringing a flashlight to shine on the laundromat wall in the alley.

As the school came into view, she took her last puff, hearing the nagging sound of the principal in her head warning her not to smoke on school property—she already had enough detentions to fill her week. Keeping her head down and her hood up, she walked across the wet lawn to the side entrance, close to the woodshop classroom. Once inside, she grabbed her stool and shoved a chocolate wagon wheel in her mouth before Mr. K. walked in.

Her recent project was going pretty well—an oak entry table with two drawers and long legs that she would later carve with some type of filigree detail, but she had yet to design it. Robin was eyeing the work, sucking chocolate and cream from her teeth, when she caught sight of Mr. K. approaching. She tried to stay calm, to not look affected, but this couldn't be good since he usually started in front and worked his way to the back.

"Looks like you figured out the issue with the sticking drawer," he said as he tested the left side.

"Yep." Robin nodded and pointed to the drawer in question while she swallowed her sticky breakfast. "I had to cut in a little more on each side and reattach the rails, but it seems to be pretty smooth now." Robin gave her most enthusiastic smile, knowing the nicer she was, the more teachers would likely leave her alone.

"You've, ugh, got some wagon wheel to finish there, Miss Rodriguez." Mr. K. gestured to his own teeth, then headed towards another student. Robin quickly reached for her phone to check her teeth in her camera. *Ugh, so embarrassing.* She dug a painted nail between her two front teeth and wiped her whole mouth with her sweatshirt sleeve.

Still sucking air and spit through her teeth and gums, Robin got back to work, checking the table's proportions and making plans for where she would start carving the detail into the legs. She could usually imagine the finished product so clearly in her mind and be able to execute it, most times even better than she thought. She never planned out her street art either, but it usually came out okay. But the mural had thrown her and made her question her entire repertoire of creative ability.

Robin leaned in closer to the table's legs. She didn't need her imagination this time. The final details in the wood were there in front of her—complete and carved away. The filigree spilled down the limbs of the table, and the shadows and light picked up the natural color of the wood grain. She followed the deep design as it got tighter and then all the way down to where it curved, turning into feet and claws at the bottom. It was impressive work. Robin hadn't even thought of making this a claw-foot table, but she liked the idea, even though it pissed her off that someone thought of it first and had the nerve to take over her piece.

She snuck a look around the Shop class to see who might be watching and maybe guess who might have messed around with her table. But, of course, everyone was busy with their own projects, and Robin honestly couldn't think of anyone other than herself that was capable of such detail.

She turned back to inspect the table once again and moved her hand out to touch the curling carvings at the feet, but there were no carvings to see. Instead, the leg was smooth, fresh wood and was back to the plain, unfinished hunk of wood she'd left there the day before. *Weird*, she thought. But, then again, it wasn't entirely out of the realm of possibility for an artist like her. With painting street murals at night, shop, and music class during the day, maybe she was really rounding out her artistic brain and activating a new, hallucination-like part of her creative abilities.

Robin took a minute to sit back and look over the table as a whole once more. It was fresh, untouched, and ready to be carved.

"Claw feet," she spoke quietly to herself. She had a smug grin as she grabbed her tools and got started.

2

MILA

"Hi honey," her mom shouted from the kitchen before Mila could get her key out of the front door. "Come in and tell me about your day."

Mila huffed as she threw her pile of new textbooks beside the stairs and shuffled towards the back of the house. Her mom was unwrapping plates and glasses from boxes marked FRAGILE. Her little sister, Gemma, was on the floor with crayons, happily coloring on the scrap newspaper as it fell.

"I got the screws for your bed, so we can put it together tonight, okay?" Her mom said, smiling.

"K," Mila answered flatly, joining Gemma on the floor to draw and color, thinking back to when she had a simple life like Gemma's.

"I guess school was okay?" Her mom asked cheerfully.

"Fine," Mila mumbled, grabbing the navy crayon and darkening the outline of a bird. Her mind wandered to the best part of her day when she stumbled upon the school library.

Earlier, at lunchtime, she followed the crowd towards the cafeteria, but halfway there, she got curious about what was at the end of the hall where she could see natural light hitting the floor. She walked against the crowd, hardly avoiding the elbows that flew into her sides, and then scooted around a corner to see more light streaming in through the top of four doors.

As Mila approached, she had to squint her emerald eyes against the light. As she got close enough to peer in, the grand, arched windows at one end came into view. Continuous glass framed the walls next to the ceiling making the room warm and bright. Her eyes adjusted to the light streaming in, and she started to see the edges of the stacks. She'd found it. But would she be disappointed by the selection in the suburban high school library? She chose to stay positive and walked in. Cautiously, she moved past the turnstiles, scanning the room filled with heavy wooden furniture and the comforting smell of paper and ink. Walking around the low shelves, Mila started to feel the first sense of ease since her day, and possibly her whole week starting at Blackrock. It felt like forever since she felt comfortable after moving here from the city. While scanning the reference materials, she noted some titles she had never seen before, especially some texts in Latin. *"Might need to visit this one at some point,"* she whispered to herself, thinking of her earlier mistranslation. Looking around the library further, she also noted lunchtime seemed a good and quiet time to be there. Aside from a librarian rustling in a back office, she was completely alone, just how she liked it.

Back on the kitchen floor Mila ran her hand through Gemma's curls a couple of times, admiring the golden-blonde color, as opposed to her own gaudy auburn that she always likened to dark rust or crusty dried blood. But her musings on the library reminded her of reading, so she gathered her things and started on her way to her bedroom.

"Did you even hear me, Mila?" Her mom called to her as she walked upstairs.

"Sure, Mom," Mila answered, even though she hadn't.

~ * ~

Mila woke to a soft knocking on her bedroom door, lost as to why she wasn't hearing her hooting owl alarm clock.

"What?" She shouted as politely as possible for her first words of the day. Gemma waddled in, fully dressed and smiling.

"I'm weady. Why aren't you dwessed, Miwa?" She asked, tilting her head to the side.

"Should I be?" Mila moaned and squinted at her phone to see her alarm hadn't gone off yet.

Gemma walked further in and put her hand on Mila's back. "You have to take me to daycaw today. Don't you wemember?"

Mila flipped over and rubbed her eyes, realizing that was probably what her mom was talking about the night before when she was busy not listening. "Go and watch a cartoon, Gemmie Bear. I'll be down in five minutes."

Walking Gemma to daycare meant Mila would definitely be late for homeroom on her second day. *Late or skip? Late or skip? … skip.* She decided she would rather miss a class than walk in late to a room of critiquing strangers and didn't want to do anything that would make her stand out more than she already did for being the new girl.

On their walk, Mila took Gemma's hand, half-listening to her babble on about the friends she had in daycare already and why she loved the sandbox the most.

"What do you wuv the most at yow school, Miwa?" Gemma asked, looking up innocently.

"The library," Mila responded instantly. "Without a doubt."

~ * ~

Later, thanks to the chat with her four-year-old sister, Mila knew exactly where she would hide out for her skipped lesson. The librarian was at her desk this time, doing a newspaper crossword. Mila hoped to skirt by without her noticing. And fortunately, the turnstile gave way without a sound as she slowly pushed it over. The librarian continued to sip her coffee, and Mila made it in without getting a look. She perked up, walking as tall and confidently as she could, hoping to fool everyone into thinking she was a senior with a homeroom spare, not a junior skipping class on her second day.

She liked the look of the reference section and found a large table to take over. Mila didn't have a lot to make her look busy since her homework was finished, and she was all caught up on the school reading lists she had been given before arriving in Blackrock. Mila started to read her Fitzgerald but was soon distracted by her curiosity about the library. The stacks were much taller than at her previous school. These were big, old, and made of real wood—*no wiry, metal racks here. Nice.* Some of the stacks were even adorned with illustrative carvings on their sides. Mila delighted at the sight of Virgil, Dante, Peter, and Wendy. There were more shelves set into the walls all the way around the room, where most of the reference materials were kept, neatly arranged in their rows, and completely free of dust, which Mila's allergies appreciated.

It was a library exactly how all libraries should be, like something from a historical novel where powerful and ancient books lived, and hidden passageways could be triggered by an innocuous book no one would ever check out. As Mila walked around the carpeted floor, the sun rose up to the high windows, and sunlight poured in with a silent blast. There were a few senior students in there, probably for legitimate reasons, but they didn't seem interested in her. Mila made a quiet wish that she could see this every morning and be surrounded by all this knowledge and stories instead of being stuck in boring homeroom math class. She sighed and let her hand fall limply behind her, bumping along a trail of hard book spines.

At the other end of the stacks, Mila found herself in the science section. Journals and leather-bound books crowded the shelves among the more modern covers of out-of-date textbooks of years gone by. The contrast between the boldly colorful modern books and the well-kept muted soft covers made Mila smile. One small brown journal, in particular, pushed farther back, almost unnoticeable, caught her eye. She pulled it forward to be in line with the others, and the title on the spine became clear, *Illness and Greatness: How Great Men Found Ambition When Faced with Death and Disease* by Archer Lemon. She was never particularly interested in science or medicine, but she was intrigued by the size of the little book and pulled it down from the shelf.

On the faded cover, there was a symbol Mila wasn't familiar

with. It knotted around itself and came to several triangular points, but it wasn't anything Mila had seen associated with medicine before. The same symbol was repeated several times as Mila flipped through the first chapter—The Fear of Death and Dying in Great Men. Mila's fiery eyebrows perked up—*pretty heavy for a first chapter, Mr. Lemon,* Mila thought to herself. She placed the journal back carefully in line with the other titles, just in time for the bell to ring for the second period.

Mila grabbed her things from her table and headed for the exit. She moved swiftly through the turnstile but was stopped suddenly as her hips crashed hard into the locked metal bars. A soft, high-pitched beep sounded, and Mila saw the librarian on her way over.

"Open your backpack, please." The librarian huffed and gestured to Mila's bag.

"But I didn't take anything out," Mila pleaded.

The librarian pursed her lips and pointed to Mila's bag. "Open."

Mila spun her backpack around to let the librarian peer in to see that she hadn't done anything wrong and the stupid machine was probably on the fritz. It was going to make her late for her next class. The librarian dug her hand into the bag and pulled out all of Mila's textbooks, then stopped a moment to look over her copy of Fitzgerald's *This Side of Paradise*. She thumbed through the rest of Mila's texts, and there, between math and history, was a little brown journal. The librarian opened the book and turned it to Mila, the Blackrock High stamp and barcode facing out from the inside cover.

Mila's mouth fell open. "Honestly, I have no idea how that got in there."

The librarian looked from Mila, then down to her books and her neatly done homework, taking note of a Fitzgerald novel not on any class list, and then back again at Mila, who looked confused and truly ashamed.

"I'll let this one slide since this doesn't seem like something that would interest you," she said, holding up the Fitzgerald specifically and then placing it back in Mila's bag. Mila breathed a sigh of relief as she left the library but wondered if she would ever feel comfortable going back there again now that she was a fugitive. Behind her, the librarian thumbed through the journal quickly and placed it on a cart to be reshelved.

ROBIN

Robin slumped down on the stool in the percussion section for music class, ready to focus on something like a steady beat to take her away from the day she was having. Mr. K. was on her about the entrance table, and she was still struggling with how to execute the detail, especially after her imagination had laid out the intricate possibilities. Plus, she was out again all night at her back alleyway mural, still unhappy with how it was turning out. At least in music class, she had to focus on her parts and performance and could deal with the other stuff later on.

The entire set of chimes sounded suddenly as her section partner, Gary, oafishly walked over to join her. He gave her a silent nod as he put his backpack down and started tuning the drum kit. Robin sighed and followed suit, getting the chimes set back to how she liked them and finding her favorite timpani sticks from her secret hiding spot in the sheet music cupboard. Then, just as she was standing up with her sticks, readying herself to test the tuning on the timpani, Gary came up close beside her.

"Hey," he greeted, his minty breath hovering in her space.

Robin moved backward to create a more comfortable distance between them. "What d'ya want, Gary?" She put a suspicious edge to her words. Gary never spoke to her, so *he must want something.*

"I wondered if you would let me have a go on the timpani today. You can have the drum kit." He gestured proudly to the drum kit like it was sitting in some sort of divine light.

"Well, I haven't really worked on anything over there for a while, Gary." Robin threw extra sass over his name, loving the opportunity to throw it in Gary's face that he had basically taken over the drum kit for most of the semester, leaving Robin to the much less cool instruments like the timpani, bongos, and chimes. She wasn't going to make it easy for him.

"I just thought it was time to share, and we both can learn the other drum parts." Gary held a nervous and goofy smile as he made his proposal, and Robin shrugged in casual agreement, moving over to the drum stool. This would be the perfect thing to keep her focused. It had been months since she had played real drums, so she would really have to concentrate on what she was doing instead of thinking about all her other projects that were going wrong.

Robin picked up the other drumsticks, which were much lighter and cooler than the timpani strikers. She tested out the snares and then the kick drum. Surprisingly, everything seemed to be tuned properly. *Maybe Gary wasn't such a goof after all*, she thought and wondered what game he was playing, wanting to switch after all this time. *Nobody ever just offers to be nice*, she thought.

Starting with a warm upbeat, Robin kept it simple and quiet as she tried not to disturb the flute and clarinet players who were getting set up and tuned as well. Quickly, she looked ahead to find and go over the challenging runs before Mrs. Bletcher came in with her usual cynical and serious gaze. Robin always wondered how she became their music teacher when she didn't look like a creative person at all. In her tight navy-blue suit and smart black shoes, it was hard to imagine she could actually play every instrument in the room. It was easy to picture someone like Mrs. Bletcher as your bank teller, not someone who could wail on the drums.

"Let's get ready for scales," she announced, hitting the top of her music stand with the wand. She did a short double-take as she noticed Gary and Robin had switched. She nodded at Robin wearily, perhaps readying herself for disappointment.

During scales, the percussion section was supposed to provide a steady beat, which was no problem for Robin, even though she was a little rusty. Then it was time for the first official piece of written music from *The Lord of the Rings*, which all the nerds had voted on the first day of school the week before. Robin didn't really care, but as the piece played out, she started to grasp why Gary might have wanted the switch. There were a lot more interesting parts for timpani than regular drum parts in this piece. Robin, in fact, was getting quite bored, and it wasn't helping tame her wandering mind that kept going back and forth from the unfinished entrance table to the even more unfinished alleyway mural.

As she played, her hands moved while her mind focused on finding more exciting parts throughout the piece, searching for something that could challenge her. While looking and looking, she saw there were some cymbal crashes here and there—between the timpani rolls, of course. She always loved those timpani rolls, and after looking over at Gary, she could say he did too. She sighed. *Outwitted by Gary. Shameful.*

Robin kept playing, moving, and following, but it was just all so easy and regular. She kept even control of the beat and held it steady even though wanting to chuck her drumsticks at Gary's stupid head. Then, as the flutes were having their moment, Robin did soft drumrolls on the snare, gradually getting louder, and saw a big moment when she could crash some cymbals and pound a little harder. They had reached a part of the song where she could let loose a little, maybe even take some creative liberties. It all reminded her of how much she actually had missed playing drums, and she began to really dive into the moment, using the opportunity to pound out her anxieties.

Everything was coming to her so easily as she started to breeze through the pages without effort, and she dared let a smile come onto her face even when she caught sight of Gary in her peripheral. She struck with perfect timing, passion, and even a little flair. It was like she had been playing the piece since birth. She knew what rhythms and changes were coming next instinctually, it seemed. Her strikes were a balance of style and precision like red and yellow paint mixing to be the perfect vibrant orange. She worked her way up through a masterfully executed drumroll that vibrated through her hands and up her arms leaving her exhilarated and exhausted all at once. She crashed the cymbals explosively one last time, and the song was over.

"So much for no practice," Gary grumbled as he ran his fingers back through his fine, ginger hair like he'd just been blown away. Mrs. Bletcher and the rest of the class were beaming back at her, giving her thumbs-ups and high-fiving each other.

"Miss. Rodriguez, I see you've been practicing," Mrs. Bletcher said, sounding impressed for once. Some of the other students nodded in agreement.

"Ugh, ya. Totally. I love *Lord of the Rings*." Robin shrugged, only slightly panting.

"Well done to you as well, Mr. Barns. But perhaps a little more time on the timpani should get you caught up to Miss Rodriguez's speed?"

Gary was quiet and held his drumsticks in front of his crotch. "Yes, Mrs. Bletcher," he mumbled.

Throughout the rest of class, Robin continued to effortlessly run through the music like never before. Her mind was far away from her entrance table—her little brother and sister stubbornly not wanting to get dressed in the morning, and her mom somehow found her stash of spray cans and tossed them away. *Maybe I'm supposed to be a rock star drummer after all.*

At the end of class, Robin collected her things and headed for the door, pretty pleased with her performance and apparent natural ability to just take up the drums like riding a bike. Gary had left quickly, along with the other students who'd also had great performances as a result of the heightened drum energy. Robin was the last one left in the hall and was taking her time to leave while she reflected on her performance. *Where did that come from?* She wondered silently to herself as she shifted her backpack further up her shoulder and started walking out of the class, passing the rows of metal chairs for the brass section. Then, at the edge of the third row, the first chair on the end started to wobble. Robin looked over the ordinary metal chair, leaned it back towards her, and set it down again. It gave one last shake as it fell into place. She blinked hard—and stared again at the chair, but it was definitely back to being ordinary and still. She continued to walk but again heard a vibration like the shaking of a chair on the floor behind her. The same chair was starting to rock back and forth again. Robin walked up and squatted down to see if there was something next to the chair, like a small animal that got in or someone's lost cell phone going off. But there was nothing, and the chair was shaking before her eyes like a finished kettle about to blow. She took a small step backward to get out of the way, and it was enough room for the chair to lean over towards her and then rock all the way back to fall on the one beside it, creating an actual domino effect in the music room. One chair kept leading to another, shaking and pushing its neighbor. Robin couldn't put together what she was seeing as they all came crashing down. About halfway through the toppling over, she wondered, *did I do this?*

When all of the chairs in the row had fallen over like furniture dominoes, Mrs. Bletcher was back in the doorway, checking in to see what was creating all the clatter.

"Well, rock star, you can start with picking it all up, and then we'll see you in detention tomorrow."

MILA

The teacher walked around throwing worn copies of *To Kill a Mockingbird* on everyone's desk. *Plunk… plunk… plunk.* Mila took one of the ragged paperbacks but was glad she had her own copy at home, somewhere in one of the moving boxes. She was just thankful they were reading something she had already read, and it wouldn't matter that she missed the first week of classes where the teacher had gone over the background and history of the novel and the biography of Harper Lee. Mila had already done it all the year before in tenth grade and could probably teach the class herself. *American South, Black and White, ignorance, an iconic child's voice as the narrator, blah, blah, blah.*

"Scout?" An athletic-looking boy chuckled as he flipped through the first pages. "Who would name their kid 'Scout'?" he loudly voiced to the room.

"Who would name their kid 'Javaris'?" A pretty girl jeered from across the room.

Javaris answered back by throwing the eraser butt of his pencil at her.

Mila rolled her eyes; *every school is the same.*

"Enough. Let's get going," the teacher called before taking a seat behind her desk.

The first chapter sounded off, sentence by sentence, up and down the rows as everyone took turns reading. Mila knew the first pages practically by heart, so her eyes relaxed and went in and out of focus as everyone read, though her lips kept moving over the words silently. When it was her turn to continue, she thought she knew what was coming: *"The Radley Place was inhabited by an unknown entity, the mere description of whom was enough to make us behave for days on end; Mrs. Dubose was plain hell."*

But that's not what was on Mila's page. Not even close.

She almost read aloud: *"I shall enter here some of my notes, as they may refresh my memory when I talk over my travels with MILA."* Mila gawked at the text, especially at her own name in ink. The chapter started in Scout's voice, the story of her brother's injury and then a specific summer, but then Mila caught the sudden narrator change into another character she knew just as well—Johnathan Harker in *Dracula.*

Mila flipped the school copy over in her hands. She knew this purple cover: the typical school issue of *To Kill a Mockingbird,* but it had been tampered with. *What a ridiculous joke,* Mila thought. Whoever it was must have spent a lot of time finding just the right paper and then retyping the page to look authentic. A perfectly good copy had been ruined just to play a dumb prank on the next student to pick it up. But she was also puzzled at how they had somehow set it up just right to embarrass the new girl and cleverly replaced MINA, Johnathan Harker's love in *Dracula,* with MILA.

The teacher cleared her throat, waiting for Mila to continue. Mila quickly recited the lines by memory, and her turn passed. Of all the pranks someone could play, messing with books against Mila would get you nowhere. But, she'd bested them. Still, when she finished the last of the lines, *"making Boo Radley come out,"* she sank in her seat, not feeling like she had won at all. She didn't dare look around to see who it could have been—who wanted to humiliate her in front of the class. She stayed scrunched in her seat for the remainder of the chapter and the rest of the class, doing her best to remain small and not cry. *They're all the same.*

$\mathcal{S}$oo

Off the edge of the science class stool, Soo's long narrow feet dangled and relaxed. Swim practice had been another battle that morning, but at least she had improved her time, and more importantly, she had beat out Tessa again. The praise from the team and Coach Riley had given her an adrenaline rush right before science class, but when the high wore off, she flopped into her seat and sprawled her torso over the lab table for a power nap before the teacher arrived. Her face stretched out as she rested her cheek in her hand, not noticing she was facing Tessa and her boyfriend, Todd, who was giving Tessa a shoulder and neck rub. Tessa scoffed at seeing Soo's open mouth pointed in her direction.

"Jealous much?"

Soo startled. Tessa was right about one thing—Soo was definitely jealous. She was starting to feel her own shoulders seizing up this week from the extra strain she had been putting on them, and a shoulder rub would be amazing. But she quickly turned, wiping the drool from her mouth, and sat up just as the teacher walked in, carrying a clinking tray of test tubes. All the students leaned closer to see just what the murky liquid was inside. *What did they have to stick their hands into today?*

"C'mon, people. Grab a tube and take it to your microscope," the teacher announced. The noise of screeching stools and shuffling teenagers erupted as they all got up at the same time to take a specimen. Soo hung back and waited to get hers and then lazily made her way back to her station, eyeing the dark floating bits of rock among the corpses of small bugs. She didn't need a microscope to see this was gungy, Lake Blackrock water.

"Spill a drop onto the slide and carefully place it under your lens."

The test tube was as thin and delicate as a pastry shell, so Soo took extra care to hold the tube close to her body as she popped open the top. Then, carefully, she spilled just a drop on the lens and placed it onto the microscope's stage. She gently replaced the cap and sat it in the crease of her textbook so it wouldn't roll and break on the floor, like last time with diatomaceous earth.

"This is a first-year task, people, as a review to get you back into form for the rigorous junior year I have planned. Let's get moving. Get the information, label the diagram, and hand in your notes."

Soo squinted one eye at the microscope eyepiece to see the bubbles and particles at play. She completed the molecule diagram easily, naming the two hydrogens and one oxygen and creating a list of the particles she saw in the lake water. The teacher was right—it was an easy enough task. Maybe too easy. There was still a lot of water left in the tube for some other assignment, but she was too tired to guess what it could be.

"With the rest of your sample, we'll be testing it for particles and creating a breakdown of the sediment and, most specifically, the oblivian content."

Tired moans floated around the room. Everyone hated the word '*oblivian*.' It was what Blackrock was famous for—the black rock foundation the town was built on. By eleventh grade, you were especially sick of hearing about it in all your classes. In geography, they taught you about the oblivian metamorphic plates that converge at the town center and how the cliffs beyond the lake had pushed up, forming gleaming black walls of hard, igneous rock. In history, you learned how the settlers discovered the valley and used the surrounding oblivian hills and cliffs as a defense against intruders as well as bad storms. Soo had often thought it was too much glory for boring rocks.

The word had become white noise, and her mind was too busy being elsewhere to care about what dumb experiments they had to do to get class over with. Schoolwork was just a duty, and then there was swimming. No science experiment would bother her or distract her from her goal. She wanted to win at the county tournament in two weeks, and she was well on her way if she could just stay awake in her classes.

Everyone else had a partner, so she worked alone to observe and test the water as they were told, jotting down her notes and recording her procedure in her notebook. But then, suddenly, the ink of all her letters started to bleed, getting longer and fading from the paper. She sat back to see water spilling all over her desk. The test tube had a crack all the way down the side and leaked through all of the pages of her textbook and over to her own notebook. She tried to sop up the water discreetly with her shirt sleeve, but the teacher caught her in the act, walking over with paper towels and a new tube of water.

"Soo Kim, why can't I ever leave you with a test tube?"

"Sorry, Miss," Soo said quietly, looking over her soggy books.

"This is the last one," the teacher said, holding out a new tube.

Soo took the tube and did her best to find some dry pages to start over. She held it in her hand this time while copying her original notes first as best as possible from what could be read. She tried to ignore the giggles from around the room, and the taunting looks from Tessa.

OBLIVIAN -1.9%

OTHER SEDIMENT - 0.4%

Before she could finish copying her findings, the tube exploded in her hand, and a huge shard of glass punctured her palm while the rest smashed and splattered as it fell to the ground. She let out an automatic scream and held her hand where the jagged glass had stuck in, just under her thumb. A thick stream of blood was falling onto the floor, mixing into the pool of Lake Blackrock water.

"Guess you can now test the blood content," Tessa called over.

"To the nurse, Soo." The teacher sighed.

3

ROBIN

Detention wasn't anything special for Robin. She was infamous for skipping gym class… and history… and science… and basically, everything that wasn't art, shop, or music. She had also practiced the art of talking back to her teachers when she felt like a little excitement in her day. So, it wasn't unusual for her to forget why exactly she was in detention on any particular afternoon, but on this day, she knew. Robin remembered the weird rumble in music class and how the chairs fell into each other. She remembered being blamed for something she was pretty sure she didn't do. Not completely sure, but pretty sure. She couldn't explain it otherwise and was taking the detention on the chin.

Robin grabbed her usual spot at the back and got into the normal routine of completing her homework from all those other boring classes she hated to sit through. It was actually a perfect plan since it was never peaceful and quiet at home to do any homework with Enrique and Esther around, her five-year-old twin siblings that acted like, well, five-year-olds. So, if she wasn't getting them washed up or cooking them dinner, she was listening to them play together, noisily, until putting them to bed. But if she was honest, she didn't really mind all that much as long as her mom was home from her second job by midnight, and she could sneak out of the house to complete her 'art pieces' around the neighborhood.

As she got out her math assignment, Robin scanned the detention lab to see who else had rebelled this week. Some of the usual suspects were there—a couple of jocks thrown in for fighting, some smokers Robin knew, and Casey Ponnick with her tutorial-like makeup who managed to be late to every class but still be well-liked by most teachers. Then, just before the bell rang to start, a red-haired girl she was sure she had never seen before walked in, clutching her books tightly to her chest. It was always slightly satisfying to Robin to see some goody-goody nerd in detention for the first time, and this girl reeked of it.

The girl sat in the first seat of Robin's row and took out a novel, of all things. She couldn't see the title, but the author's name was clear: F. Scott Fitzgerald. Robin admired the girl's auburn hair that went with her eggplant dress and matching glasses and the fact she was reading something that wasn't on the English department's reading list. *What nerdy thing could this girl possibly have done?*

Robin turned back to her work. *You have to get a passing grade to get out of this hellhole,* she reminded herself, even resenting the fact that she would never need algebra when she was a famous rock star or working at a prestigious gallery in Italy or New York.

The monitor came around for everyone to check off their names on the day's naughty list. Except for the scratching of pencils and faint typing on one senior's laptop, the room was completely silent. Someone coughed. A chair leg squeaked as someone shifted forward. Paper shuffled, and pages turned. Awkward quiet. There was some stuttered movement from the new girl, and Robin looked over. The new girl shifted in her seat and changed her leg position a couple of times. She fidgeted with her ponytail and let out a deep sigh. *Definitely not used to this,* Robin thought.

Then, it was quiet again.

Robin continued working while she twisted her wavy black hair around her finger all the way to the green ends. She let it all unwind when the new girl made a sound that Robin couldn't place. A squeak? A moan?

Suddenly, the new girl slammed her book on her desk, startling the whole room. Everyone was now gawking at the girl who was moaning and rubbing her eyes. *Weirdo.* Some people laughed while others shook their heads. The monitor glared at Robin with a look for her to focus on her own work.

Then the new girl groaned like she was on the toilet after too much pizza and breadsticks and grabbed her desk *hard*. She leaned forward and pushed her face right up against the pages of her book. First, the Fitzgerald novel flew off her desk with an angry swipe right into the radiator under the window; next were her glasses. She then slapped her hands back over her eyes.

"Is there a problem, Miss? Ughhh..." the monitor said as he scrambled nervously with the attendance list. "Miss... Mila?" he called.

The girl groaned, her hands still stuck to her face, pressing on her eyes and breathing heavily. She pressed and rubbed, moaning frantically like someone who touched their face after picking hot peppers.

Something was wrong. But what were they going to do about it? What if this girl had problems or issues or something? The monitor kept his eye on her, and Robin tried to get back to her work.

"Miss Mila!" he shouted while looking out to the hallway, maybe for another adult who might know what to do.

Robin stood, readying to run out for someone, anyone who knew what this girl's deal was. But just as she was about to climb over her desk, the girl put her head down on her desk and broke into a regular cry like she was giving in. The monitor gave a clueless shrug and cautiously walked toward the new girl with a box of tissues. The girl jumped at the touch of her forearm but took the tissue and whispered, *"Thank you."* Then, she slowly leaned over and stretched to pick up her book and glasses by the radiator. When she sat back, she looked around, blushed, and slumped down in her chair.

"Sorry, everyone," she said, showing off her northeastern manners and accent as she pushed her glasses up the bridge of her nose. Then, she turned and stared out the window for the remaining time in detention. When the bell rang, Robin was slow to collect her things. It was only her and the girl left in the classroom.

"You all right?" Robin asked, feeling compelled to say something. Plus, she was more than a little interested in the creepy freak-out.

"Sorry. I'm just… I started this week, but I guess I'm having trouble… adjusting," she said, pushing up her cat-eye frames even further. Robin smirked at the nerd move. They both simultaneously fixed their backpacks around their shoulders and walked out of the classroom together.

"I have PE next. You?" the girl asked Robin through sniffles.

"Computer Science," Robin answered, feeling guilty somehow for having to leave this girl on her own in PE, of all things.

"Okay, well, I guess I'll see you around," the girl said with a sigh before turning to walk off.

"See ya," Robin said, feeling sorry for New Weirdo Girl.

~ * ~

Sometimes Computer Science was creative and interesting, like when they learned about animation. Robin had created a dinosaur world where a great comet hits the earth, all the dinosaurs burn up, and extinction ensues in slow motion. *Creative and informative,* she had thought. "Ridiculous and halfway executed," her teacher commented in the notes attached to her final grade of C+.

Regardless of the teacher's opinion, Robin still enjoyed the class for its creative potential. She didn't care about the grade, really, just that she passed and maybe even learned another way to express more of her angst through art. However, Robin got the feeling from the teacher's expression that it wasn't about to be a particularly passion-igniting lesson.

They were to read and copy two sets of code in a program and note the stylistic differences. *Snooze,* Robin thought, even though she knew she would probably be good at this type of assignment. She was pretty good at noting differences in individual styles, from signature graffiti tags to more traditional art. She could quickly tell you which songs on the radio were more influenced by the

Beatles than the Rolling Stones, and she was particularly adept at identifying false designer handbags. The last one she did for fun because it always pissed off the popular girls.

Vivian Voorhees had been Robin's most recent victim of this at Spring Formal. As part of detention last semester, Robin was asked to oversee the committee, and, against her will, she also had to attend the dance. That night while Robin had been excused from her post for a break, she ran into Vivian in the girls' bathroom.

The two girls faced forward over the pink sinks in the gymnasium locker room. Robin washed her hands as Vivian fixed her lipstick. Robin used her hair to cover her face in hopes it sent a message that she wasn't into making conversation, but before she turned away, she couldn't help but notice Vivian's designer clutch on the shelf above the sink.

"Like it?" Vivian asked, noticing Robin's gaze.

Robin rolled her eyes at Vivian's arrogance and put her skills to work. "Sure. Too bad it's not real," Robin said.

"What do you mean? Of course, it is. My father bought it on his last business trip to *Paris*." Vivian stressed 'Paris' like an old pro, exercising the same muscles she used to flaunt her money or tease the less popular kids like Robin. Robin only slightly flinched and then did her best to hide her deep and longing desire to one day visit the home of the Louvre.

"Well, I just hope he didn't pay full price," Robin managed with composure. "It's as fake as your weave," she said as she walked out, leaving Vivian's painted mouth unhinged.

$\mathcal{S}$oo

Soo couldn't wait to tell her parents that she beat Tessa at practice for the third day in a row. She had so much energy lately that she sprinted outside. Her mother's car was waiting in the parking lot in the cool autumn air, and she jumped in the passenger seat without losing breath.

"I did it again, Mumma!" She said as she got in.

Her mother said nothing but sent her usual icy stare Soo's way. It was the message to settle down, compose herself, and remember how she was raised. Soo coughed as she corrected herself, wishing more than ever that it would be her dad picking her up. He was always happy to hear about swimming and sports and never made her feel like she was either too much or not good enough.

"No, Mumma, it's not bad. I beat the team captain again this morning in swim practice," she said, gaining the usual composure she was to have in front of her mother.

"Oh, swim practice," her mother said dryly as she pulled out of the parking lot. "That's nice. Your father thinks it's nice. I still think you should focus on being top of the class in science, math, and history. You have to get good grades to get into an Ivy League and become a doctor."

"I could also get a swimming scholarship," Soo mentioned, for what seemed to be the millionth time.

To which her mother said, "Mm." Which meant, *"That's the end of this conversation."* And they drove home in silence.

The rule at home was for Soo to complete her homework in the dining room, and then she could go to her bedroom when her father got home from work. Usually, though, Soo stayed downstairs a little longer to talk to him. He'd want to know she made it three in a row and, like clockwork, Soo's father walked in the house just as she was cracking open her history textbook. *Saved!* She screamed inside, putting it away.

Standing at the edge of the dining room, she watched as her father entered the kitchen and nodded to her mother. Her mother nodded back to him silently in return and went back to sipping tea and reading her book at the table.

Soo bounced up and down in the doorway. She wasn't supposed to move from her homework prison, so she waited for him to look her way. When he did, he saw her smile and then held up three fingers accompanied by a questioning grin. Soo fiercely nodded back with a beaming smile and three fingers up to confirm. He fist-pumped the sky behind her mother and then made the gesture of jogging and pointed to his watch, meaning *"later."* Soo happily went back to the dining room table for five more minutes to fool her mother into thinking she was finishing her history work and then made her move upstairs to stretch and get into her running gear.

Soo was stretched, getting comfortable, and even a little sleepy as she visualized her next day's swim. Her father hadn't come upstairs to change yet, so she quietly crept downstairs to check on him.

From the staircase, Soo could see his office door was closed, and she could hear him talking on the phone in Korean. Her Korean was limited, but from what she could understand, it wasn't a friendly conversation. A minute later, he came out, looking around nervously like he'd lost something. His head was down, and his short haircut was messed up. He stopped short when he saw Soo waiting on the stairs.

"Oh, honey. Sorry. I've got some things I really have to look at. Have you seen my keys?"

"Everything okay, dad? You look worried," Soo said softly, knowing he probably wouldn't tell her about it anyway.

"Everything's fine," he said, forcing a smile as he brought his briefcase from the kitchen. "I need to go back to the office for something."

He walked up to Soo and whispered, "Are you okay with going alone?" Soo's mother never approved of her being out alone, even insisting on driving Soo to and from school every day though it was only a short walk away.

"Ya, I'll be okay," Soo said with her most assuring smile. Her father kissed her forehead quickly before going back into his office, shutting the door tightly behind him. Soo quietly sneaked outside and was careful to close the front door softly. She swung her arms around to loosen up again and walked a little down the street as she planned her route. The longer roads and newer streets had fewer shady trees and more street lamps to light her way to Blackrock High and back. It was getting to be evening, and she wasn't taking any chances running alone. *Oh no, I'm starting to think like my mother.* She shook the thought away, pressed the timer to start on her watch, and began her run.

Soo breathed in the fresh air of the early evening and let her muscles do their work. Her swimming achievements had given her an extra boost, and she was reveling in the feeling of being at the top of her game. Her body felt strong and healthy, and she ran with ease. Coming up to the midpoint, Blackrock High, Soo checked her watch to see she was definitely ahead of her usual pace. A burst of pride turned into an adrenaline boost that pushed her up the school's lawn to smack the flagpole, marking her progress before she turned around to go back home.

Before she turned to leave, she noticed all the lights were turned on inside the school. Every. Single. One. *Strange for this time,* she thought. Though as soon as she noticed, they all shut off simultaneously. Soo stood still for a moment to consider what she thought she had seen. The flagpole was an arm's length away, but before she reached out to touch it, a deep laugh began from somewhere in the school and quickly faded like a slowed-down recording. Soo quieted her panting to hear if there was more, but there was only the silence of the streets—some late birds chirping and a train whistle far off in the distance. Then, finally, several lights in the school's basement went back on, and she hopped backward toward the street. She waited for them to shut off again, but they stayed on this time.

Forgetting the flagpole, she started to move down the lawn again, but she struggled to move forward, and her running shoes were half in mud. *Was it muddy when I ran up here?* She tried to remember. She tried to take a step, but jerking her legs up did nothing—she couldn't take her feet out of the sludge. It was as if she had stepped into cement, and it was grabbing hold of her, and the hold was getting even stronger the more she pulled. And someone was *laughing.*

The more she strained and struggled, the more she almost lost balance. She really didn't want to fall and not be able to get her entire body out. Something was definitely determined to pull her down or keep her stuck. She searched the area in a panic to see if there was anyone around to help her, but she couldn't see much past the dimly lit front lawn. No one even drove by on the street. It would probably be useless to scream. She kept pulling at her feet, but they were becoming even more glued in place. Then the laugh continued—not from inside, but from nearby, though she couldn't tell exactly where. Straining through the dusky evening light, she couldn't see very far in front of her to see if anyone was coming for her—to find her in their trap. Her heart raced at the thought of being taken or captured by whoever was doing this. Tears were starting to form out of fear, but before she gave up, she gave out a desperate call for help to the janitor who might still be in the school.

"Is someone there? Please, please!" It was all she could manage while trying to remain upright. The mud had nearly swallowed her shoes, and they were sinking deeper into the ground the more she tried to grab onto them.

"Hey, what are you doing there?" A man in coveralls called at her from the front doors. When she saw him, she gasped in fear and wiggled as hard as she could. She dug down deep for more strength and finally felt a release. She stumbled slightly and had to resist putting her hands out to stop her fall, or she'd be back to square one. Then, once she gained traction, she was able to skid away and run home as fast as she could without looking back.

At home, Soo was seriously out of breath, and her heart was pounding. She hadn't planned on making her jog a full-out sprint. She checked her time, even though it would now be completely useless after being stuck in the mud for five minutes or more. *What was that?*

"Soo," her mother's sharp voice startled her out of her musings, "Why are your new trainers covered in mud?"

"I ugh… I went for a short jog around the block, but someone was…" Soo thought quickly, "putting down new grass, Mumma."

"Did your father go with you?" her mother asked.

"No, Mumma, but that's why I didn't go far." She was sure to plead this part clearly.

"Take those shoes outside and get upstairs. No TV. You know the rules for jogging alone."

"Yes, Mumma," Soo mumbled. Her chest caved, and her head hung down automatically. Then, as she opened the front door to throw her mud-encrusted shoes outside, she carefully looked around and, taking a skip back, turned both locks as fast as she could before running upstairs in her dirty sock feet.

In her room, as soon as she lay on her bed to relax, thoughts of what she felt in the mud crept back in. Soo sat up before she began to sweat all over at the thought. It was all so strange, like *impossible*. Thinking back on everything, she even wondered if it had all really happened. Maybe she was just not paying attention or got too caught up in the lights going on and off to concentrate properly on pulling herself out. *That must be it*, she thought as she gathered her pajamas. In the bathroom, she turned on the tap to heat up the water for her shower but just as quickly turned it off again. Her mind rushed to the memory of the shower in the locker room that burned her hands earlier that week. It was strange that she had almost forgotten about it until now. She sat on the edge of the tub and paused, turning over her red palms that were still slightly scorched. She rubbed her thumb over the bandage on her finger from the accident in science class. She hadn't thought these were anything but fluke accidents and hadn't had any reason to put any of it together. So, why were these things happening? She wasn't usually so clumsy or accident-prone. Was something wrong with her? Now that she was getting the attention she had always wanted on the swim team, was she about to lose it all?

MILA

Mila read the chart as the doctor instructed, "T Z O D, P E C F D"

"And the last line?"

"L E P O D P C T"

"Good, Mila. It seems like your prescription might be okay, but let's take a closer look into those peepers," the optometrist said, leading Mila to the *phoropter* while turning down the lights. Mila remembered the name of the eye testing machine from when she looked the word up after her first appointment, back when she was seven years old. But even after so many eye exams over the years, she was nervous to sit down at the whirring machine. Reading had been impossible for several days, and the headaches were getting worse. There had to be something the doctor would find wrong with her eyes, but at the same time, she wasn't sure she wanted to hear the answer.

In history class, she had been asked to read a chapter aloud, and all she could do was read what she saw, knowing it wasn't right.

"This was a glorious massacre?" she began, pausing when everyone in the class giggled. It took her a moment to think back and realize what she had said. The teacher cleared his throat as a first warning.

"This was a glorious massacre as if ordered by Satan himself. There were rows and rows of bleeding bodies covering the ground. It was a delight to play in the pools of blood."

"Mila, stop this immediately," the teacher scolded.

"I'm not… I'm trying… I can't," she moaned and lifted her glasses to press her hands to her eyes, attempting to squeeze out what she saw, knowing it couldn't be right. She rocked back and forth, hoping she could press her top and bottom eyelids together hard enough to reset everything. She tried again and again but ended up saying more in detail about the countless dead bodies strewn and blown apart with intestines swirling like red serpents escaping to the earth. The description went on to glorify the First World War, and Mila continued, "It was a beautiful and perfect genocide. Purification of sinners on all sides."

"Enough, Mila!" the teacher shouted like a parent would. The other students laughed at what they thought was a joke. Mila began to shake as she tried harder and harder to see the page for what it was, but she couldn't. Then she couldn't stop reading at all. Her mouth moved on its own, and the words spilled out. The putrid descriptions of the war, the blood, and death in the fields, the way the enemy slit throats and piled bodies in senseless hate.

Finishing the assigned page to the end, Mila finally felt something let go, and she fell over her desk and cried. By the end of it, she hardly knew what she had said or what had happened, but she was kicked out of class and given detention.

Not being able to read her novel was one thing, but reading descriptions that belonged in a horror movie from a history book was another. She had honestly read what she saw on the page—just like in English class when she almost read the lines of *Dracula*. It was completely bizarre. Mila liked glamorous, easy texts that whisked her away to the roaring twenties of carefree living and high society. Where was this dark side coming from? And why did it have to come out in her class in front of everyone? She would have worried about that even more if she had a reputation to ruin. Reading was what she always depended on. It was her go-to sanctuary. Who would she be if she couldn't read and be good at school? As she went over everything that had happened, she answered the optometrist's prompts dutifully: "Better, worse, better," Mila said as he moved and changed out the lenses. Thicker glasses than she already had would be the icing on the cake after having just moved to a new school, but it would be worth it if she could get back to reading.

"Are you sure, doctor?"

"I'm sure. Your eyesight is fine," he affirmed, smiling and wheeling away the squeaking arm of the machine. But Mila wasn't sure this was the news she wanted. Now she really had to wonder what was happening with her eyes or maybe her brain. She tensed up at the thought but made her way to the waiting room, where her mom was reading a magazine, and Gemma was playing with the colorful wire and bead maze on the table. The doctor called Mila's mom into the room to have her own annual check-up while they were there.

Mila joined Gemma on the floor, grabbed some beads, and started moving them across the wires.

"Miwa, what's yow favowit color?"

"I like yellow."

"I like wed."

Mila giggled at Gemma's simple happiness and wished so hard to feel any kind of joy as close to the delight she always saw in her little sister. Mila moved the colorful beads up and down the plastic wires and thought about just how much she hated being a teenager. She hated her new life, her stupid new school, and her stupid eyes that were playing tricks on her. She almost started to cry but thought better of it, not wanting to upset Gemma too.

~ * ~

In the car on the way home, Gemma slept, and Mila's mom was quiet. Mila loved silence, but her mom loved to talk— even during movies and funerals, she always had something to whisper. So, it was strange not to hear her babbling about anything.

"Mom? Everything okay?" Mila asked.

"Well," she started.

This won't be good, Mila thought.

"The doctor said your eyes are fine, but maybe we should take you to a psychologist if things don't improve."

"What? I don't need a shrink," Mila scoffed, though wondering if maybe she sort of did.

"We can talk about it more later. Let's just take some time to get used to everything," her mom said, getting back to her more usual optimistic tone. "It's a lot of change to handle."

"I guess," Mila agreed and turned away to look out the window. "Just call me Zelda from now on," she mumbled.

"What?"

"Nothing," Mila said quickly. Her mom wouldn't understand the reference to F. Scott Fitzgerald's wife, who ended up in several insane asylums. Mila stayed quiet the rest of the way home, stuck on the possibility that she would be the second woman Fitzgerald had driven into madness.

4

Soo

Soo's winning streak was officially over. She couldn't get her energy or enthusiasm back up; it had been more than a week since she'd had a proper night's sleep. For one thing, the nightmares wouldn't stop. Several times every night, she was waking up with either hot sweats or quivering chills, and her head reeled at everything from boiling water in the girl's locker room to the exploding test tube in science class. But mostly, they were about reliving the panic and confusion of the gripping cement mud at the front of Blackrock High.

Lately, Soo had wanted to skip swim practice and avoid school altogether. In the mornings, she didn't want to get out of bed and even tried to fake being sick one morning when her mother whipped out a thermometer, seemingly out of nowhere, and shoved it in Soo's mouth to prove she was okay.

But her nerves were getting the better of her, and it was starting to show physically. The circles under her eyes were growing darker by the day, and her trademark ambition was replaced by sluggishness and disinterest. She barely came close to her record times in the pool the week before and stopped even looking in Tessa's direction for a challenge. Strangely, Tessa hadn't even bothered to tease her about it. Soo started to look so down and miserable that everyone, even Coach Riley and her teachers, gave her a break to deal with whatever was happening.

In her classes, she was struggling to concentrate—always listening beyond the teacher's words to see if she could hear any laughter coming from the school's basement. A few times, she thought she heard it and jumped up, only to realize she had been startled by one of those nightmares that feels like you're falling into a dark abyss. Since the flagpole, she hadn't had any other incidents but was still wary of dismissing it. She had gone back the next day to look all around the flagpole, but there was no mud—nothing but lush, green grass.

The county swim meet was happening in two weeks, and it should have been her top priority. But she wished, somehow, she could escape it. Unfortunately, it was plastered all over the school hallways and in the morning announcements, but deep down, she truly wanted it and just didn't know how to get the rest of her body on board. If she wanted to do well, she had to handle all this weird stuff and get proper sleep. *Where did all the magic go?* Soo wondered. How could she get back to those few days, just a week before, of her best times and amazing mornings of out-swimming the entire team? How could she have changed so much in such a short time?

On Friday, Soo knew she had to go to the afternoon swim practice and push harder than she had all week, even if she didn't have the energy. *This is Counties,* telling herself, and somewhere within, she would have to find her drive. Surprisingly as Soo reached the pool area and the chlorine smell hit her, she felt much better. And after a week of moping, it was the first time she actually wanted to be in the water. She desperately hoped a few laps would clear her head.

In the locker room before practice, Soo got dressed alone. None of the other girls even said hello to her. She guessed she deserved it by how she had been acting so distant. Then, out on the deck, she tried to at least smile at Faye and Ava. They politely smiled back, but it was more a look of *'pity on the poor girl who almost became the strongest swimmer on the team but couldn't cut it in the end'.* Soo hated pity, and she never wanted to be thought of as anything but strong and capable. But she also knew she wouldn't regain a good reputation after just one good practice. She would have to take things slowly.

Dutifully, Soo put on a stern face, marched to the pool, and began with a slow swim to warm up. It felt good not to hurry through the water and just concentrate on her form, the pace of her breath, and the weightlessness she had missed. At the end of her first few laps, Coach Riley bent down at the top of her lane, speaking gently, "I like the focus but still want to see your goggles facing the bottom of the lane on every stroke, Kim."

"Ok, Coach," she said, diving away, appreciating the gentle pep talk that normally would have been a lot worse. Soo did a few slower strokes to over pronounce her face-down form to get the feeling Coach Riley was looking for. She focused her eyes all the way down to the bottom of the pool, each time finding the dark blue lines of her lane and the edges of the horns of the Ram mascot. Rhythmically breathing out almost all her air, hearing the strong swell of bubbles blast beside her ears. As she got into a good rhythm, her muscle memory took over, and she was able to give more and more. But as her arms and legs moved in harmony and flow, she felt her other senses being left behind. Soo no longer heard the bubbles rush past, and the bottom of the pool suddenly became blurred. She did a few strokes with her eyes closed, turned at the end of the lane, and pushed herself back, strong like a missile in the water. But as hard as she tried, she couldn't get her eyes focused on a target. Instead, Soo felt a wave of nausea flow through her, making her stop mid-lane to tread water while checking her goggles. As she kept herself up, a vibration entered her whole body, from the tips of her toes, moving upward and shaking her from the inside. It startled her, and she tried to pull away, swimming back to the edge at the start of the lane, but her arms were heavy sacks, and she could barely pull herself forward. The water was too deep for her to touch down, so she kept treading in place with her slow-moving arms and legs to keep her head above water. She moved her head to see the side of the pool, two lanes over. Could she make it?

She pushed with her legs to straighten out, then pulled with all her strength to make a single stroke, but she could barely move forward and was going under. With every move she made, the water was thickening, like she was swimming in thick soup, molasses… or *cement.*

Oh, God. It's happening again. Soo could hear the muffled bubbling and gurgling of the water from below. Or was it *inside her?* She couldn't hold herself in the water any longer. *Step one, when you think you're drowning…* flashed through her mind, but she couldn't even move to get into a floating position. As she began to sink further, water splashed over her face and went down her throat, along with a wave of nerves and fear. It was as if all her training had left her, and her mind went blank. She splashed and struggled to keep afloat, gasping for air and trying to rise up against what felt like a hot and heavy blanket over the top of the water, engulfing her. She coughed and choked under the water that was pulling her down until she was no longer able to make a sound. And then everything went dark.

~ * ~

The next thing she knew, she was on the pool deck with Faye Gilbert's mouth on hers. Faye sat back when Soo's eyes opened. Soo coughed heartily and sat up to get more air into her lungs. The whole team was around her, murmuring things she couldn't quite hear beyond her water-logged ears.

"What happened?" Soo snapped off her swim cap, and the team took a step back at the sudden movement, but she didn't dare to look up at them through her dripping black hair.

"I had to pull you out. You were… you looked like you forgot how to swim," Faye said softly, crouching down, her head tilted to the side.

"I… I haven't forgotten," Soo coughed back, trying not to sound ungrateful for having her life saved. But she couldn't thank Faye when she was so embarrassed. The pool stood empty and calm as everyone remained around her. "Someone had me… it was boiling, I—"

Coach Riley pushed the team back and went to Soo. She covered her in a big towel, and they walked to her office while she coughed out the remaining water from her lungs.

"What's going on, Soo? Last week you were swimming the fastest I've ever seen you, and now you're…" She folded her hands on the desk and sighed sympathetically. "Just tell me what I can do."

"It's something… I don't know, Coach. Everything is like hot cement, thick and boiling. It stopped me and was taking me in."

"Soo, you're not making sense," Coach Riley said, closing her eyes with genuine concern.

Soo kept quiet with her head down on the verge of tears.

Coach Riley sighed with sympathy. "Let's call your mother."

ROBIN

It was just after midnight when Robin heard her mom's keys in the door. Robin used the sound of her mother coming in to slip out of her own bedroom window. Her room being on the main floor allowed her to hop into the side garden, but she still had to be careful not to ever land on the water meter… again. *God, that'd hurt.* Her black cloth bag was full of spray paint cans. She held them close, making sure not to let them rattle together while scurrying downtown to her spot behind the laundromat.

In her all-black clothes and fitted wool hat, Robin was invisible in the night, aside from the low light of the glow sticks she flashed on the wall to get cleaner lines on the outline of her mural. There was still one side she couldn't balance. It needed to be thicker toward the middle, so the 'M' in 'FREEDOM' curled up into a question mark that punctuated the ending. But even the light of the glow sticks wasn't helping. The shadows they caused were more eerie than anything and made her more nervous that she would get caught, which ended up disturbing her lines even more. Finally, after about an hour of filling in the other letters that she was happy with, Robin stood back, looked over what she had completed, and shook her head. The creative juices that had been flowing so easily in shop and music class were clearly gone. *This is stupid,* she decided, then carelessly and noisily threw down her spray cans. She gathered the rest in the satchel, tossed the glow sticks in the alleyway dumpster, and abandoned the mural for another night.

The next morning, Robin couldn't get the failure out of her mind as she walked her brother and sister to school. Enrique and Esther kept each other occupied, chattering on about the puddles they were stepping in on the way while Robin zoned out.

"Hey, don't splash me, you little monsters," Robin snapped. Both of their innocent faces fell, and Enrique looked like he was on the verge of tears. Quickly, Robin stuck her tongue out and made a teasing face to let the twins know she wasn't actually angry. They giggled and ran ahead of her up to the school. Robin sighed as she watched them go in, Esther pushing with both hands to open one of the big doors for Enrique to go ahead. Robin smiled at how cute they were when they weren't fighting or playing loudly.

Before she turned to leave, something caught her eye at the side of the school—a messy auburn ponytail she recognized was blowing in the wind. She walked closer to see if it really was that weird girl from detention standing at the daycare entrance. A curly-haired cherub gave the girl a hug and waved goodbye. Robin again felt a pang of regret for the way she'd snapped at the twins. She'd be sure to hug them later.

Robin stood on the sidewalk where Weird Girl would have to pass by to walk toward the school. As she approached, Robin held strong, blocking the way. Weird Girl's face was so far in her book she was sure to walk right into the trap.

"Hey, watch it!" Robin squealed with dramatic flair.

"Sorry," Weird Girl said, barely reacting and not looking up from her book.

Robin couldn't believe how into books this nerd was. She cleared her throat dramatically, hoping to get her point across this time.

Weird Girl looked up and turned. "Oh, hi!" she said, laughing awkwardly and pushing her glasses up her nose. She let the novel drop to her side.

Robin grabbed the novel from the girl's hand and checked the cover for anything special. "Uhhh, hi! What's up with this book? You're always with your face shoved in it," she jeered, throwing it back.

Weird Girl stumbled as she caught the book. "It's just been taking me some time to read lately," she answered back, grabbing the book and holding it strangely close.

"That sucks," Robin said plainly, putting her hands in her pockets. "Was that your sister?"

"Ya, that's Gemma. What are you doing here?" Weird Girl asked, her eyes bright and blinking with curiosity. Robin was thrown off for a moment. No one really asked her anything, least of all the peppy kids who weren't jaded by Blackrock life.

"I walk my brother and sister to school," Robin shared, feeling like she wanted to say more. She wished she could tell someone the fact that her brother and sister were twins, which made everyone love them immediately, and it drove her crazy. She also wished she could tell even one person, beyond her family, that her father died four years ago, and her mom works two jobs, so she doesn't have a choice about babysitting a lot of the time. And today, she snapped at her adorable siblings for playing in puddles because sometimes she wished there were no little kids around to worry about.

But she could never talk about those things. So, instead, Robin took out her vape pen.

"I'm Mila, by the way," Mila offered, pushing up her glasses again.

"Roberta," Robin said, exhaling. "But call me Robin."

Mila

Mila still couldn't believe she had talked to anyone at all, let alone someone who seemed halfway interesting. It had been two weeks since starting at Blackrock High, and she hadn't made any friends unless she counted the librarian or the senior who helped open her locker. It was easy talking to Robin, and she hated to ask for a rain check when Robin asked to hang out.

"Are you for real? Who says 'rain check' besides old people on TV? You're too classic." Robin said, laughing to herself.

Mila smiled. "I'm just not used to telling people, 'I have to go to therapy'. Is that too weird?"

"Yes, actually, it is. But it's cool. And don't worry—it's not like I have anyone to tell," Robin assured her, rolling her eyes and gesturing toward the students loafing around on the school's front lawn.

Robin was funny, but Mila still wanted to wait to get to know her a little better before she told her more. She had fallen for that trap before with other so-called friends at her last school, and it hadn't turned out well. She would definitely wait a little longer to mention that she was seeing words in books that weren't really there, and her imagination was filling in the space with gory descriptions from classic horror novels.

"I'll catch up with you maybe tomorrow?" Robin asked as she put up the hood of her black sweatshirt and started towards the school's side entrance.

As Mila watched Robin leave, she thought about what it would be like to tell someone else, out loud, all of the weird things that had been happening. What would the therapist really think? *What if they think I'm really crazy and I have to be locked up or put on medication for the rest of my life?* She was starting to regret that she had agreed to go. But her mom was adamant that this might be the only way to find an explanation for her reading troubles. And reading was all Mila wanted to be able to do. Desperately.

At the end of the day, Mila's mom picked her up, and they drove to a really nice part of Blackrock where the trees were taller, houses bigger, and the air became cooler and damper as they got closer to the lake. The streets were lined with old-fashioned iron lamp posts that weren't much taller than their SUV. *How helpful could those really be in the dark?* Mila wondered. They pulled up to a large, bone-white historic home with black shutters. The house fits into the classy neighborhood perfectly except for the swinging sign on the front post that read:

DR. ANDRA PAVI

PSYCHOLOGIST, PSYCHOTHERAPIST.

Inside, a tall woman with smooth brown skin was collecting files from an assistant in the office hall. Mila recognized her as Doctor Pavi from the online profile she had found. The doctor was quite slender and had perfect posture like she used to dance and probably does yoga. Mila hugged her arms around her soft middle.

"You must be, Mila. Are you ready to get started?" Doctor Pavi smiled and gestured for them to go into the private office, and Mila sheepishly followed.

The office was nothing like she expected. It was more like a large living room or library than a doctor's office. Mila's eyes expanded, and her arms fell to her sides as she admired the full, floor-to-ceiling shelves of books. She tried to take in as many as possible but doubted she would ever be able to look over them all. *They really know how to do libraries in this town.*

Doctor Pavi leaned over Mila's line of sight to get her attention and gestured for her to sit on the couch. Mila grimaced when the leather squeaked as she sat. She kept her feet flat on the floor, thinking it didn't seem appropriate to start divulging deep dark secrets while sprawled across the sofa on her first visit. So, she sat up as straight as possible, attempting to rival Doctor Pavi's posture.

"Your mother says you're having trouble concentrating," Doctor Pavi began.

"Not concentrating, really. Reading," Mila corrected.

"What's the difference?"

Mila paused, taking a moment to think, and let the doctor know she wasn't going to spill her guts right away. "I always *want* to read, but the letters won't stay put on the page. They get mixed up, and it's like… like I have to chase them to put them together properly or—." Mila stopped herself from saying more. *So much for not spilling your guts,* she thought.

"Or what?"

Mila tried again to slow down her thoughts and not give too much away, but oddly, she found herself feeling quite comfortable with Doctor Pavi. Maybe it was all the books in the room. Or maybe the quaintness of the house or the cozy, overstuffed furniture. But more likely, Mila assumed it was some special psychiatrist training that made people feel like they wanted to blab out their darkest secrets. *That way, they can find the real psychos.*

"Or they'll just spell out strange things like stupid stuff that makes no sense," Mila added. Doctor Pavi scribbled down her notes, and Mila squirmed.

"Can you give me an example of what kinds of things you see spelled out?"

Mila cleared her throat, pushed up her glasses, and thought back. Did she really want to share the mixed-up messages? This was always the part in books or movies when the doctor would press a secret button, and two large orderlies would come in with cattle prods. Would they take her away and lock her up? Mila froze at the places her imagination was taking her. She just wanted to read again and escape all of this. Getting back to reading and being able to do her homework was all she really cared about, so she was going to take the chance.

"It's weird stuff like in my history class. I don't even know what I read, but the teacher sent me to detention. Then, when I was reading in the school library, I had trouble getting through the last pages of my novel because all the pages were covered in the word STAB, over and over again."

Doctor Pavi took more notes. "Does this ever happen at home?"

Mila paused. The only times she had trouble reading at home were from her being worried something would pop up or if she was too exhausted from trying to read all day at school. *No,* she realized and let out a simultaneous gasp. *It all happened only at school.* When she looked up at Doctor Pavi, the doctor tilted her head to the side and gave Mila a sympathetic smile.

"How *is* the new school, Mila? "

~ * ~

Mila sat in the waiting area for her mom, who was getting the psychologist's official report. She wondered if she should try to read a magazine or something on her phone to test the doctor's theory that nothing would happen outside of school, but there was another girl with her mother waiting there, and Mila didn't want to risk a freakout. The girl sat slouched in the chair while the mother sat straight, her arms curling around a stylish black purse on her lap.

When Mila's mom returned, she had a sad look on her face, similar to the sympathetic smile the doctor had shown her. Mila sighed and knew she would have to endure her mom's pity, probably another lecture on making friends and another suggestion that she go with her to her stupid aerobics class. But Mila had to admit she was relieved that everything could be explained by the stress of starting at a new school.

As Mila stood to leave, her eyes followed the other girl in the waiting room as she walked into Doctor Pavi's office. The back of her jacket read BLACKROCK RAMS SWIM TEAM, and something about it made Mila's breath quicken.

~ * ~

At lunchtime the next day, Mila went straight to the library. She and the librarian made their usual polite exchanges, and she headed for her favorite table. Even though reading was a challenge, Mila was determined to calm her nerves and finish her novel. But when her usual and very favorite reading spot was occupied, she stopped in her tracks, thinking of giving up on the idea altogether. But where else would she go? Begrudgingly, she sat at the next table, which was more out in the open than she liked, but she settled in to sip up the last words of *This Side of Paradise*.

As the last line was read easily, and thankfully, without 'interference,' Mila closed the book and slid it gently across the table in accomplishment. She leaned back, arching her body over the chair, and looked up at the carved wooden ceilings with a sigh of relief. An intricately carved tableau capped the room. The figures were a little unclear, even as she squinted and tilted her head for a better angle. It looked like some sort of colonization tableau—one group of settlers approaching a group of natives in a camp on the edge of Lake Blackrock. It seemed like an odd choice for a school library, but Mila chalked it up to everything in Blackrock being strange and new and, well, the patriarchy. Cursive writing beside it read: *'Rising Hell'*. Out of habit, Mila closed her eyes tight and knew she would read something different when she opened them. There was no way that was the actual name. But after closing her eyes tight and looking again, there was no change. She realized that was the actual name of the cliffs that surrounded the town. The edges of Mila's mouth curved downwards. "Rising Hell," she whispered to herself.

Then she remembered she wasn't alone in the library and cleared her throat in case anyone had heard her talking to herself. She corrected her posture and shook her head to clear before taking a quick look around to see if anyone had noticed. There weren't many people around anyway. The librarian was back at her desk, and the girl at the next table was deep into a science textbook. Mila did a double-take at the girl's face. She couldn't be sure, but it looked a lot like the same girl she had seen at Doctor Pavi's the day before.

Mila got up quietly to act as if she were getting a book from the next aisle so she could take a look at the girl's jacket that was hung over her chair. Mila peeked through the stacks and saw she was right—BLACKROCK RAMS SWIM TEAM. Mila's mind flashed to her mother and Doctor Pavi urging her to make new friends. But what would she say, *'Hi, I saw you at the therapist's office yesterday. I guess we both need therapy. Wanna be friends?'* Mila gave a soft laugh at the idea, pushed her hair behind her ears, and continued walking around the stacks, maybe to find a new novel to read. She had read almost everything on Fitzgerald except one, but there wasn't a copy of it here. *I guess I could start something new*, she thought. But too many things were new, and she wasn't ready to branch out as far as a new author too.

Sitting back at her table, she started to collect her things to maybe grab a snack at the cafeteria when she heard a *'pssst!'* sound behind her. At first, she ignored it, thinking no one would be trying to get her attention.

"Hey," Mila jumped from the touch on her arm. "Did I see you yesterday? Doctor Pavi's?"

The girl sat down eagerly at Mila's table and leaned in close to talk.

"I… just started," Mila whispered, unsure how to sound casual about it. "My mom's making me go."

"Mine too!" The girl said a little too loudly. From the girl's athletic build and excited eyes, she wasn't accustomed to library life, Mila suspected.

"I'm Mila."

"Soo Kim."

5

Soo

Determined to continue hiding and even more desperate to skip swim practice, Soo was happy to show Mila the bookstore in town instead of attending their last two periods. She couldn't understand why anyone would want to skip gym class as badly as Mila did, but she was happy to get away from Blackrock High for any reason.

"So, where did you move from?" Soo asked enthusiastically.

"Miller City," Mila answered sheepishly while curling her hair around her ear.

"Whoa, that's far. Why did your family come here?" Not being anywhere besides Blackrock, Soo struggled to imagine why anyone would choose this small town to live in after living in a big city.

"My mom's job is here, and we needed a change," Mila said with a forced smile.

"What about your dad? What does he do?"

"He's not around. We don't know where he is, actually." Mila shrugged, and Soo went quiet. Her parents weren't exactly the happiest couple, but she had no idea how she would survive without her father around. He was her rock and her favorite person, especially when her mother got on her case for not being diligent about her homework or manners. Her father was the only one who seemed to understand her.

"Sorry," Soo said finally.

"It's okay. It's my mom, my little sister, and me."

Soo smiled and realized it had been a while since she'd had a good talk with any of her friends and even longer since she actually made a new one.

Downtown Blackrock was mainly one street of historic buildings and a newer plaza that was further down the road at the bottom of the hill. As Mila and Soo walked, the sidewalks slowly transitioned to having curbs, and before they knew it, they were up on the landing in front of the general store. A little further on, Soo stopped and opened a bright blue heavy door belonging to the bookstore that chimed as they walked in. Mila giggled with excitement as she skipped over the threshold, letting the warmth and the smell of paper and coffee warm her cold face. She stood dead still in the doorway and breathed it all in with her eyes closed. Soo watched her, smiled, and thought about how she does the same thing when she could smell the chlorine from the pool when she walked into the school.

"So, what are we looking for?" Soo asked, waking Mila from her moment.

"F. Scott Fitzgerald," Mila announced, clearing her throat.

The girls walked to the left side of the store, where a large sign on the wall read, 'fiction.' The old floors creaked as they walked over, releasing more of the scent of old wood and paper. Mila knelt low at the bottom of the 'F's. On the shelf, right before *The Great Gatsby*—with its smooth cover, art deco font, and a coral-pink title, there it was: *The Beautiful and Damned.* Mila flipped the pages, closed her eyes again, and let more of the paper-fragranced breeze blow into her face. Maybe Mila *was* a little weirder than Soo had initially thought, but any quirky indulgence was okay with her. She even envied Mila for being able to obsess over something that wasn't for the betterment of her grades and future college applications.

Soo scanned the room while Mila fell in love with her book and thought about taking a look around for something she might like even half as much. She always knew this shop was here, but not being allowed to read books for pleasure, she had never been inside. Her mother's voice echoed in her mind as she browsed, scolding her for even thinking about reading anything besides a school textbook. But if she was going to miss more swim practices, she might need something to read while she hid in the library.

As she creaked around the room, she couldn't believe she was thinking of skipping more practices, but how could she go back? How could she ever get in the water again and not wonder if she'd make it out alive?

She let her arms relax, and her hands bumped over the smooth spines of some hardcovers in the sports section, but she kept walking, going further back in the store. A thick bright yellow book caught her eye as she walked near the generic non-fiction. She tried to pull out the heavy yellow book, but as she did, a small, brown journal fell to the ground in front of her instead. *Illness and Greatness: How Great Men Found Ambition When Faced with Death and Disease* by Archer Lemon. Squatting down, Soo picked it up and raised her eyebrows at the symbol on the front cover. She flipped through the pages, but it looked too much like something her mother would *want* her to read, so she placed it back on the shelf. Mila was finishing up paying for her novel, so Soo walked to the front of the store, and the girls returned to the cool but sunny September day.

"So, what do you think of Doctor Pavi?" Soo asked, hoping it was a good time to bring it up.

Mila shrugged awkwardly. "She's nice, I guess."

"Tell me if I'm being too nosey," Soo started. "I get it if you don't want to talk about it. But I'm not sure how I feel about the whole therapy thing. I just wondered—"

"I know," Mila offered, trying to keep the conversation comfortable. "I don't know how I feel about it either, to be honest. I don't like sharing too much with her yet, y'know? But I love reading books more, so I kind of have to give it a chance." Mila kept her head down and kicked some stones as they walked.

"What does reading books have to do with it?" Soo turned to her with a scrunched face.

"Lately, I've been having some trouble with words getting

confused, which makes it hard to concentrate or read anything at all. Doctor Pavi says it's probably because I'm new to town and at a new school, and maybe it's just stress. How about you?"

Soo hadn't really been good at explaining what was going on up to this point. Even with Doctor Pavi, she couldn't explain what was happening to her without sounding like she was losing her mind.

"I'm kind of seeing things too. Well, more like feeling things that aren't there, like water getting hot and feeling like I can't move."

"Whoa." Mila turned her whole body toward Soo as they walked. "What did Doctor Pavi say it might be from?"

"Stress too. I have a big county swim meet coming up, so I could be 'self-sabotaging' or something like that." Soo air quoted her diagnosis, and Mila gave a snort.

"Being a teenager sucks," Mila said as the girls walked back toward the school.

"Totally," Soo agreed.

"Anyway, thanks for coming with me today. I guess we'll get to hang out again when we get detention for this," Mila said with a shrug.

"And maybe even more afterward if my mom doesn't kill me for skipping school first."

They laughed and parted ways, but deep down, Soo's stomach sank at the thought of all the ways death was coming for her lately.

ROBIN

Well, this is a new one, Robin thought as she eyed Mila coming into after-school detention again, this time chatting with one of those tall jocks from the swim team. Mila smiled in her direction, and Robin smirked back, moving her eyes from Mila to the girl in the SWIM TEAM jacket before sending her a questioning look. Mila shrugged in response, and Robin hoped to get the full story later on.

When the monitor started detention by taking attendance, the three girls learned they were going to be the only ones in the room.

"Must be a slow week," Robin said arrogantly, doing her best to antagonize the monitor.

"Shhh!" Was the only response she got.

Robin knew it would be too quiet for her to even whisper to Mila to find out why: *One*, Mila was in detention yet again. And *two*, how she became friends with the preppy jock. So, when the bell rang, it was as if Robin could finally get some relief. She had so many things to say that she bombarded Mila with questions and caught herself sounding like someone who cared about gossip.

"Mila, seriously. I thought you were a goody-goody nerd. What are you doing here again?"

"I skipped gym class, and Soo and I went downtown together instead."

"I'm Soo." Soo waved.

"Got that," Robin snapped, not even looking all the way up to Soo's face. Instead, she tried to pull Mila from Soo to ask more.

"It was fine, actually," Mila said, standing firmly. "Soo and I go to therapy together." Mila gestured to Soo, who shrunk and hid her hands in her windbreaker pockets.

"Oh, Soo! I'm so sorry I spoke for you." Mila held a hand to her mouth and another out to Soo.

"It's okay," Soo said as she shrugged. "The whole school knows, anyway."

Robin's eyes fell on Mila's hand, touching Soo's arm. Her teeth gritted together, and her neck began to get hot. *How close had they gotten already? Who makes friends at therapy? And why would Mila be friends with anyone on the swim team?* Yet, Robin understood that if she wanted to be friends with Mila, she might have to suck it up and be nice to this Soo person. She took a breath and spoke in her friendliest voice—the one she often used to win over her teachers.

"Hey, so what are you both doing today after school? Maybe we could hang out or something?"

"That would be cool, Robin, but actually, we both have therapy sessions this afternoon," Mila said, smiling up at Soo.

"Oh, right. Cool. Maybe another day?"

"Of course," Mila said as she skipped away with Soo, leaving Robin alone.

Robin walked through the parking lot towards home but couldn't stop thinking about how Mila hadn't even invited her to skip class with them. On the other hand, why did she care? A few weeks ago, she didn't even know Mila, and now she was jealous of seeing her with other friends? She had never cared about having any friends before—not at school, anyway. Robin was always more interested in hanging around the kids that hung out downtown— the artists, musicians, and other punks whose parental supervision was lacking, much like her own.

She just thought Mila was different— weird and not annoying, which went a long way for Robin. But she was still really angry— angry enough to want to destroy something. She thought of doing some lewd graffiti in the girl's bathroom again. *Not enough*, she thought. Plus, she had already been down that road as a freshman and immediately gotten detention for it.

No, she had the desire to burn something, like, *burn the school down to the ground*. That way, Mila and her stupid therapy buddy would have nowhere to meet. Robin pulled her vape pen from her pocket and began to unscrew the top coil before heading through the deserted hallway near the wood shop class. She needed a lot of dry wood to make a pile that would catch fire and was powerful enough to burn the entire school. *Maybe some gasoline...*

Robin's eyes darted around wildly as she thought of where she could find a gas can. The automotive department wasn't far. She made a plan to run there and back after getting some of the other materials together. First, in the dark shop class, Robin began to gather some pieces of wood from the corner when someone called her name.

"Robin?" Mr. K. said before turning on the lights. "What are you still doing here?" Robin had never stayed at school longer than she had to, especially on a Friday.

Robin was startled like a prey animal, and all at once, she shared the teacher's confusion. Why *was* she still at school? The last she remembered, she was heading home from the school parking lot.

"Mr. K… ughh… hi?"

"Robin, what are you still doing here?" he repeated. Robin didn't have an answer because she was still wondering the same thing. But she knew she needed some kind of response or excuse to keep her out of trouble.

"Well, a creative spark hit me, and I thought I'd come to check if there was wood here for me to get a head start on Monday morning." Robin flashed her biggest smile that sometimes worked on Mr. K.

He looked at her suspiciously but seemed satisfied enough with the answer, maybe even slightly impressed by Robin's initiative.

"Okay, great," he smiled, clapping his hands on his thighs. "So, did you find what you were looking for?"

"I think so. But now that I'm here, I think I'll sleep on my idea over the weekend and see if I still like it on Monday," Robin shrugged, trying not to sound too awkward as she carefully stacked the wood back in the corner.

"Sounds good, Robin. I'll see you on Monday then. Enjoy your weekend." Mr. K. opened the door for Robin to leave as he shut the lights off. Robin smiled politely as she walked past him and scurried down the hall and back out to the parking lot, where it was now almost dark.

How long was I in there? She thought. The last thing she remembered was heading home from the side exit after talking with Soo and Mila. She kept trying to recall while walking home against the autumn wind and light drizzle. She reached in her pocket for her vape and then stopped dead. Her hand quivered as she pulled it out without the coil attached.

"I was going to burn the school down," she said out loud to herself, just to be sure she heard it. Then, she stopped and looked back at the high school in disbelief, realizing what she had almost done. The thoughts of how angry she had been for no reason swept over her, along with the feelings of how determined she had been to set a fire in shop class with wood, gasoline, her lighter… and with people still inside the building.

"What the hell?"

In a panic, Robin hurried home to pick up the twins, all the while hating the fact she could barely run and inhale her Cherry Jubilee at the same time. As the elementary school came into view, she took one last inhale to relieve the panic she felt for being late. Around the corner, she could see Enrique and Esther waiting on the steps like perfect angels, an assistant teacher behind them.

"I'm so sorry, thank you for waiting with them," Robin said, ignoring the unimpressed look from the teacher as she opened her arms and let the twins run into her. As she hugged them, her nerves settled even more. She bent down and gave them both a hard kiss, each on their soft cheeks. *What had she nearly done?* There with the twins, she realized she had almost lost everything and hugged them even tighter. Then, Enrique made a choking sound, and Esther made a fart noise with her mouth, and they all giggled. Robin wiped her cheeks as she stood up and held a twin in each hand as they headed home.

As soon as everyone was fed and playing quietly together in the living room, Robin grabbed her phone to send Mila a message. She didn't have many contacts, and Mila's number was still at the top from when they exchanged numbers earlier in the week.

Robin: U HOME FROM THERAPY? NEED TO TALK. URGENT

Mila: JUST GOT IN. WHAT'S UP?

Robin: ANY CHANCE YOU CAN MEET ME LATER?

Mila: WHAT TIME?

Robin: 12:00

Mila: 12?!

~ * ~

Robin met Mila halfway between their houses at a closed café downtown. Besides the faint rustling of trees after the rain, the streets were quiet and deserted. Blackrock wasn't the kind of place you'd find a lot of people around after dark. Nightlife mostly consisted of families spending time together, neighbors sharing potlucks, or moms drinking a responsible amount of wine at their book clubs.

Robin reached the café first and sat on a wet chair on the dark patio. She continuously blew giant white clouds of vape smoke into the night to calm her nerves, shivering from the dampness. She scorned the eerie quiet of Blackrock that lacked the buzz of a big city—nothing in the background to drown out the rattle of shaking up her spray cans. She always had to either shake them slowly or muffle the sound under her jacket. The quiet wasn't any more welcome as she waited alone for Mila. Her mind started to wander toward the flashes of her earlier in the day, what she could remember about setting a school on fire. Her jaw tightened as she thought about how much she'd lost control. While she was trying to search for answers, a pattern of sound began in the dark, and Robin turned toward it. Clomping, wet footsteps were getting closer, and a bug-covered streetlight shone over a shadowed Mila.

Robin pushed out one of the heavy iron chairs, and it screeched across the cobblestone like a train on hot tracks. Mila sat and wrapped her arms tight around her against the cold. They sat on the dark patio with only the dull glow of Blackrock's historic street lights shining on them, lighting up their fogging breath.

"I can't believe I'm out here at midnight," Mila said with a shiver, pulling up her hood and rubbing her hands together for warmth.

The cold forced Robin to get straight to the point. "Look, I don't know if you'll want to tell me this, but I have to ask," Robin started. "When your stuff with reading is happening, do you ever lose your sense of time or end up somewhere you don't remember getting to?"

Mila furrowed her brow. Robin knew it all sounded crazy and like she was really losing her mind, but she was desperate for an explanation for her thoughts earlier that day. She couldn't have been in her right mind when she was planning to burn the school down, could she? She needed Mila to say she was dealing with the same thing. She needed someone to say it was fine. She needed Mila to understand.

"I don't think so, Robin… why? What's going on?"

Robin slouched, winded by the answer. "What about your friend Susie?"

"You mean Soo?"

"Whatever. Does she have the same thing as you? Does she ever lose time?"

Mila chewed the inside of her cheek before she answered. "Not every time, but the last time she woke up unconscious on the pool deck after one of her teammates pulled her out of the water."

Robin sat back and thought with her black-painted fingernails in her mouth.

"Robin, seriously, tell me what this is about. I can't stay out here for too long." Mila bobbed her knees and looked around into the night.

"Okay, okay. But I think something happened to me today. And now that I'm thinking about it, there's been something going on for a few weeks, but I didn't pay it much attention because it was all good things—great things actually, before today. But today was bad—really, *really* bad, Mila. I don't know what came over me. I got… really angry like I wanted to *hurt people*." Robin whispered the last words, put her hands in her pockets, and gazed down at her boots. "Then I lost track of where I was and how long I'd been there. Does that sound like what you have? Do I need therapy too?" Robin couldn't help her eyes from welling up as she met Mila's gaze.

Mila looked back at Robin sympathetically, but Robin knew she wasn't going to say what she wanted to hear.

"Well, it's not like what I have, but Soo has something different going on too. Maybe it's just puberty or hormones or something."

Robin gave a tight smile. Obviously, Mila was just trying to be nice. "But don't you think that's strange? Why would the three of us all of a sudden not be able to do the things we're good at?"

Mila told Robin more about Doctor Pavi's theory—that it's probably all stress-related. And the fact that all the incidents happened at school might mean they're dealing with specific stress related to their classes, grades, making friends like Mila, or achieving goals like Soo with swimming. Robin couldn't think of how she was stressed at school, but she had to hope Mila was right. A damp wind blew in from the lake, and Robin knew they both had to get home soon.

"That's true, I guess. Everything that's happened to me has happened at school," Robin said, thinking back but not feeling any better.

~ * ~

The three girls agreed to meet downtown in the afternoon that Saturday. Not surprisingly, Mila suggested meeting at the bookstore. Robin and Mila sat with their coffees, and Soo had an herbal tea and a cookie. The store was busy around them with Saturday shoppers and smelled more like pumpkin spice than ever. All the tables around them were full, so it wouldn't be easy to have an open conversation.

"Soo, right? Look, I know this is weird, but Mila and I were saying maybe we should all share what's going on with us to see if there are any things in common. Maybe that way, we can help each other somehow." Soo wasn't taking the hint that Robin wanted her to talk first.

"Okay, I'll go first," Robin offered, stopping herself from rolling her eyes. She started with the carvings she saw on her table in Shop class, then her amazing drum playing in Music class, and how the chairs fell like dominoes. She hesitated slightly as she got to the part about wanting to set fire to the school, but she continued on.

"What made you angry in the first place?" Soo finally spoke.

"That's not important," Robin dismissed the question quickly, not wanting to admit her jealousy of Soo and Mila's friendship.

"But Mila said you lost track of time too, right Soo?" Robin asked the question in earnest to distract away from herself.

"Well, sort of. I think I actually passed out from almost drowning in what I thought was boiling water."

The girls fell silent for a moment and let the buzz of the people in the store fill the space. Hearing Soo's story somehow made Robin feel better, like maybe there really was something going on at the school that was affecting all three of them, like lead paint on the walls or something. But it also made her feel really sorry for Soo. She'd heard the story being passed around, and people were saying terrible things. Sure, she was an awkward jock who was messing up her new friendship with Mila, but she didn't deserve to be taken apart by Blackrock High gossip.

"What about you, Mila?" Robin asked. "Any other things happen to you like that?"

"I don't know. Mine isn't as bad, I guess. I just get words wrong and read messages that aren't there—nothing illeg—." Mila stopped mid-sentence. Soo gawked at Mila with a cookie half in her mouth, waiting for her to finish.

"Well, I did get into trouble once, actually," Mila remembered. "In the library. A book I thought I put back ended up in my backpack, and it set off the alarm."

Robin was slightly amused for a moment as she took in that Mila's version of 'illegal' was having too many books in her backpack.

"What book was it?" Robin said with a teasing smile.

"It was this weird, small journal that had something to do with being sick and dying. Something… *Lemon*?"

Soo's eyes widened to the size of her cookie. She got up from the table like it was a test of agility and jogged to the back of the store to the big yellow hardcover. When she skipped back, she plopped down the same brown journal in front of Mila.

Robin could see this meant something as Mila's face lost all its cheery pink color.

"How did you—?" Mila said with a slack jaw.

"It fell off the shelf in front of me when we were here the other day," Soo mumbled through the cookie crumbs she let fall to the floor. Robin bent her neck to look all the way up at Soo's stunned face and then back to the book. Mila had moved back from the table and pressed her hands into her thighs. Nobody seemed willing to touch the book again, but Robin reached out for it. Mila breathed in a small gasp as Robin grabbed the journal, *Illness and Greatness*. It seemed harmless enough, Robin thought as she leafed through it—pictures of anatomy, some diagrams, and some tables. It was like a boring school science book.

"I don't get it," Robin said, turning the book to the other girls. The page she opened was a diagram with the same strange symbol from the front cover.

"Maybe we should buy it," Soo suggested.

"I'm not buying it," Mila said, now turning her whole body away. "It freaks me out!"

"I'll buy it," Robin announced. "I've just got to get a refill first." She got up from the table and walked to get in line at the coffee counter. While she stood waiting, she slipped the little journal into her bag.

6

MILA

Mila hated carrying around the creepy book. But after two days, Robin wasn't getting anywhere with its overly formal text and medical terms, so she passed it on, saying, "it probably only speaks to bookworms." But after not getting any answers from the eye doctor, Mila wondered if she could really help. She was reading as much at home as possible because, at school, the cryptic messages continued to come in. As one plan of action, she began making notes about everything she thought she saw, but still, none of the messages that came in made any sense or gave her any clues. Sometimes the words appeared in Latin, like a translation, and other times the words were jumbled and repeated over and over on the pages. Not only was she frustrated, but she was starting to worry about her grades. If she couldn't get a handle on whatever was happening, she'd have to figure out another way to get all of her work and reading finished away from the school, and it didn't seem like that was even possible at this point.

In Doctor Pavi's office, Mila pulled the journal from her bag and looked it over. She flipped through the first pages, hopeless about anything else standing out to her. She hadn't found any online results for an author named Archer Lemon or a record of the book anywhere. There was no publication date or place of printing. It was like a ghost.

Mila actually welcomed her time with Doctor Pavi to get

everything from the week off her chest. She'd be able to put the book out of her mind and perhaps focus on the stress that was likely at the root of her problem. But as much as she wanted to blab about everything that was happening, like what Robin had told her about almost setting the school on fire and now the coincidence with Soo and the book, she was still closed about revealing too much to the doctor. It wasn't fair that she would probably tell her mom everything said because she wasn't eighteen yet. And maybe they'd even make the decision to send her away or to some sort of juvenile asylum—she'd read enough books to know what happens to young girls that share their strange visions. So, she was careful to give just enough information to get the doctor's opinion without getting put on anti-psychotic medication or sent away to a 'hospital' out of town.

"So, how was last week for you, Mila?"

Mila paused to consider. "I guess I'm finding ways to cope in class and only had a few times where I had trouble reading some text messages from my friends. Nothing too major."

"So, you've made some friends?"

"A couple. They're kind of having a tough time too. One of them is your patient, actually. Soo Kim?"

"Soo Kim," Doctor Pavi said as if she had lost her train of thought. She scribbled some notes, and Mila could see she made two sharp underlines. Mila tried to sit up taller so she might see what Doctor Pavi wrote.

"So, you're the friend that also saw the book." It wasn't a question.

Mila's eyes opened so wide she could feel their edges go dry and start to burn. *How could Soo tell her about the book? They hadn't even figured out what it was yet or if they were just overreacting to a coincidence.*

Mila decided not to answer. What would she even say?

"Do you not believe in coincidences, Mila?" The doctor asked.

Mila kept a gobsmacked look on her face. Had she been thinking aloud? No, she was sure she still hadn't said anything. She considered Doctor Pavi's question. She had never heard that someone could *believe* in coincidences. She'd always thought they just existed, and that was the end of it.

"I don't know," Mila started. "I guess? I mean, I first saw the book in the library. We thought it was strange that we both knew what the book was."

"Where's the book now?" Doctor Pavi asked, shifting forward in her seat.

Instinctively, Mila clung to her backpack and pulled it tighter to her chest. Sure, Soo had told the doctor about the book but showing it off was a different story. Why did she want to see it anyway? It was only a weird little book. Then Mila thought about how they got it. She knew very well that Robin hadn't paid for it. She really hoped Soo hadn't told that part.

"Are you afraid to show me? Are you afraid I'll take it away?"

Mila was startled by the questions. "No," she said, though she was getting more nervous with all the questions. Mila crossed her arms around her backpack even tighter and then slowly shifted her gaze back to the doctor. "Maybe."

Doctor Pavi sat back.

"Mila, I only want to help. Maybe I can help you girls figure out what this book is. It could be helpful to get an adult's perspective." Doctor Pavi seemed casual but sincere. On the one hand, Mila wanted to tell her everything, but on the other hand, the thought of institutionalization wouldn't allow her to relax.

"You report to my mom. I'm a minor, so you can tell my mom anything I do or say, right?"

The doctor smiled sympathetically. "Mila, our conversations are protected by doctor-patient confidentiality, like anyone else. The only time I have to report what you say is if you are going to hurt yourself or another person. I'm sure that's not the case here, is it?" Doctor Pavi crossed her long slim legs and waited for Mila to make the next move.

Mila thought about how too many of her beloved fiction books and movies had led her astray. She even felt a little guilty that she had ever been attracted to the trope of the young girl being sent away unfairly only to come out on the other side of the ordeal empowered and vindicated.

Admittedly, it may have been a little far-fetched that she would be thrown into an asylum straight away, but she had felt there was something about the journal that made her cautious about revealing how it had come into their lives, just in case.

Her hand slowly reached inside her backpack, and she grabbed the small brown book and pulled it out. As she removed it and showed its cover, Doctor Pavi's dark eyes froze on the front symbol and focused as if Mila wasn't even in the room.

"I can't believe it," Doctor Pavi stammered. Mila remained guarded as she held the book's cover up for the doctor to see from across the room.

"Mila," Doctor Pavi began, "that's a very rare book." The doctor paced her words, but she couldn't hide her shock as she leaned forward. "They were all allegedly burned many years ago. "

"Well, there's at least two of them around," Mila said plainly.

"Two?" Doctor Pavi almost spat.

"There's another one in my school library," Mila told her.

"Mila, you have to get it out of there."

"Why?" Mila said, thinking about what kind of trouble she'd be in if she tried to check it out after seemingly trying to steal it. "What's so special about these books anyway?"

Doctor Pavi squared her face to Mila's. "They're Summoners."

"Summoners?" Mila scrunched her face waiting for the doctor to explain.

"Spellbooks. For summoning demons."

Demons? Great. She's nuts too.

"Demons?" Mila repeated, this time out loud, looking for any signs of Doctor Pavi's face cracking into a joking smile.

"Look, Mila, I know you don't believe me right now, but if these books are following you or trying to get your attention, it's for a reason and probably not a good one."

"Are you crazy?" Mila squinted and pushed her glasses up her nose. "Are you even a real psychiatrist?" Mila sat back with her arms crossed, proud of her confrontation. *They always say psychiatrists are the ones who need help the most.*

"Listen to me, Mila. This is why I'm here in Blackrock. I've seen all of this happen before. I know this book and what it can do, and how it speaks to young girls. You have to trust me." Doctor Pavi's voice had lost its slow, soothing tone. "In the town where I lived before, I had clients report similar things to what you and Soo are telling me. My research led me to this same book at one point, but I was told all copies had been lost or burned, so I stopped looking. Eventually, the demons left town, but I found ways of tracking where they went, and I followed them here to Blackrock. I was sure if I set up a practice again, someone would come to me and report similar things as before. So, when Soo came to see me, I immediately recognized it was happening again. I almost didn't notice your symptoms as being connected, Mila, until Soo told me the two of you were friends."

Doctor Pavi moved to the couch, but Mila stood up and walked away from her to stand next to the doctor's desk. Everything she was hearing was impossible and ridiculous, and she felt like screaming and laughing at the same time. This crazy woman was saying unbelievable things, but at the same time, she was terrified she might be right. Deep down, Mila knew this was all somehow true—the doctor had no reason to lie, and there was something else. She could just *feel it.* Everything she felt happening had a darkness to it, and *demons* weren't the worst way to describe it.

"So, what do we do now? What are the 'demons' going to do to us?" Mila cringed as she air-quoted the word *demons.* She felt ridiculous asking these fantastical questions, but Doctor Pavi didn't even blink.

"We have to use the Summoner to ask them. First, get the other Summoner from the library as soon as you can so it's safe. Then the three of us will meet, and I can show you what to do."

Mila's eyes rose to the ceiling while giving a heavy sigh, realizing another coincidence. "Halloween is this week."

"I know," Doctor Pavi said, taking a long breath with her. "And it's a full moon. Hopefully, we can use it all to our advantage."

Mila scrutinized the doctor's actions and expressions even more closely now. Her ironed gray pants and white blouse was nothing to cause alarm bells to go off. She had a pretty face, beautiful brown skin, and a bright white smile that popped a slight dimple on one side. *Normal-looking*, Mila thought. *Until she started spouting off her knowledge of demons and spellwork.* But she was so knowledgeable and spoke so confidently about it all that it didn't seem as crazy as it did at first. It was starting to feel like it could be a step towards relief, and Mila could soon forget all of this and get back to reading regular books.

As Mila started to walk out, she wondered how Robin would react to all of this. Would she laugh in her face or be curious enough to at least come and meet the doctor? How would she even start to explain that her therapist thinks demons are real, and they have to supernaturally summon them to find out why they're causing mayhem in their lives? Robin was cool, but probably not *that* cool.

Before she reached the door, Mila stopped and called back to Doctor Pavi. "There's one more of us you'll have to meet. I'll bring her along." As Mila left, she shook her head at the idea of bringing Robin to meet the doctor. *Well, Robin, you're going to therapy after all.*

Soo

After the near-drowning incident, Coach Riley and Soo's parents decided that a break from the team would be best for her. At first, she put up a fight, but she knew it was probably the right thing to do in the end. It was the only thing to do, really. The problem was she had no idea if it was going to be a short break or if she would ever be able to swim again. Since everything happened, she wondered if she'd ever get into a pool and not worry about having another attack.

With all of this going on, she was glad to talk to Doctor Pavi, even if it was on a Friday night. But without swim practice, she had nothing better to do, nothing to train for, and maybe nothing to live for. She sighed at herself for having such dramatic thoughts as her father pulled the car up to Doctor Pavi's home and office.

"You know this is only temporary," he said, shutting off the car.

"I do?" Soo balled her hands into fists on her lap.

Her father leaned back in his seat, and for a few moments, Soo held her breath while she waited for him to say something else.

"Everybody gets stressed sometimes. Even me. Things can be hard to handle, and our minds can only take so much."

Soo didn't respond, only slowly exhaled.

"Try and enjoy this break while you can, and you might find you'll be even better than you were before." Her father smiled and gave her a double pat on her knee.

The pep talk didn't make her feel much better, but she smiled as best she could at her father for trying. She took her time walking up to the house to see Doctor Pavi, drooping her arms like a rag doll and barely lifting her feet. She could feel her father's eyes on her as he watched her walk in. Was he just as disappointed as she was in her failure? Had he noticed how unlike herself she had been feeling? Would he notice that she wasn't wearing clothes that said SWIM TEAM on the back?

Inside, Soo expected to have to wait in the lounge outside of Doctor Pavi's office, but a card on the assistant's desk read:

SOO, COME ON IN.

As she opened the door, she stopped halfway, not believing her eyes. Mila, Doctor Pavi, and *Robin?*

"Come in, Soo, we're just getting started," Doctor Pavi said, coming around from the desk with an open arm.

"Um, started what? What's everybody doing here?" Soo waited to hear the explanation and involuntarily balled her hands into fists once more. She liked her new friends and everything, but she was really looking forward to having Doctor Pavi all to herself. With all of her latest swim team drama, dealing with her overbearing mother, and not getting enough time with her father, she really needed to talk it all out.

"Come in and sit down. I'll explain everything in a sec," Doctor Pavi said gently.

Soo eased down into the chair she usually sat in for their sessions and turned her nose up, smelling the room as it filled with the scent of black licorice candles. Mila smiled over at her from the desk a couple of times like she was somehow enjoying the get-together. She and Doctor Pavi were organizing objects on the desk, lighting candles, and stacking papers. Robin was in Doctor Pavi's chair, her dark lips in an innocent pout, thankfully looking just as confused about why she was here, but neither of them bothered to speak to one another while they waited.

Finally, Mila came and sat cross-legged on the floor. Her purple skirt billowed around her legs, and she didn't seem to have a problem with Archer Lemon's journal in her hands anymore. When Doctor Pavi joined them, Soo leaned forward, ready to hear what was going on.

"What's been happening to you girls has happened before," Doctor Pavi started. "Before I came to Blackrock, I was in an even smaller town, if you can believe it."

Robin scoffed at the joke, but Mila gave her a look to pay attention.

"I was working as a psychologist there too, and all of my clients were young women, like you three. They all had experienced different incidents like you—Claire was tortured by the sounds of howling dogs and would beat her ears until they bled. She eventually had to be confined to her bed in a straitjacket to stop her from hurting herself. Lauren had terrible visions of people who weren't there and demonic figures telling her to commit terrible acts of violence, like stabbing herself, attacking her family, and even lighting places on fire."

Robin shifted and let go of the twirl of green hair around her finger.

"But Meghan experienced the worst of it." Doctor Pavi's words were slow and even. "She had numerous attacks that caused her body to contort and writhe to the point that left her paralyzed. The doctors claimed it was epilepsy, but no medication had any effect. Her family went so far as to hire a priest to perform an exorcism, even though they weren't a religious family in the slightest. It didn't work, and she ended up dying this past summer."

Soo felt a chill go up and down her spine. *She died?*

Robin put out her hand. "Doctor, sorry—but did you say *exorcism*? As in Satan spitting pea soup kinda stuff?"

"Just listen for a minute, Rob," Mila urged, reaching up from the floor and patting the top of Robin's foot.

Doctor Pavi went on. "It seemed like the next step was performing an exorcism on the remaining two girls, but their families were against it because of what had happened to Meghan. So, I researched other ways of talking to demons and came across the mention of a secular spellbook written roughly a hundred years ago by Archer Lemon."

Soo sat back, remembering she had told Doctor Pavi about the book in their last session.

"Only a few within a certain inner circle of knowledge, at the time, would know the meaning of his… or her… pen name. It took a while to get access and find people in the circle who would tell me anything, but eventually, I got in. But by the time I found out more, I learned that all of Lemon's books had been burned—some accidentally, and the rest on purpose because of their content. I did the research for months but couldn't track down even one copy and, sadly, Claire and Lauren…" Doctor Pavi trailed off.

"But now we have two," Mila piped up with some optimism, looking at both Soo and Robin. Mila separated the books in her lap to show she actually had two copies on top of each other.

"Hopefully, we won't need them both," Doctor Pavi said.

Soo had a million questions and accusations against Doctor Pavi. *Demons? Seriously?* Mila and Robin were both nodding along like this all made sense and were completely on board with all of this exorcism talk. And with all the storytelling and candle lighting, it was clear that a book reading was coming next. The room was heavy, ceremonious even, and didn't leave a lot of room for questioning. At least not yet. For the moment, Soo decided to keep quiet and go along with it all. But only for the moment, just because Mila seemed to be okay with it all so far, and she trusted Mila.

Doctor Pavi led them to her desk that was alight with more candles. Mila handed one of the journals to the doctor, and she held open the book to the page with the same symbol as on the front cover. It was a geometric flower of triangles, specifically drawn, with measurements in each corner and along each line. More triangles converged beneath the top, creating a dizzying image that Soo found hard to follow, but it was also near impossible to look away from.

"You're about to see why so many of these books burned accidentally," Doctor Pavi said as she started to work. "I have to be very careful to only heat the paper and not light it completely on fire," she said, waving one page of the book slowly over the candle's flame. "The heat will reveal the notes under the images."

The three girls looked on in anticipation, their faces lit by the candlelight glow. They watched the brown tarnish of the citrus ink revealing words and notes on the page as it wove all the way through and around the triangle flower. Soo had no idea what this meant, but Robin seemed blown away in recognition, smiling as she leaned in even closer to watch the process.

"We totally used to do this to pass notes," Robin said excitedly. "Lemon juice works like invisible ink."

"Exactly. Our writer knew this secret, too, and hid the spells behind the symbols on the pages. If we do it right, the spell we need to talk to the demons will be revealed. And if that's what's really going on here, we can all get some answers."

Answers from demons? Soo still didn't want to say anything rude since it seemed like she was the only skeptic now. But was she actually hearing her psychiatrist talk about summoning demons with spells? And how was Mila still so cheerful and unfazed by the fact that their psychiatrist was actually turning them to the occult, witchcraft, and demon summoning? Soo wished she could be as cool as Robin or as enthusiastic as Mila, but it was getting too weird. One minute she was coming in to talk to her therapist about her crappy week; the next, she was getting involved in some satanic ritual.

Doctor Pavi continued to wave the book over the candle flame very carefully, being sure not to get too close to the actual flame. "You can see how many of these books were lost to negligence and impatience," she remarked.

"Does it have to be black candles?" Soo asked, letting her irritation get the better of her at last.

"No, but it's what I had on hand." Doctor Pavi stayed calm at the question and continued her measured movements.

She 'just happened' to have tall black candles on hand and was now revealing words to a spell that could talk to the supposed demons possessing them. It was too much for Soo to believe or take in. There was enough on her mind with everything going on at school without adding this craziness to her life. Dramatic exits had never been her thing for fear of being rude, but she needed to get out.

Without a word, Soo moved to grab her things and headed for the door. The other girls called to her, but she didn't look back. Instead, she skipped out to the car where her father was waiting and got in.

"That seemed quick. Everything go okay?" He asked, putting his phone down and starting the car.

"Just go, please." She leaned her seat down as far back as she could and closed her eyes all the way home.

ROBIN

Robin ran out after Soo, but the car had already pulled out onto the road.

"*Soo!*" she called after her as she ran to the gate. She stood for a moment, watching the car drive away down the wet, black road. Robin raised her hands to her head to think. *Maybe they should have been more careful with Soo, or she needed more time,* she thought while kicking the gravel around on the driveway under her boots. It was a lot to take in for all of them, but she knew Soo was dealing with a lot on top of everything else happening. She had to know about the rumors that had started at school about why she was off the swim team. Whispers of everything from steroids to mental breakdowns. Robin suddenly felt guilty about how she treated her when they first met.

Plus, Soo wasn't as used to hearing about demons as Robin was. When Robin was young, her grandmother talked about demons like a regular, everyday conversation: "*Wear your crucifijo, Roberta, to keep the devil away,*" she would say. Or, "*You know your primo struggles with the demon, Alcohol.*" The word 'demon' was thrown around all the time at home and in church, but it was always just a story—a way to talk about regular bad things that happen, like her cousin Filipe who always smelled like mouthwash.

Robin wasn't sure of how she felt about the idea of demons being real either. She was really pissed that she might have to face the fact her *abuela's* rants about praising Jesus Christ and rejecting the devil were all true.

But she tried not to think about that since it felt like she, Mila, and Doctor Pavi were just playing with invisible ink and getting information at the moment. Then they'd do some sort of ceremony and hope for the best, like a prayer. It was no different than a baptism or First Holy Communion, really. And she had survived both of those.

Robin walked back inside, where Doctor Pavi and Mila were hunched together like innocent students studying for a big exam. There seemed to be a larger pile of books out on Doctor Pavi's desk. Most of the candles were blown out, but the scent of smoke was still lingering. Robin hung back a little. She wasn't too sure if she wanted to get sucked into demon studies for no extra credit.

"Robin," Doctor Pavi called without stopping her frantic flipping of pages. "How's Soo?"

"She left," Robin answered while swinging the door closed. Then she dropped into one of the armchairs and let her bulky army boots dangle at the ends of her skinny legs like burnt marshmallows on campfire sticks.

"So, you never got to speak to these demons before, right? How do you know they're actual demons? How do you know what these weird books do?"

"I don't. It's just been my theory this whole time. And trust me, I know how it sounds. It's all kind of crazy to me too, Robin." She didn't look up, but Robin smiled to one side. Adults weren't easy for Robin to get to know or trust, but Doctor Pavi was a little different. She seemed smart, genuine, and even funny in her own way. In a weird way, Robin found herself wishing she could have therapy with her, like Mila. *Talk about demons…*

Robin was about to ask her next question when Mila chimed in, "Every other part of Doctor Pavi's theory has been true, and she even followed them here with a witch's spell for specifically tracking demons."

"Witches too?" Robin slapped both sides of the armchair. She didn't know how she felt about heaven or God, but if her *abuela* was watching from heaven, she would be wagging a finger at Robin, saying, *"I told you so,"* which sucked for many reasons. She always gave her *abuela* a hard time about religion, heaven, and hell and was always a little rebellious when it came to sitting quietly in church. Now her *abuela* was gone—maybe in heaven *if that's real too*—and she couldn't tell her she was sorry.

Shaking her head to rid her thoughts of family problems, Robin got up and joined Mila and Doctor Pavi, who was still working on revealing the hidden messages in the journal. Robin approached the desk with her dark, doe-eyes on the last candle flame, still somewhat distrustful of herself getting too close to the fire. Mila was completely engaged and in her element. She was reading the lemon-juice spell at her usual slow, concentrated pace but simultaneously cross-referencing, researching, and taking notes. Robin's face softened as she watched Mila working among the books and information. It gave her hope that maybe this crazy stuff was the answer to what was happening to them all, and they'd be back to their normal lives soon, albeit with more knowledge of the supernatural than any of them could have ever imagined.

Doctor Pavi opened her desk drawer and pulled out a brown bag with the hardware store stamp on the front. She handed it to Robin along with one of the Lemon books that had three bright pink sticky notes hanging out of the side.

"Robin, I need you to paint the symbols on each of these pages on the floor, under the rug. Can you do that?"

Robin peered inside the bag to see three cans of spray paint. She snorted to stop herself from laughing full-out in the doctor's face. "Ya, I can do that," she said.

Sliding the furniture gently over and pulling the rug out of the way, Robin revealed more of Doctor Pavi's gleaming hardwood floors. She had vandalized before, but it was on things like dull cement walls or deteriorating old brick, never on something so pristine. She caught Doctor Pavi's eyes once more to double-check that she had her approval to destroy her home, but Doctor Pavi nodded and waved Robin on.

Robin went over the first symbol—the one from the cover of the book. She stared at the lines, noting the numbers inside of the angles, mentally measuring the length of each line. Then, reaching for her backpack, she pulled out her protractor and made small pencil marks on the floor. Her tongue stuck out slightly as she checked and reviewed the degree of the angles from the symbol and double-checked her measurements. A slight bout of nervousness came over her only when she remembered her mural behind the laundromat was still unfinished and not going the way she wanted it to. She hoped she wouldn't have the same problem getting things right here. It was probably pretty important, to be precise.

Once Robin had all three symbols mapped out on the floor, she began to shake up one of the paint cans. The familiar rattle inside reminded Robin of her secret life in dark, dirty alleyways. It was now extremely odd to hear the sound filling the immaculate library of one of Blackrock's more beautiful historic homes. But strangely, it gave her more confidence for what was about to happen because if Doctor Pavi was willing to spray paint runes and symbols on her floor, it felt like the real deal—not a practical joke or something childish. So, crouching down, Robin happily went to work, painting the first lines of the summoning symbols on the floor. As she did, her nerves settled, and the flow of painting took over.

When she was done, Doctor Pavi came over.   "Perfect, Robin. Really great work." Robin had no idea what she had actually painted, and she was a little vexed that this had been her first official commission, but she appreciated Doctor Pavi's praise. She had never been praised for anything she spray-painted before.

"Thanks, but what are these anyway?"

Doctor Pavi sighed like she, too, was running on faith that all of this would work the way they hoped and the symbols would do anything at all.

"The middle one is to call demons in general. The one on the left will hopefully bring them out and away from the school, maybe for good."

"And the one on the right?"

"That's so we can talk to them without becoming possessed ourselves."

The word 'possessed' raised the hairs on Robin's neck. Up until that point, she hadn't realized it was a possibility, and all at once, her Catholic upbringing hit her in the face. She had been told about lesser demons that lead you to alcohol and gambling or the one that makes you cut off all your hair when your baby dies—or so her *abuela* said. But *possession* was a whole other level that made her mouth go dry.

Doctor Pavi noticed Robin go pale. "It's okay to be scared, Robin. I'm scared too."

So, they were all in over their heads. These weren't the demons that most people have inside—Doctor Pavi dealt with that kind every day. These were legit, outside-of-the-body, directly-from-hell demons that had been playing tricks on them. Robin realized that the choice to believe was no longer a choice—either she believed in what they were doing, or she would have to admit she was a psychopath who really wanted to burn a school down and the people inside along with it.

From the desk, Mila called, "Are we really going to do this without Soo?"

It was a good question. What if they got answers, and the demons agreed to set them free? Where would that leave Soo?

Doctor Pavi looked right through Robin as she considered the question. Robin didn't move in case she disturbed the doctor's thoughts.. And after what seemed like a long staring contest, Robin blinked, and Doctor Pavi luckily had the answer.

"No, we have to try and make contact now. Let's see if this works, and we'll be able to help Soo better if we know what we're dealing with."

Mila came to join Robin and Doctor Pavi with the other spellbook. The doctor started lighting more candles around the freshly painted symbols on the floor while Robin and Mila watched the room light up.

$\mathcal{S}$OO

At home, Soo sat in the kitchen on the island stools, dangling her long feet and quietly watching as her mother cooked dinner. Her mother hadn't said much since the near-drowning incident, which Soo expected since she knew her mother didn't really 'do' feelings. But, on the good side of things, she had been cooking a lot of Soo's favorite meals lately and not giving her such a hard time about school work. She hadn't even asked her to move from the kitchen island to the table to eat her *mandu-guk*.

Her phone beeped and vibrated on the countertop while she was eating. She figured it was Robin or Mila again, trying to get her to come back to Doctor Pavi's. Her mother turned from the stove with a raised eyebrow, so Soo picked it up to turn the volume down but noticed a message from Faye. Something about a party. She clicked it open.

"Your friends again?" Her mother asked.

"A girl from the swim team, actually. There's a Halloween party." Soo turned her phone over dismissively, knowing her mother would never let her go to a party if she didn't know the parents.

"Finish your soup," her mother started sharply. "And then get dressed. I'll drive you to the party."

Soo almost choked on a dumpling and wondered for a moment if demons had decided to possess her mother too. "Really?" She managed with a full gob.

"You need to be with your friends, Soo Na. Maybe have some fun and calm your stress."

Soo messaged Faye back and got the details. But when she got back an answer, Soo slumped in defeat—the party was at Vivian Voorhees's house in Blackrock Heights. She would have to go back to the same part of town as Doctor Pavi's office.

~ * ~

Faye was waiting for Soo in the driveway, wearing a cute denim skirt and fuzzy pink sweater. Soo's face flushed in mortification under her full face of white clown makeup.

"No drinking," was all her mother said as she opened the door. Soo climbed out of the car awkwardly and was careful not to ruin her mermaid tail. She wobbled as she walked up to the house in her half-clown, half-fish creation.

"Clownfish!" Faye smiled and skipped up to lock her arm in Soo's. "So glad you came."

"I thought it was a costume party," Soo said, using her other arm to bring around her tail and using it as a distraction to not look

Faye in the eye.

"You look great. Don't worry about it," Faye said finally.

They walked up the stone walkway arm in arm, Soo's tail rustling behind them.

Then, on the doorstep, Soo continued to fuss with her costume, but Faye used a soft hand to turn Soo's face to look at her.

Soo grimaced uncomfortably. "I can't believe you invited me."

Faye gave a small giggle. "I know what it's like to be under a lot of pressure," Faye said, now reaching out to hold Soo's hand. They could hear the music pounding inside the house.

Soo felt like she should say something nice. "Y'know, I never got to properly thank you for saving my—" But she was cut off mid-sentence as two laughing teenagers came storming out the front doors, breaking Faye's hand away as they ran between them.

"Come on," Faye called and waved Soo inside. Soo followed, shuffling her feet with her tail dragging behind her.

Inside there were people everywhere. The music was blaring, and, as Soo had already expected from seeing Faye, no one else was in a costume. Some people were dancing in the living room, and others were playing drinking games in what the Voorhees' probably called the parlor. Behind all the teenagers, Soo could see that the house was not only enormous but beautifully kept, without a Halloween decoration anywhere in sight. She hoped Vivian knew what she was doing by having all these people here. *Try to relax and enjoy it*, she reminded herself.

Faye led Soo to the kitchen, where some of the other swim team members were hanging out, away from the smoking and drinking. Tessa was sitting on the countertop beside her boyfriend, Todd, a sprinter on the track team. They were both sipping on some sort of pinky-red power drink instead of alcohol, and their lips were stained to match. Then, Tessa's face dropped as Soo walked in. Luckily, Todd grabbed and kissed her, preventing her from spitting out any number of taunts that could make Soo feel any more uncomfortable than she already did.

Soo's tail wiggled and swung out as she crouched to sit with

Faye in the breakfast nook, where a few of Faye's other friends were hanging out. No one paid any attention to Soo. Instead, they all started chatting and laughing with Faye, which was completely fine. It was at least better than being asked for the millionth time about what happened in the pool, how she was enjoying therapy, or why she was such a mental case. She was happy to sip her bottle of water and listen to them discuss their favorite bands, the best horror movies, and who they thought would barf first at the party.

~ * ~

In another part of the house, Tessa had led Todd away from the kitchen to continue their kiss. They found an empty office, though it was more like a library with rows of books on polished wooden shelves. And with its oversized leather sofas, it was about to become the perfect make-out room.

Tessa led Todd over to one of the sofas, held him down, and kissed him hard. Todd had his hands on Tessa's strong, bare waist as they laughed and pressed themselves together more, kissing and giggling. But before it could get any more heated, the door to the office slid open.

"Guys, this room is off-limits. You can't be in here." Vivian had asked her two friends, Jacee and Celeste, the other two most popular girls in school, to help her keep people out of her father's office. But they hadn't done their job, and Vivian was now standing there, doubly pissed. She marched into the room and turned on the lights without thinking, which showed off her own slim figure, long brown legs, and perfectly set dark hair. She stood tall with her arms crossed, waiting for the couple to leave. Tessa adjusted her shirt and scurried past Vivian with her head down. Todd followed her out, "Sorry, Vivian," he said as he passed by her, trying not to ogle Vivian's pushed-up breasts and bare midriff.

As Vivian turned off the lights and was about to leave the room, she heard a *thump* like something had fallen behind her. She walked back into the dark office to investigate, hoping the intruders hadn't broken something.

Her father spent most of his time in his office though Vivian was rarely welcomed inside. It felt strange to be in there without him. She usually only heard him from the outside, making calls and having powerful men from the city join him for a drink. Her father, Langston Voorhees, had his hand in most of the architectural projects in Blackrock and even connections overseas, where he was at the moment, allowing Vivian another rare occasion to see the inside of the office for herself.

The dim shelf lights that were always on helped guide Vivian behind her father's desk, where she had heard the drop. She was thankful she didn't have to touch a light switch. As she walked behind the desk, she came upon a small, tattered journal on the floor. All of the other materials her father had were pristine, well-kept, and neatly displayed. This didn't seem to fit. Vivian was slow and careful about turning on the desk lamp and breathed a sigh of relief when it switched on without incident. Sitting in her father's chair, she held the little journal in front of her and felt compelled to flip through the pages as the party continued in the rest of the house. Her mind raced to find meaning in her father having a book on death and disease in his collection. He didn't seem sick. In fact, her father was one of the healthiest men she knew—powerful, smart, and strong.

Vivian closed the book and read the title aloud. "*Illness and Greatness: How Great Men Found Ambition When Faced with Death and Disease* by Archer Lemon." Something about it unnerved her.

She knew she had to keep a closer eye on her father once he got back, but she was sure it was nothing. He was rarely sick a day in his life. It was probably just an old book he didn't even know he had. *Probably.*

Vivian sighed and sunk deep into her father's desk chair. The party raged on outside, but she was in no rush to return. At first, she had been really excited to have a big party after a long and frustrating week of technology failing her—like her entire essay erasing from her laptop, the small microwave fire in home economics, and shocking herself on her phone. But before she could feel completely sorry for herself, she was interrupted by someone else walking straight into the office.

"Who are you?" Vivian charged, leaning into the light of the desk lamp to show her face.

"Ugh… I'm Soo. Soo Kim."

"What do you want?" Vivian felt her neck get hot.

Soo stammered, "I was looking for the washroom, and I saw the light on here. I heard no one's supposed to be in here, so I was just checking…"

Vivian was silent and gave no indication that she appreciated Soo's vigilance. Soo turned to leave, but before she did, she made an awkward stop in the doorway.

"Uhh, I know you don't really know me, Vivian, but is everything okay?"

"Yes, I'm fine," Vivian snapped. "You can go back to the party now."

Soo stepped back bashfully to leave, but not before stumbling slightly on the tail of her costume, making her exit like a court jester who had displeased her queen. Soo took one last apologetic look at Vivian, who was now holding up a book in front of her face, hopefully blocking Soo from saying anything more, but Soo stopped dead in the doorway.

"Oh, no! Not you too!" Soo shouted. And before Vivian could answer, Soo had run right up to the desk and was reaching out to grab the book.

Vivian snapped the journal away, clutching it to her chest, glaring at Soo. "What the hell, *freak*?"

~ * ~

Soo balked a little at the insult but quickly remembered she did look a little freakish in her costume.

"Look, this book is… is something. It's important, but I can't tell you about it here," Soo said, checking the door.

"Seriously, you need to get out of here. You're freaking me out," Vivian said, closing the journal but keeping it tightly in her hand.

"No, Vivian, listen to me. Has anything happened to you lately

91

that you can't explain, like trouble reading, feeling out of control, or seeing things that aren't there?"

Vivian glanced at the desk lamp and hesitated slightly, but she barely let it show. Then she turned, looked at Soo straight in the face, and exerted her power as host. "You need to get out right now."

Soo hesitated, not wanting to leave Vivian without telling her more, but she had an idea.

Soo left Vivian behind the desk, gawking at her as she rushed out from the office, out of Vivian's front door, as fast as she could— all the way to Doctor Pavi's office. It wasn't far by car, but a good jog on foot and an especially daunting task in a full clownfish costume.

Soo's mind raced as she made her way through the streets. *What was happening? How could Vivian Voorhees have the book too? And how had she been there right at the moment she was reading it?*

It was all too much of a coincidence, like magic. Or… *demons.*

Soo continued to fumble along the dark winding streets and down a hill that led to the therapy office. The office light was still on, so the girls must still be inside. She burst into the office to find Mila, Robin, and Doctor Pavi sitting on the floor around weird symbols painted in red paint. Mila sat right up, startled, as Soo ran in, "Soo! You're back!"

Soo bent over, catching her breath. It had only been two weeks of not training, but she could feel herself not being in top form. Sweat had made her clown makeup smudge and begin to drip from her face. She did her best to talk. "There's another one," she managed.

"Another what, Soo?" Doctor Pavi asked, handing Soo a towel and a glass of water.

"Another one of us."

7

Vivian

Vivian watched as the girl ran from the office and, hopefully, straight out of the house. *Who invited such a freak?* The situation had broken her concentration on the journal, so she put the book back on her father's shelf and, once again, carefully and slowly reached for the lamp to turn it off. Even though it hadn't yet happened at home, she was still wary of all electronics, getting sick and tired of being shocked by everything she touched.

As she was sliding the office door closed to rejoin the party, someone grabbed and hugged her from behind. It was Cameron. He kissed her soft neck with his spongy lips and rubbed his smooth cheek beside hers. Vivian giggled and turned around. Standing on her toes, she kissed him and breathed in the smell of sweet cologne mixed with the scent of his leather football jacket.

She pressed herself into him more, looked into his eyes, and froze. Her eyes widened for a short second, and then a strong shock rushed through her torso, pushing her back to slam onto the floor. Vivian's limp body slid over the polished marble floors until she hit the wall and smacked her head on the corner of the office door frame.

"Vivian!" Cameron yelled in vain as the music kept playing loudly in the background. He slid down across the floor to Vivian's side, lifting her head and still calling her name, but she was out cold.

~ * ~

Vivian woke in her bed, Jacee and Celeste beside her, though both were lost in their phones. She could faintly see Cameron at the window.

"What happened?" she said, slowly sitting up. Jacee and Celeste looked up from their screens, and then the fuzzy form of Cameron came closer into Vivian's focus at the side of the bed.

"Viv, I don't know. You flew across the floor like you were electrocuted. I think it was because of my cell phone. I took it apart, but it seems fine. How do you feel?"

"I... I don't know. My head hurts. How long was I out? Is everybody still here?"

"Don't worry, we kicked everyone out who hadn't already left once they saw you unconscious," Celeste chimed in. She emphasized *unconscious* as if Vivian had been a drunken embarrassment rather than a lightning rod for a freak accident.

"Ugh... okay. Thanks, guys," Vivian huffed, wincing as she tried to blink away what felt like a fog over her whole bedroom.

"Do you need anything?" Jacee joined the conversation.

"Aspirin... and maybe ice. My hip..." Vivian managed, adjusting her position in her bed, trying to find a way to sit up comfortably.

"Oh no! Your Winter Formal dress is backless!" Celeste exclaimed in horror. "I'll get you that ice pronto. That bruise cannot show!"

Celeste left, and Jacee followed, giving Vivian some time with Cameron. He sat closer to Vivian on the bed, looking at her with concern.

"That's the second time this week you've gotten some kind of zap like that. I thought the first time it happened in home economics was a fluke. I know you hurt your finger pretty badly, but you didn't pass out anything, right?"

Vivian was rubbing her hip, taking it all in and trying to catch up after losing time from the hallway to her bedroom.

"I... I think... I don't know... ya. I feel like something strange is going on, Cam."

"I'll say."

"No, really. There was this book... and this weird girl," Vivian said weakly, trying to remember the details but struggling to make sense as she tried to explain.

"Sounds like a concussion dream to me," Cameron said with a smirk. He'd been knocked out before on the football field and knew what it was like to wake up feeling confused.

"You really need to rest. And if you don't feel better tomorrow, we might have to go to the hospital."

Vivian lay down to relax and let Cameron adjust her blankets and pillow. She had never seen Cameron act so caring before. She wanted to relax, she wanted to feel safe and let Cameron take care of her, but something kept her awake. Something wouldn't let her rest.

MILA

Mila hadn't stopped reading and researching since the night before. She took a few books home from Doctor Pavi's collection and spread them out to get to work. The spell hadn't worked, and while she and Doctor Pavi had a few theories of why, Mila was determined to find out for sure. Maybe, in the process, she'd also learn more about what they were dealing with.

What they had done—the half of a spell, the symbols on the floor—shifted something, and the interference had officially left the bounds of the school. Mila was definitely feeling it as she struggled to read through the research splayed out on her bedroom floor. These were ancient and creepy texts, but she knew for sure they were in English, yet Latin and ancient Greek words were poking their way in as she read. She did her best to catch the outlier words when they appeared and quickly jotted them down, hoping they'd lead her to something. But as she read over her notes, she could still see no connections.

To slow everything even more, Mila had to keep throwing everything under her newly assembled bed every time her mom knocked on the door. First, she came to announce that dinner was ready, and then later, she came asking if Mila was okay, suggesting over and over that she should go hang out with her friends on a Saturday night. Mila's response was what she always said: she had a lot of homework and felt like staying in to read. It was always what she said because it was always what she preferred to do, but her mom never stopped asking. Mila didn't see what was so great about going to parties like Soo did. She was perfectly content to continue reading and struggling to find something that would help them learn how to do the spell properly, to get the answers they were looking for, as soon as her mom would leave her alone.

Then Robin messaged her.

Robin: HEY, WHAT ARE YOU DOING? READING THOSE BOOKS?

Mila: TRYING. EACH PAGE IS TAKING ME AN HOUR

Robin: WHAT IF I CAME OVER AND HELPED?

Mila: YOU HATE READING

Robin: BE THERE IN TEN

Robin arrived in comfortable jogging pants, a hoodie, and pink socks with blue rubber bats on the bottom. Mila was in sweats, too, so it all felt like it could be a fun sleepover, minus the demonology study-group theme.

"Aren't you two just adorable," Mila's mom commented sweetly. "Should I bring up some snacks?"

"No!" Mila and Robin answered together.

"I mean, no, thank you," Robin said charmingly. "I already

had dinner, and we have a lot of work to do."

"We can get snacks if we need them later, ok mom?"

"Ok. Have fun," her mom called up the stairs as they scuttled away.

Mila's mom did a happy dance in the kitchen.

Once in the room, Mila brought the books out again from under the bed. Robin lay on her belly to read the texts as Mila took notes.

"This one says something about different kinds of demons. Do you think that's important?" Robin looked at Mila, who was already scribbling down the information.

"What do you mean by *kinds*?" Mila stressed the 'sss' sound in the plural. The idea of more than one type of demon needed an immediate explanation.

"Well, in this book, there are apparently nine levels of demons."

"Nine?" Mila whined, now somewhat regretting asking.

"Nine," Robin confirmed and then continued. "And then there are some specific jobs they do. One type is like a boss or *dominus,*"

"*Dom-i-nus,*" Mila mumbled as she wrote, trying to move on from the idea of nine separate kinds of demonic nightmares.

"But there are other jobs and levels too. Some negotiate with humans, some play tricks on people, and others control hellfire."

Robin stopped there and sat up. "Hellfire. Well, I guess we know what kind of demon I've got."

Robin pulled the book back onto her lap and continued reading in silence for another minute. She let out a sigh, slamming one of the books shut. "In that other book, they said there are four types, and now they're saying nine jobs. This is so confusing, Mi."

Robin moved the books to the side and stood up to stretch. Her black t-shirt lifted over her waist as she raised her hands nowhere near the top of the room. Mila smirked at how Robin's huge attitude certainly didn't match her petite size.

"Come on," Mila said, trying to speak softly to calm Robin

down and get her to focus again. "If we know what kind of demons we're dealing with, Doctor Pavi says, we have a better chance of getting rid of them. Can you help me find anything on summoning demons and what happens?"

Robin huffed as she sat back down and pulled one of the biggest books onto her lap. "I'll look again."

As the night went on, Mila could see how studying with Robin could be fun if the final exam wasn't summoning a demon. They giggled and made jokes despite the topics they were reading through—possession, blood spells, sacrifice. They were not only being productive but having a good time until they were interrupted by a small voice at the door.

"Miwa?" It was Gemma, standing in the doorway rubbing her tired eyes. *Oh no*, Mila thought, *had they been too loud?*

"Gemma, it's okay. Go back to bed," Mila whispered gently, hoping her mom wouldn't hear that Gemma was awake and it was probably Mila's fault. The lights in Mila's room flickered, and Gemma's small three-year-old form was only a tiny shadow in the doorway.

"I can't go, Miwa. The man said I have to tell you somefin."

Robin dropped the heavy book she was reading and pushed herself back towards Mila's bed with her mouth open. Mila's mouth went dry, and she could feel the pulse of her heart in her stomach.

"What man, Gem? What did he tell you?"

Gemma cocked her head to the side, her lips pulled over her few teeth like a feral dog, and she gave a deep growl. *"He said, 'No permission for young souls, girls. Our offer is not forever, so hurry.'"* Gemma's voice was low and smooth—not her own.

It felt as if all of the air had left the room. Mila didn't want to breathe or make any noise or movement. Her little sister was threatening them, baring her teeth. *What was she even saying?*

Then, as if she were sleepwalking, Gemma turned, waddled away from the doorway, and went back to her room. Robin came up to Mila's side, and they huddled together for a moment. Then Robin pointed at the door, and Mila followed beside her as they crawled from the room to look down the hall to watch Gemma get to her room and climb back into bed.

Mila sat back, shaking uncontrollably as Robin tried to hold her. Mila tried to speak and cover her mouth at the same time, in disbelief at what she saw. "That wasn't her, Robin. That couldn't be her voice." Robin tried to hold Mila up and stop her panicking, not wanting to disturb Gemma again or alert her mom downstairs.

Robin was eventually able to steady Mila and bring her back inside the bedroom. Mila felt like her feet were barely touching the floor, feeling like what she just saw didn't actually happen to her baby sister. The lights in Mila's bedroom had returned to normal, and the girls wearily sat back down on the floor.

Robin silently handed Mila her pen and paper. "Let's write it down, okay?"

Mila nodded and took the pen with a shaky hand but suddenly stopped. She turned to Robin and hugged her full-on, taking a deep breath so she wouldn't cry.

"My sister, Robin. My little sister," Mila's voice shook.

"I know, I know," Robin whispered, rubbing Mila's back softly.

When they finally broke, Mila sat back with a sigh and pushed her glasses up. Then she started to write what had just happened.

"No permission for young souls. Our offer is not forever, so hurry," Mila mumbled as she wrote. "*Well, I could hurry if you'd let me read,*" Mila said through her clenched jaw and gritted teeth.

"Mi? This means they can possess children without a spell or summoning—*without permission,*" Robin said slowly, her intense worry showing on her face. Mila knew she was thinking of her own little brother and sister.

It was Mila's turn to be the strong one. She steadied her voice, "That's why we have to hurry. We have to figure out what the hell they mean by an 'offer'."

Robin agreed, and they somehow got their focus back to continue working, though Mila went out to check on Gemma every ten minutes to see if she was still sleeping… and breathing. It wasn't a fun sleepover any longer.

In the morning, Robin was gone, and Mila woke up to see all the books and paper shoved neatly back under the bed. There was a note on her desk:

SEE YOU AT DR. P.'S

Mila instantly remembered Gemma and rushed to check on her, but when she opened her sister's bedroom door, she was gone. Thankfully, she instantly heard the familiar sounds of Sunday morning laughter of her mom and Gemma from the kitchen. She decided to take advantage of the moment to go into Gemma's room and check for anything lurking in the corners. Something had been in here and *inside* her sister.

Mila walked in further, cautiously looking around, lifting stuffed animals and blankets. She had no plan of action if she found anything there, but she had to look. At the closet door, she hesitated before sticking her head inside, but her heartbeat calmed when she noticed a stuffed bear on the closet floor. It once had been hers, but she had given it to Gemma at some point. She picked it up and hugged it tight. She was the big sister, after all.

Thankfully, everything was as it should be—some toys and crayons were out, probably from when Gemma woke up that morning, but nothing seemed out of place or particularly demonic. Mila grabbed a green crayon from the floor and wiggled under Gemma's bed on her back. It was a tight fit, but on the bottom of the wooden frame, as big as she could, she drew one of the protection spells she'd learned from her research. Guilt washed over her for not thinking of it sooner. She drew the triangles and circles that overlapped and did her best to reach her arms wide, making the lines thick. If she had been scared at all since this all started to happen, it was all gone now. Now she was angry.

ꝏocror Pavi

Doctor Andra Pavi was tired after two long, heavy nights smothered in demonology lore and teenager drama. But the reality was calling her back to fulfill her other duties as one of the only psychologists in Blackrock. Sundays at the hospital were for checking in on a couple of her patients in the psychiatric ward and then volunteering her time for a mental health group therapy session.

At Blackrock General, she signed in with her ID badge and made her way through the main building into the brightly lit common room of the psychiatric ward. One of the perks of the common room was the amazing view of the whole downtown of Blackrock itself. Immediately below the wall of windows, a soccer field and two impressive baseball diamonds were lush and still green. Large trees turning red and orange surrounded the park and loomed over the downtown area behind. She glanced at the view outside once before starting her check-ups. It was one of those clear days when you could see all the way to the lake.

Her first patient was an elderly man named Joseph, who was diagnosed as schizophrenic and sometimes got aggressive toward the nursing staff. But she'd never had any problems with him.

"And Ben. Never forget Ben." Joseph said.

"Why is that, Joseph? Who's Ben?"

"Ben Astra. Everyone knows Ben Astra. They're all gone now. And poor Kenny O'Toole. They're coming back to school soon. You tell them hello for me, okay?"

"Sure, I will," Doctor Pavi promised, smiling and taking notes. It was always the same with Joseph. He'd mention names of schoolmates he knew in the 1950s.

Doctor Pavi made her observations and left Joseph sitting in the sun in front of the window, staring outside. At the front desk, she passed her files to the orderly and was about to prepare for group therapy when a nurse rushed into the ward and approached her.

"Doctor Pavi? Doctor Monroe wondered if he could speak to you in Emergency." The nurse continued to walk backward out of the ward as she talked, knowing Doctor Pavi would follow her. Down on the first floor, the nurse directed her to the bed of a pretty young girl with expensive highlights and perfectly manicured nails.

"Doctor Pavi. Thank you for coming down," the young doctor addressed her. "I wonder if you would observe for a moment and tell me if there's anything here that falls into your line of work."

The girl's face was slack and unresponsive. The dark circles under her eyes didn't match the rest of her smooth dark skin, neat hair and manicured nails. The nurse adjusted her pillow and the wires attached, but the girl had no reaction, only stared off to the side and blinked like something was irritating her eyes.

"Of course," Doctor Pavi said, moving back to be a fly on the wall. The nurse adjusted more tubes on the girl as Doctor Monroe started to ask questions.

"Vivian, are you experiencing a headache?"

The girl slowly licked her lips and breathed heavily. "No," she said finally. "My head… is fine… it's electric."

Doctor Monroe glanced at Doctor Pavi, who leaned forward in interest.

"It's electric," the girl said again, seeming as though the words were taking a great effort and concentration. Then, a look of confusion began to shadow her face as though she wasn't sure of what she had just said.

"What do you mean, 'electric,' Vivian?" the doctor asked her.

"I don't mean to say… I can't… *Electric!*" Her voice was suddenly clear and powerful. She groaned and flung her arms so the wires flew and tugged on the machines. She pounded her fists into the hospital bed and began a scream that turned into a frantic cry.

The nurse and doctor held Vivian by the shoulder to lie her down. Vivian's eyes were wide and wet, but she didn't fight back. Her breathing settled as a nurse placed a cloth on her forehead before injecting something into her IV line. Tears streamed down

Vivian's face as she closed her eyes.

Doctor Pavi followed Doctor Monroe beyond the blue curtain, where he lowered his voice. "Her boyfriend brought her in after what he described as an electrical shock from a cell phone. He said she also injured her head on a door frame as she fell. And all she's been saying is this stuff about electricity and her head being 'electric.' " The doctor closed his notepad and looked at Doctor Pavi.

Doctor Pavi took a moment. "It could be a temporary amnesia or even shock, but I'd have to run a few more tests and observe her a little more."

Doctor Monroe agreed to let Doctor Pavi take some time to look closer.

"I have other patients right now, but I'll be back. You can take as much time as you need, and I'll return when I can." Doctor Monroe left the curtained stall to check on new patients coming into the emergency ward.

As Doctor Pavi moved into the room again, Vivian looked directly at her with no visible signs of disturbance. She looked relaxed now. Doctor Pavi smiled sympathetically at her, and Vivian gave a polite smile in return. *Interesting.* Doctor Pavi took a moment to check the vitals on the heart monitor and took down some initial readings. As she did, the levels became increasingly erratic, changing and increasing rapidly. Doctor Pavi looked from the monitor to Vivian, who hadn't moved from the bed and was sitting still. The monitor showed Vivian's heart starting to race at impossible levels though Vivian appeared fine—relaxed and breathing normally while the monitor was starting to beep in alarm. Doctor Pavi's stomach churned as the pointed heartbeat graphics smoothed out to a flatline, though Vivian still sat unchanged with sad eyes, her eyebrows furrowed.

Sneakers patted the floor towards them, and the room became crowded with two nurses and Doctor Monroe once more. He leaned Vivian forward to hear her lungs and heartbeat. "Completely normal," he said, looking at Doctor Pavi with relief. The two doctors left the room again to let the nurses get Vivian comfortable and remove the haywire heart monitor.

"Is the boyfriend still here?" Doctor Pavi asked.

"He's in the waiting room, I believe." Then, at the sound of a call alarm going off and a voice on the intercom mentioning him by name, Doctor Monroe perked up and flashed a smile. "Thank you, Doctor Pavi. We'll catch up later," he said quickly before he jogged off. Doctor Pavi watched him jog away and gave a short prayer of gratitude that she hadn't gone into traditional medicine.

~ * ~

The waiting room was full of people, but the handsome teenage boy on his phone was a dead giveaway.

She bent down to get his attention. "Hi, are you here with Ms. Voorhees? I'm Doctor Pavi, a psychologist here at the hospital."

The boy jerked his head upward and stood to greet her.

"Is Viv okay? She was saying such weird things I didn't know what to do," he said rapidly, all in one breath.

Doctor Pavi gave her most comforting smile to hopefully calm some of the boy's nerves. "You did well bringing her in. Do you mind if I ask you some more questions about what happened?" She gestured for him to take a seat as she quickly checked her watch and sat beside him. She had some time before her group therapy session began upstairs.

Cameron retold the event as he remembered, but he didn't know what Vivian had been doing before he saw her come out of the library. He only saw her after.

"So all of this happened at a party?" Doctor Pavi asked.

Cameron nodded shyly as he admitted it all to an adult. "Her parents are out of town, and she's had a rough week, so…"

She remembered Soo had run from a party where she saw another book and another girl who might be having incidents like the rest of them. Doctor Pavi tried to get more information from him before she made any conclusions about Vivian being connected to the other girls. "Why was she having a rough week, Cameron?" Doctor Pavi asked.

"Well, first, she got shocked pretty badly from a microwave at school, and then it caught on fire. Then her cell phone stopped working, and, like I said, her parents are both gone right now, so she's had no phone all week. Kind of annoying, y'know?" Cameron clapped his phone between his two hands.

"Yes, I can imagine," Doctor Pavi tried not to chuckle. "Do you happen to remember some of the things she was saying before you brought her here?"

"At home, she was babbling about a girl and a book... and a dream about... lemons or something. But it was the way she was saying it—it made no sense. It was like she was talking to herself but getting confused. But then she was pretty quiet on the ride over here. I think she was sleeping, actually."

Doctor Pavi thanked Cameron and told him to go home and that they would call if there was any news. She made her way back to Vivian's bed in the emergency ward and peeked at her through the curtain. Vivian was asleep and breathing normally. Doctor Pavi sighed as she peered in. *Why was this happening to them,* she wondered. *Why does it always have to be young, innocent girls?*

Walking to the elevator to return upstairs, she called Soo.

"Soo, it's Doctor Pavi."

"Are we meeting today?" Soo asked boldly, clearly chewing something on the other end as she talked.

"Yes, we are, but I have a question first. Was the girl you were talking about named Vivian?"

"How'd you know?" Soo's voice cleared as she swallowed.

"I can't say right now, but I need you to find out exactly what happened at the party. Can you see if there's anything on social media or someone who was there that can tell us more? I need you to be caught up on what happened there after you left."

Soo was obviously confused but agreed. "Ugh, sure. Okay, Doctor P. Anything else?"

"Ya, don't call me Doctor P.," Doctor Pavi playfully scolded.

"Gotcha. Sorry. I'll see you later, Doctor *Pavi*," Soo said with exaggeration and a small laugh before hanging up.

After a productive group therapy session, Doctor Pavi went once again to the emergency ward to see Vivian, but she was gone. Checking at the front desk, the same nurse who had gotten her earlier said she had been moved to a private room.

"Her parents are the Voorhees', Doctor," the nurse said, looking above the rims of her glasses. "Private. Room."

"Gotcha," Doctor Pavi said. "Where is she then?"

8

VIVIAN

Cameron called Vivian's parents to tell them about what had happened. Neither of them could get back right away, but Vivian's father put in a call to have her placed into a private room until he could get back from China.

Vivian had a nice window that looked out over the soccer field and a television of her own. *Just don't fall asleep again, no sleeping,* she told herself over and over. *No dreaming. No nightmares.* Tears pooled in her eyes as she looked up at the speckled ceiling. Then her head snapped down and forward when she heard someone walking in. Her eyesight was still a little fuzzy from the concussion, but as the figure came closer, Vivian could see it was the pretty doctor from before. Vivian hoped she would have some good news or at least stay with her a while for some company. She smiled brightly because it was all she could do.

"Vivian? It's Doctor Pavi. I see you've got a comfortable space here," the doctor said, looking around at the large room. "Can we talk?"

Vivian sat forward, smiled, and nodded at the doctor. She wanted to say so much more, but all she could do was nod her head 'yes'. She tried harder and harder to speak, but her voice was gone, or *taken...* She stared into Doctor Pavi's eyes directly to let her know there was more she wanted to say but couldn't. *Why couldn't she talk?* It was one thing to have her voice hijacked, saying nonsensical things, but not being able to talk was definitely more terrifying. Out of frustration, she started to cry silently—no moans or screams, only tears streaming around her open mouth.

"Okay, okay. Let's calm down. I understand. We can do this a little differently. If you can nod yes and no, we can do this. Can you show me a nod again, 'yes'?"

Vivian nodded more gently now, calming down as Doctor Pavi sat on the bed.

"Good," Doctor Pavi had a calm, soothing voice, and Vivian appreciated it while wiping the last tear from her cheek.

"Can you shake your head, 'no'?"

Vivian shook her head gently from side to side, her black and copper hair flowing easily with her. She could smell her own coconut shampoo, and the familiar scent calmed her even more.

"Okay, Vivian, do you remember being at your party?"

Vivian nodded.

"Do you remember being shocked and having a fall?"

Vivian nodded.

"Do you remember what you were doing before you were shocked?"

Vivian nodded.

"Were you reading something?"

Vivian nodded slower, suspicious of where this was all going.

"Was it yours?"

Vivian shook her head, not taking her eyes off the doctor. She really hoped this woman wasn't working for her father, which was always a possibility in Blackrock. But strangely, Vivian somehow felt like the doctor genuinely wanted to help her and wanted her to feel comfortable. And she never felt that way around anyone who was associated with her father, or her father himself, for that matter.

"Was it a book of symbols?" Doctor Pavi continued.

Vivian's head moved back, and her whole body stiffened—*there's no way she could have guessed that,* she thought. And in that second, Vivian wanted to get away. Her hip hurt too much to move from the bed, but she pushed the blankets with her good leg toward the doctor and moved backward, creating as much distance between them as possible.

"Vivian, calm down… I'm here to help you. I swear," the doctor assured her, showing the palms of her hands. "I think I know what's going on with you, but I need you to answer my questions so I can help you properly."

Vivian stayed back from the doctor at the head of her bed, breathing heavily and looking around for a way to get out.

Doctor Pavi continued, "I know this is strange, but it's all connected to the book you were reading and the girl you kicked out of your house."

Vivian flinched, and her eyelashes fluttered. *That weird girl she called a freak? The girl that was in her dreams or nightmares every time she closed her eyes since Friday night when this all happened?*

Doctor Pavi pulled the blankets over Vivian's legs and sat on the bed close beside her. She spoke softly and slowly. Vivian stayed still, eyeing the doctor as she moved closer.

"Soo is a patient of mine too. Similar things are happening to her and two other girls your age at your school."

Vivian flinched at the word 'patient'. She didn't want to be anybody's *patient.* She just wanted everything to be over so she could go home. But looking at the doctor's pleading and kind face, she tried to relax and listen. Doctor Pavi helped her fix the blankets even more and straightened the pillows behind her.

Vivian took a deep breath and gestured eagerly for Doctor Pavi to continue.

"Was it a book of symbols?"

Vivian nodded and prepared herself for what she might learn next.

Soo

Soo: HEY, ARE YOU MAD AT ME?

Faye: NO, NOT MAD… BUT WHERE'D YOU GO ON FRIDAY?

Soo: SORRY. MY MOM CALLED ME TO COME HOME RIGHT AWAY—SORRY I DIDN'T SAY GOODBYE

Faye: NO WORRIES. THE PARTY FINISHED SOON AFTER YOU LEFT, ANYWAY

Soo: REALLY? IT SEEMED LIKE IT WAS GOING STRONG

Faye: SOMETHING HAPPENED TO VIVIAN, AND WE ALL LEFT

Soo: WHAT HAPPENED?

Faye: SHE GOT ELECTROCUTED AND FELL AND HIT HER HEAD. IT WAS HORRIBLE. SHE WENT TO THE HOSPITAL

Soo, reread the message to be sure. This had to be what Doctor Pavi wanted her to find out.

Soo: OMG, THAT'S AWFUL. IS SHE OK, NO?

Faye: NOBODY KNOWS. HER BF CAMERON HASN'T SAID MUCH. I THINK SHE'S OK NOW. BUT YOU KNOW HOW SECRETIVE RICH PEOPLE CAN BE. ANYWAYS, IS EVERYTHING OK WITH U? HOPE IT WASN'T SERIOUS

Soo: IT'S OK NOW.

Faye: MAYBE WE COULD DO SOMETHING AGAIN… SOMETIME?

Soo: YA, FOR SURE! TALK LATER?

Faye: ABSOLUTELY, HUN. BFN:)

Soo wanted to know more about that 'hun' part, but she had other things to deal with at the moment. Her parents would never believe she was having therapy on a Sunday, so she had to lie and say she was going to watch swimming on TV at a teammate's house.

Pedaling over to Doctor Pavi's to meet the other girls, she had time to think about everything going on and tried to put together everything that was happening lately—*How did Vivian fit into all this? Why was Faye so adorable? Did Vivian hate her? Did Faye call everyone 'hun'?*

Soo's daydream came to a sharp end as she reached Doctor Pavi's house. Maybe once all of this was over, she wouldn't need to go to Doctor Pavi for therapy anymore. The thought tugged at her mind with disappointment. She liked therapy, actually. She didn't have anyone else to really talk to about the pressure she was under on the swim team, her parents' strange relationship, and her insecurities around cute girls like Faye.

She sighed at her overabundance of thoughts and parked her bicycle before going inside. But her steps halted in mid-stride as she found Robin and Mila spread out all over the demonic symbols on Doctor Pavi's floor, scoffing down burritos and extra-large drinks.

"What's up?" Robin asked with her mouth full. "Want some nachos?"

"Um, no thanks," Soo said, dropping her backpack. "But I got some news about Vivian."

"Oooh," Mila said after she swallowed all her food and brushed the crumbs from her hands, "What did you find out?"

"She's in the hospital. Something about being electrocuted. Faye didn't know much more than that."

"Faye? Who's Faye?" Robin asked with a teasing voice.

"Robin, focus!" Mila scolded on Soo's behalf, which Soo appreciated. Then Mila continued, earnestly looking at Soo. "So what are we supposed to do now?"

"Is Doctor Pavi not here?" Soo asked, looking around.

"No, not yet," Mila answered, checking the time to see Doctor Pavi was a few minutes late.

"Well," Soo began, "I'm going to guess she's thinking what we're thinking…"

"That we all have to be together for the summoning spell to work," Mila said, finishing Soo's thought.

"Let's just hope Vivian is the last one," Robin added. "This is the weirdest thing to ever happen at our school."

"Ya, since that fire in the sixties or whenever that was," Soo added.

"Oh ya. The Blackrock High Maaaassssaaacre…" Robin said in her best ghost story voice.

"What massacre?" Mila asked with scrunched eyebrows and a mouthful of burrito.

"A really bad fire broke out at a dance, like, sixty years ago, and almost everyone in the junior class was killed," Soo said dryly, snagging one of Mila's fries. Mila didn't even notice.

"Mi, you okay?" Robin asked.

Mila gave her head a small shake. "Ya," she answered with some pause. "I just remembered that I've heard this story before. There's a picture at the school, but I guess I didn't make the connection that they were just juniors… like us."

"It's been sixty-*six* years, actually," Robin mumbled, lettuce spilling beyond her lips.

Mila squirmed.

"Right. But I doubt any of the stuff that's been happening to us has anything to do with that. That was so long ago, and nothing's happened since," Soo said, attempting to assure Mila and maybe even herself.

"Nothing really happens in this town at all," Robin added with a scoff.

"But one of the books was *at* the school," Mila said, wide-eyed.

"Are books all you think about?" Robin teased, quickly stealing a french fry from Mila's container.

Soo chuckled as Mila gave Robin a fake angry face. Then they all laughed and went back to chomping on their food and waited for Doctor Pavi.

"Hey guys, just a thought," Robin started slowly as she casually dug back into her burrito. "If we all got here because we all were shown the books, how come I don't have a book of my own? Do you think that'll matter?"

It was a good question. Four girls but only three Summoners. Soo turned to Mila for the answer because books were her forté, after all.

Mila chewed the inside of her cheek for the answer. "No, it won't matter!"

Startled by Mila's volume, Robin squeezed her burrito, and special sauce dripped from the bottom.

"Why not?" Soo asked, seeing Robin was dealing with burrito guts on her pantyhose.

"We're four girls with only three Summoners because one of us can't read." Mila sharply pointed two thumbs at her own chest and then slumped into a pout.

Soo immediately recognized Mila's frustration of not being able to do her favorite thing. She knew how defeated Mila felt about not being able to read books. Just like Soo would do almost anything to get back to swimming.

"And one who can't speak," Doctor Pavi called from the doorway, walking in with a limping Vivian Voorhees.

ROBIN

"What the hell, Doctor P.?"

"Please don't call me Doctor P.," Doctor Pavi groaned as she brought Vivian to lie down on the sofa.

"Hi Vivian, I'm Mila," Mila introduced herself with a cheerful wave.

"She can't answer you, Mila," Doctor Pavi said, trying her best to sound sympathetic to Vivian.

As she looked around the room, Robin couldn't help but share her skepticism. "So, she can't talk, you can't read—what is this, The Helen Keller Society of Demons?" Robin laughed to herself.

"That makes no sense," Mila scolded Robin in a sisterly tease.

Vivian lay on the sofa uncomfortably, looking at all the girls and then at the demonic symbols on the floor. She rolled her eyes, scoffed, and turned her head away to the back of the sofa.

"Vivian? I'm Soo." Soo said, peering over to catch Vivian's eye and introducing herself. "I was at your party? We, ugh, met in your library?"

Vivian's head lifted. She moved slowly, signaling she wanted to sit up. Soo held out her hand to help, and for a quick second, Robin noted the difference in their hands. Despite the hospital bracelet on her wrist, her dark skin still glowed. Her nails were delicate and perfectly manicured. Soo's hands, in contrast, were large, chapped from chlorine, and her nails were cut as short as possible.

Vivian sat up slowly with Soo's help. There were dark circles under her eyes, but they were the only blemish on her otherwise 'Ms. Perfect' face. Vivian gestured for a pen, and Mila handed her a notepad and pencil.

SORRY, I YELLED AT YOU BEFORE. IS THIS FOR REAL?

She handed her note to Soo, and Soo chuckled as she read.

"It's for real," Soo confirmed, nodding.

Robin rolled her eyes as she watched Vivian and Soo exchange love notes. Then she turned her attention back to Doctor Pavi, who was flipping through the third Summoner, cross-checking for any inconsistencies.

"Where'd that one come from?" Robin asked.

"The Voorhees' library," Doctor Pavi said with one eyebrow raised, nodding towards Vivian.

"So you went there after you broke Vivian out of the hospital?" Robin asked, tilting her head towards Doctor Pavi. Robin wasn't doing a great job of keeping their conversation quiet, and Mila gave Robin a pleading look from across the room to go easier on Doctor Pavi.

"Vivian signed herself out, refusing care," Doctor Pavi said firmly. "I just offered to give her a drive to her house. She invited me inside, where we chatted about her father's library and—"

"I thought you said she can't talk," Robin cut her off.

"She can gesture yes or no, and she can write," she pointed to Vivian and Soo on the sofa.

Robin couldn't help feeling feisty and uneasy. She didn't want Doctor Pavi to calm her down with her 'doctor voice.' She had a rotten history with Vivian Voorhees and her popular entourage over the years.

"But why are we helping her?" Robin pleaded, still not bothering to quiet her voice at all. She didn't care if Vivian heard. Vivian, along with Jacee and Celeste, were horrible to Robin growing up. They teased her all the time for being poor and used to call her 'Robin Raw Beans' and sing *La Cucaracha* when she walked by. They looked down on everyone like they were superior just because of who their parents were. But to Robin, Vivian was the worst of all. Robin couldn't understand why she would join in the racist teasing with two white girls. Didn't she have any self-respect?

"She's having a hard time, just like you, Robin," Doctor Pavi softly scolded.

"She's nothing like me," Robin snapped. "She's a total rich bitch who could rot inside the hospital forever for all I care." She was sure Vivian heard her that time.

"Robin, please," Doctor Pavi half scolded and pleaded for her to be more reasonable.

Robin quickly glanced at Soo and knew what she had to do. She dashed past Vivian and Soo, grabbed her vape from her coat, and stormed out of the room, not bothering to close the door behind her.

How could they be so blind? And how could Vivian even be one of them, Robin wondered. *She was always so perfect, and her father could probably buy back her sanity anyway. And who's to say it isn't all a setup for her to get into their nerdy club and tease them for believing demons are real?*

Not long after Robin's thoughts stopped spinning, Mila squeaked open the screen door and came to join her on the porch, hugging herself in the cold. "Something's gone on between you two before, hasn't it?" Mila's teeth chattered as she spoke.

Robin squared her eyes with Mila's. "She's a bully, Mi. You have no idea."

Mila leaned against the porch rail. "There were popular kids at my other school too." Mila paused. "But we need her, Rob. And if you let her get in the way of all of this, she'll hurt you again. We need to do this spell to find out how we can all get over this and move on with our lives."

"I know," Robin exhaled, feeling calmer being outside with Mila. Then Mila reached out to Robin awkwardly, feeling like it was maybe a hug-it-out kind of moment. Robin was caught off guard at first but then fell into her, surrendering. It had been a long time since she had a friend to hug. And she had never had someone who would check on her when she was upset.

"Please come back in. It's freezing out here!" Mila smiled and went inside. Robin took a minute to get herself together again and ready herself to deal with Vivian, feeling a little better knowing she had a friend on her side now.

Robin decided not to speak to Vivian directly since she had nothing nice to say to her. She so badly would love to tell her where to go—tell her exactly what she thought of her and her idiot sidekicks while she had no one here to defend her and no way of talking back. But then again, she barely wanted to look at her stupid rich face and expensive hair and nails. She really was beautiful, and her hair still shone after all she had been through. Even her hoodie and track pants were designer labels. *She probably has no other problems in the world,* Robin thought.

MILA

"Should we uncover the spells in the third book, Doctor?" Mila asked as the two of them separated and cut pieces of dried sage for the summoning to purify the space before and after the spell.

"I think we have enough with the two, and we can keep this one safe in my locked cabinet."

Mila gave a small nod and worked her courage up to ask her next question. She didn't want to hurt Doctor Pavi's feelings by asking, but she was so curious about what she had gone through before coming to Blackrock.

Mila cleared her throat. "How are you feeling now that we've found three books here in a short time when you were at a loss before… to find even one?"

Doctor Pavi gave a surprised smile like she all at once hated and appreciated the question. "Well, I feel like Blackrock might have more secrets than I originally thought, and it feels good to be on to something."

Mila smiled. She didn't really know much about Blackrock either. Before her family decided to move, she hadn't done any research on the town at all. She hadn't been very excited to know more about a place she didn't want to be. And considering what she was doing now, it wouldn't really have mattered anyway. No Internet site would have warned her about the demons that possess adolescent girls at the local high school.

Mila stood at the desk and double-checked they had everything they'd need. Doctor Pavi had the two books with the spell revealed on her desk. Next to them were the smudge sticks of sage and raw cinnamon to burn for strength and protection as they recited the spell. The black candles were lit all around, creating a soft glow and warming the room. Incense, candles, and extra cinnamon sticks lay in a small basket to the side. Doctor Pavi reached into her desk, pulled out a small wooden bundle resembling a figure, and held it out to Mila. Mila took the twigs wrapped in red yarn and stared at Doctor Pavi blankly, awaiting an explanation.

"Rowan wood. Extra protection for the reader. Put her in your pocket," Doctor Pavi explained, and Mila carefully placed the makeshift doll in the waistband of her skirt.

"We're ready, ladies," Mila announced. She carried over the books, a bundle of sage, and a chunky candle to place on the floor.

Soo and Robin got up to help bring some of the candles closer to the circle.

Doctor Pavi went to Vivian, "Can you try to stand? I'll help and hold you up for the ceremony so you can join hands with the other girls."

Vivian moved slowly, and Doctor Pavi supported her to stay upright. Robin waited for Soo to go between her and Vivian, then Mila could hold Robin's hand and have Vivian on the other side. This was no time for Robin to create more tension with Vivian.

Each girl stood on one of the four marks Robin had painted out. Mila took a moment to glance at each of them to reaffirm why she was doing this. She wasn't sure which was scarier, summoning a demon or speaking in front of people. It was all new, and there was a lot at stake. Somehow, though, with her love for these girls, her love of reading, and maybe even a newfound love of her new hometown, she was finding strength. She was more than ready to summon some demons and get on with her new life.

The spellbook easily opened to the page Mila had been memorizing, and the words quickly began to dance and move around the page. Thank goodness she already knew what she had to say.

At Mila's signal, the girls began to chant, "*Nos autem vocamus,*

Nos autem vocamus…"

    "We call you."

She wasn't sure how many times they were supposed to say the chant, but the girls continued as Mila said the Latin spell over top of their voices.

"Demon, demons, to circle we call

We call you to circle to be known and seen by all

Show yourselves to be seen

Demon, demons, we call on you and your scheme

Show us your will, reveal your truth

Demon, demons, we call you to circle to be known

Apparete…"

Mila kept an eye out for anything different, making eye contact with the other girls who weren't breaking in their chanting. Even Vivian was attempting to lip-sync the words, but nothing was happening. A hot panic began to creep up Mila's spine, and her face flushed in stupidity. How could they have fallen for this? How could she have really thought demons were real? *Look at us—no better than girls playing Bloody Mary at a sleepover.* She joined the girls in their chanting and decided to continue until Doctor Pavi called it off.

But as Mila joined the chant, the flames of the candles grew as high as her hips. Startled, everyone stopped chanting whether they were supposed to or not, gazing into what was forming in the middle of the summoning circle. A cloud of blue fog was rising from the floor, spiraling and slowly beginning to separate. It whirled as it broke into four separate clouds and then spun into four separate shapes that stood still in the middle and faced outward. Four ghostly outlines of slim figures, the size of small children, floated expectantly, evenly spaced—one for each girl.

Besides the singe of wick and wax, the room was dead silent as everyone took in what they were seeing. One wisp of blue outline hovered in front of each of them, unblinking, waiting. If it weren't for their silent, faceless expressions and the faint outline of horns on their heads, they'd be rather precious, even cute, Mila dared to think.

Mila could see straight through her wisp to the other side of the circle to where Soo was looking through to her too. Robin squeezed Mila's hand tightly, which she knew meant, *holy crap, this worked!*

For what was only a few seconds but felt like an eternity, the ghost-like figures and the four girls considered each other, all frozen in their spots. Then, slowly, the ghostly goat-children held out one smoky arm each and uncurled all of their long, sinewy fingers in unison. The hands invisibly tugged at the girls' chests to pull a white glowing stream from each of their hearts like four spokes connected and powering a wheel.

Though there were four individual ghosts, they moved and completed the work as one. Together they moved back and became a collected cloud of white-blue fog that faded and disappeared back into the center of the symbols on the floor once again.

"Is that it?" Robin scoffed.

"Shh!" Something told Mila it was just the beginning.

Several heavy and silent seconds passed until a loud *thud* got everyone's attention. Doctor Pavi had fallen, and Vivian wasn't far behind as her human crutch crumpled. By sheer reaction, the girls broke the circle and rushed over. They helped Vivian up and off the doctor, but they couldn't budge Doctor Pavi, who was convulsing vigorously.

"Oh my god, guys, what did we do?" Soo spun around the room in a panic.

"Doesn't anyone know how to stop a seizure?" Robin yelled.

"You can't," said Mila, "We have to just wait it out!" She didn't know why they were all yelling when the room itself was so quiet.

Doctor Pavi shook on the floor in the fetal position. But the more she seized, the more it was clear she was moving—drifting closer to the center of the circle. The girls stood around helpless as they looked on.

Soo tried to step in, but Mila grabbed her arm and looked into her eyes with a warning. They weren't to go past the symbols' edges—Doctor Pavi made that clear. Soo got the message and went back to her post. The four girls stood where they were before, and even Vivian made an effort to stand on her own, though hunched over and leaning on Soo's strong arm for support.

Doctor Pavi uncurled from her position on the floor, and her eyes began darting around the room.

"Doctor P.?... Are you okay?" Robin asked, trying to tease her a little to see if she could laugh it all off.

Doctor Pavi stood up slowly but fully and confidently brushed herself off before walking the circle's borders. Then suddenly, she spun and turned on her heel to glare at Robin particularly. "She really hates it when you call her that," the voice said, adjusting the cuffs of Doctor Pavi's white dress shirt. The four girls gazed forward at Doctor Pavi, or whoever it was.

"Doctor Pavi?" Mila asked, just in case she had guessed wrong about what was happening.

"Mmm, not exactly. But I'm going to borrow your doctor's suit while we all chat. Have a seat." At the wave of the demon's hand, each girl was flung down hard onto the painted floor. Vivian winced as she landed on her sore hip.

"Firstly, I must thank you for figuring out everything so quickly. It usually takes a few more tries, but you girls are pretty... *sharp*." Its eyes settled on Mila this time, who tried to turn away from the uncomfortable stare, but no one could take their eyes away from Doctor Pavi and her new voice.

"Next, I want to give you the answers you're looking for, so let me start by summing it all up... I want to make a deal, and you're going to want to take it."

"Doubt that," mumbled Robin, and Mila gave her a 'mom' look of *'be quiet, Robin and pay attention, for godsakes!'*

The demon spun around and moved closer to Robin in smooth, graceful steps, like Doctor Pavi, yet clearly not her either. Doctor Pavi had a beautiful posture but never held her chin so high or grinned so slyly. The demon stretched down, close to the edge of the circle, and right up to Robin's nose. Robin kept a snarl on her face but didn't move away.

"Mmm…your doctor is screaming in here, y'know—she really cares for you all—so sweet," the demon said sarcastically, and then gave a small giggle, so unsettling that it made Mila shiver.

"She says you shouldn't take the deal." The demon crouched down further on the balls of its feet to speak to the girls more closely, who were all still sitting in their places.

"But here's what she doesn't know." The demon took a moment to make poignant eye contact with each of them, reveling in the news it was about to report. "You're all going to die."

"*What the f*—" Robin tried to stand up but couldn't get past a squat before she was frozen in place by a flick of the demon's finger.

Mila tried to catch her eye again to say, *Don't, Robin!* But the demon had already done something so that Robin couldn't move again. Mila, too, could feel the hold on her own body get stronger. Soo was also sitting in place, her face fixed on Doctor Pavi in a worried stare. Vivian was holding back tears, surely in part from the pain of her injuries.

Mila had two thoughts: Did it really just say they were going to die, meaning it was going to kill them now?

The demon looked deep into Mila's eyes like it had been reading her mind. "So I'm sure you all want to know what I mean." It grinned at Mila. "And to answer your questions. No, unfortunately, it's not me who's killing you." The demon walked up to Robin, who was still stuck in place, crouched like a cat about to pounce.

"It's actually another high roller. I'm sure you've heard of… Lady Destiny?" The demon reached out and ran a finger up from Robin's throat to her chin, and its voice trailed off. "And you thought demons were sadistic. Well, *She* wants you, *all of you*, before you even reach your twentieth year." It announced before walking to the middle of the circle again with a shrug.

"Destiny? You're lying," Soo said through tears, hoping it couldn't be true.

"You're…" Mila started with a stutter, hoping the demon wouldn't shut her down like Robin. "You're saying we're all already doomed to die before we're twenty? That we're all sick or something." It was more of a confirmation than a question.

"You are the smart one, aren't you, Mila," the demon said, mimicking Mila's confirming tones.

"Bull! I don't feel sick!" Robin spat.

The demon shook its head and sighed, barely reacting to Robin's remark. "Oh. You will. Soon too." It smiled and faced Mila as it spoke.

"So, what do you want from us?" Soo chimed in.

"I want to make a deal," it answered as it moved near Vivian and Soo. "Lend me your bodies, here and there, and my presence in your sickly skin suitcases will keep you alive for the foreseeable future."

"Like heal us?" Mila called to move it away from Vivian, who was already vulnerable.

It turned back to Mila on the balls of Doctor Pavi's feet. "Sadly, no." It said with an overly dramatic pout. "Demon work isn't healing, sweet, Mila." It swiveled back to Soo. "But it *is* bonding. Once you're bound to me, you can't die." It smiled slyly and gave a twirl of Doctor Pavi's hands like it was making the greatest offer the girls had ever heard.

"But there's only one of you," Mila called again.

"Yes, yes. You'll have to share. But I'm sure you'll find there's enough of me to go around."

"Why us? Why don't you stay inside, Doctor Pavi, and do what you want?" Soo charged, regaining more confidence in her voice. But as soon as the words left her lips, she regretted her suggestion of giving up Doctor Pavi to the demon.

"Like I said, she's screaming in here. And as much as I do love the sounds of a good torture, I need quiet concentration for the project I'm working on. I need bodies that are young, willing, and able. I thought you four were the perfect opportunity I just couldn't pass up."

"How do we know you're not lying? How can we believe we're

actually supposed to die in three years?" Soo asked what everyone was thinking.

"You don't, I suppose." The demon said, standing and adjusting Doctor Pavi's blazer to address them all formally. "So here's the other option: I stick around, play my tricks, and the last three years of your lives become constant torture. No reading for you," the demon said, pointing with one of Doctor Pavi's long, dark nails at Mila.

"No talking for you," it said to Vivian.

"No swimming for you, Miss Kim, and likely jail for you, Rodriguez," it said with an unapologetic shrug.

"That's blackmail! You can't do this!" Robin managed to say through stiff lips.

"I'm a demon, honey. Blackmail's kind of our jam..."

And with that, the room fell silent.

"By the way, Miss Voorhees, on this little conference call, you actually can participate. So...anything to add?"

Mila could see by Vivian's expression that she wasn't even aware she could speak. Vivian cleared her throat, "What— what would we have to do?" Her voice was hoarse, but the question was clear, and Mila had been thinking the same thing.

"You're not seriously considering this?" Robin snapped at Vivian.

"I'm just getting details," Vivian said back sharply. "If it's a deal, I want to know what the terms are and what our bodies would be... doing."

Robin scoffed and shook her head at the ceiling.

The demon took a beat before it responded. "Well, that's the thing. I can't really say."

"Can't or won't?"

"Won't, actually, since you asked, Rodriguez. It's not really your business."

"How isn't it our business if we're the ones doing the dirty work?" Robin charged.

"Well, it's not dirty, I'll tell you that much. More like… demonic bureaucracy. Paperwork, really."

Mila knew better. Demons don't possess people, so they can dot their *Is* and cross their *Ts*. But she also knew they would probably never get a perfectly straight answer. And if all of them were dying anyway, this might be a possible option until they figured out something else.

"Well, this has been nice, but I really can't stay here all night. I've been kind enough to answer your questions, so I'll give you some time to think about it. You have, let's say, a nice round number, like… sixty-six hours to give me your decision." Its voice was almost cheery and rising at the end like a young waitress saying she'd come back after you'd read the menu.

"But that's not even three days," Mila complained.

"Will you leave us alone until then?" Vivian asked, nearly begging to not lose her ability to speak again.

"You have my word."

"Whatever that means," Robin grumbled. Mila's head turned again at Robin's brazen attitude against an actual demon they had summoned from hell. She didn't know whether to think Robin was brave or completely insane.

"But remember this, Rodriguez: only you know your dark side and what you're capable of with the slightest of nudges. Wouldn't want Big Sis to lose her cool with the little ones, would we?"

Robin turned white, losing the flush of red from her frustration all at once.

"And that reminds me, Mila." The demon approached her and bent down once again to look her straight in the face. "I apologize for the mishap with little Gemma. I don't often like to communicate that way, but I had to know you were doing all you could to call on me, so we could have this nice little chat."

Mila's memory flashed to Gemma standing at her door that night. She knew the demon wasn't actually apologizing but reminding her in its twisted way what it was capable of… the vulnerability of her family… of all of them.

"Please don't hurt her." Mila tried not to quiver as she spoke.

The demon leaned in even closer, and Mila closed her eyes to hold herself still even though she was just inches away from the beast inside Doctor Pavi.

The demon whispered only to her. "Think about the deal… get all your friends convinced… and I won't have to…"

9

Vivian

The demon stepped back to the middle of the circle, walking with an arrogance Vivian had never thought possible. She'd known arrogant people before—her father and many of his colleagues could easily be described this way, but this was another level. Not a speck of humanity shone through. Standing before her was a being that was not only propelled by ego but also had supernatural powers to exercise its selfish will.

As it reached the center of the circle, it took one last silent look around at the girls. Then, tapping the face of Doctor Pavi's gold watch, the body fell to the floor like a heavy pile of laundry, and the candles went out on their own. As soon as the demon was gone, it immediately felt like the room was refilled with oxygen, and Vivian took a deep breath of relief. The girls rushed to Doctor Pavi, who was lying on the floor, unconscious.

"Is she alive?" Robin asked as Soo held her wrist and had two fingers on her throat.

"There's a pulse. Let's get her to the sofa," Soo said, supporting Doctor Pavi's body from one side.

Vivian watched the girls lift the doctor and start the work of caring for her, finding blankets and pillows and getting water. Not too many hours ago, Vivian didn't even know who Doctor Pavi was, but she already found herself caring deeply about whether or not she would wake up. Before any of this, Vivian always felt like a normal girl who had everything going for her. But now, just in the last two days, she had been hospitalized, gotten dragged to some sort of therapy cult with girls from her school she never talked to, and finished a 'chat' with an actual demon who wanted to possess her part-time. Even though she knew she could talk, she had no idea what to say about any of this.

Doctor Pavi slowly sat up and drank some water. Her voice scratched at first, "You girls know it's full of crap, right?" Her first few words landed softly on Vivian's ears after just listening to the demon's gruff drawl from the same mouth.

The girls exchanged glances while Vivian stared at Doctor Pavi. They'd never heard her say 'crap' before, and for a moment, Vivian wondered if it was really the doctor. Doctor Pavi caught her confusion.

"Girls, it's me now. I swear. And look, there's no way the demon knows if you're going to—"

"Die?" Vivian finished from across the circle.

Everyone turned to her with surprise when she spoke—partially for being so blunt, but it was also a reminder that they had been released from their individual torments, at least for the next two and a half days.

"Yes. Thank you, Vivian. Demons can't see the future," Doctor Pavi said as she took more sips of water. "At least not that far off."

"But she said—it said," Mila corrected herself. "Something about Lady Destiny. Is she real too?"

Doctor Pavi sat thoughtfully and handed her cup back to Soo while she sat straighter. "It's possible, but that's not how Fortune or Lady Destiny works either—at least in the myths. First of all, she's blind, and she doles out fortunes from the fall of her wheel, but she's not psychic—it's all considered arbitrary. So whatever the demon's talking about is some sort of trick—you're not dying."

"What about those weird spirits at the beginning of the spell? There were four of them. Why'd we only get to talk to one demon?" Robin asked. Vivian didn't want to admit it because Robin said it, but it was her thought too.

"It's been only one demon the whole time, apparently. The others, I think, are *daemons*." Doctor Pavi's voice was getting weaker as she talked, so the girls looked to Mila for an explanation.

Mila was definitely a contrast to Vivian's other friends, who were on permanent diets, rarely did homework, and had laser eye surgery before they could be caught dead wearing glasses. But she was smart and obviously the one to listen to when it came to the ins and outs of demons.

Mila sat up straight and pushed her glasses farther up her nose as she began. "From what I've read, daemons are liminal beings, meaning they aren't good or evil. Instead, they're messengers or sometimes slaves that do the bidding of different, larger, more powerful entities."

"So they work for our demon?" Soo asked.

"Oh my god, don't call it *our* demon," Robin called, putting her hands on her head as she paced behind the sofa.

"Yes, but they're separate," Doctor Pavi coughed. "They're likely soul vessels."

Vivian turned to Mila again for translation.

Mila's stunned expression clearly meant she hadn't heard the term before, but she slid gently away from the group to the pile of books on Doctor Pavi's desk. She flipped through pages of a large, leather-bound book that resembled an old atlas.

Mila spoke up and read confidently. "Oh, here! Summoning is powered by the soul itself, given to the daemon to hold and keep. Once removed, can never be replaced but unto daemon, the vessel, keeper of the summoner's light until full demon reached."

Vivian sighed in frustration from all of the old books with old language. She had to see the book for herself and help figure this out. She just wanted to go home and get back to her normal life, away from this nightmare. Finally, she got herself up and was able to stand, even through her pain. *'Demons aren't healers,'* she remembered that part. But it seemed like maybe she was a little less stiff from the adrenaline working its way through her body.

She joined Mila at the desk and read over her shoulder, skimming the text quickly to herself, but she still didn't understand. "Why do old books always have to be so confusing?" Vivian whispered in irritation.

"It means…" Mila started.

"*Louder!*" Robin called with cupped hands from across the room.

"It means when you summon a demon, they take a piece of your soul to fuel the spell, but you never get that piece back—your *daemon* holds it—forever. And if you continue to summon more and more, the daemon fills up with your soul, taking it piece by piece until one day, your whole soul is inside the daemon, and you become a demon yourself."

"So, bad idea if we want to call the demon back if we have questions, is what you're saying," Robin huffed and continued to pace behind the sofa, clicking her vape on and off.

Vivian was starting to see that she and Robin would probably continue to butt heads. Robin was angry—that part was clear—but now she was also showing her stubborn side. She was probably not the kind of person that forgives easily, maybe even a little like herself. Vivian couldn't remember exactly what she had said or done to Robin, but if it had been while she was with Jacee and Celeste, it was probably mean, catty, and not something Robin would likely let go of any time soon.

"I think I'm gonna go," Vivian announced, limping across the room. She wished she could turn quickly to look at Robin to see her relieved expression.

"Vivian, are you sure you're going to be okay?" Doctor Pavi asked weakly.

"Ya, I'll call a cab. I need to get home and think about… all of this for a bit. I need some time. I'll come back, though. I'll be here for the sixty-six-hour mark thingy."

Not even Doctor Pavi knew Vivian well enough to convince her to stay. They knew she was free to do whatever she wanted, and the other girls probably didn't need her around, causing tension anyway. Vivian gave a small, closed-lipped smile, gathered her stuff, and hobbled out the door.

MILA

"So, what do we do now?" Soo said to the room.

"Well, we have two days to decide what we're going to say," answered Mila.

"What do you mean 'decide'?" Robin sneered. "There's nothing to decide here. We're not allowing a demon to use our bodies for whatever it wants."

"But if we don't, all this stuff happening to us will continue and probably get worse." Mila sat down heavily at Doctor Pavi's desk and started rubbing her temples.

Mila wasn't the only one who was feeling a little drained, so they all agreed to go home, take a break and meet up once their batteries recharged. They had a little over two days until they had to summon the demon again, and they had to have a plan. Mila knew she needed rest, but she knew what would happen next also depended on her. There were still a lot of books to read and information from Doctor Pavi to put together. She would sleep first and then go back to demonology later. All this and she had to go to school the next morning.

At home, Mila heard her mother with Gemma in the kitchen. The noise would be too much to handle, so she rushed up the stairs. Her headache was raging on in pulsing waves like a thick balloon was filling up and pressing just behind her temples.

In the upstairs bathroom, she twisted off the childproof cap of the painkillers, and her chest drooped at the sight of one lonely tablet left at the bottom. She threw it hastily into her mouth and scooped water from the tap to wash it down. She splashed more cool water on her face and over the sides of her forehead before looking into the mirror and grabbing a wet cloth to wipe off her makeup. She started by taking off the foundation from her cheeks and neck. Most people didn't know her auburn hair came as a package—pale, sensitive skin and freckles that usually hid under layers of foundation and powder.

Once her face was clean, she put her glasses back on, facing her reflection in the mirror. There she stood, plain and pale, red baby hairs stuck down at the top of her wet forehead. She always thought she was pretty enough—everyone always told her she had a pretty face. But being around those girls, especially Vivian, made her feel like a big fat nobody. Looking at Vivian's trim figure, smooth dark skin, and perfectly set waves, Mila couldn't help but make a stark comparison between them. Here she was, plump and pale with garish red hair that wouldn't stay put unless it was in a ponytail. Vivian was the most popular girl in school, and Mila was the exact opposite.

She splashed more cool water on her face, but the heat and headache persevered. While the demon was playing its tricks, she sometimes got a headache from concentrating so hard on whatever she was trying to read. And though she could read again, her headache was still lingering even worse than before.

Mila looked down at the green-tiled bathroom floor as if it were listening. *"You said you'd leave us alone."* Frustrated by the pain still throbbing, she turned out the light and headed for her room.

Mila hid the demonology books she brought home in her closet under boxes of unpacked clothes. Then, curling up on her bed, she did her best to calm herself down, not thinking too hard about what had just happened. *We talked to a demon. The demon said she was going to die before she turned twenty years old. How could life be so unfair? But Doctor Pavi said demons couldn't be trusted. So what was the truth?*

Then, an even stranger thought entered her mind—if she was going to die as soon as the demon said, she wished she could change a few things while she still had time.

She sat up to see herself across the room in her dresser mirror. She pushed up her bushy curls, made a face, and then tried to smooth them down again. She looked more like her sister, with her hair straight.

How could she leave her mom and Gemma after everything they'd been through with her dad leaving? What would Gemma be like if she grew up without her?

The thoughts were bringing on tears, but she stopped herself, knowing that if she started crying, her headache would only get worse.

She looked at the mirror once more, again trying to adjust her curls. *"Impossible,"* she whispered, and a single tear made its way down her cheek.

Her mind continued to reel, and the pounding pressure in her head was relentless.

Soo

Every time she saw her future slipping further and further away as it became more and more controlled by the demon. When would her life be her own? The scrolling images of the demon and daemons kept her eyes from closing and started her heart pounding. Each time she got close to sleep, Soo heard the demon's voice and again the way it moved inside Doctor Pavi's body.

Around midnight, she got up to go to her bedroom window, hesitating at first to look out into the windy autumn night where the leaves would be swirling and trees would be shaking like fingers on an old lady's hand. She looked out past the fences, past the trees, and beyond her driveway, letting them fade while her mind made clearer pictures of her swimming in the Olympics and maybe becoming a coach at a high school one day, like Coach Riley.

Of course, her mother had other plans for her to attend a prestigious university and go into medicine, like most of her Korean cousins. But with the demon's premonition, everything was dark, just like the quiet streets of Blackrock. Even if she only lived until twenty, and her mother had her way, she would be in her second year of university—doing something she didn't love when she died. She'd have no time to see the world or meet her idols. There wasn't even time to fall in love, get married, and buy a house with a pool. There wasn't enough time for anything. It wasn't fair.

At five o'clock, her alarm went off and startled her from her thoughts and half-dreams. She had barely slept all night, and her eyes stung as she tried to keep them open. Her morning routine was usually her favorite part of the day—it was normally calm and her mind clear as she got ready for swim practice. But without swimming, there was no calm. Without jumping into the water on a cool morning, there was no energy in her day. Without the rhythmic pull of the water and bubbles beside her ears, she had no place to escape the thoughts about her future. There was no place to release all the anxiety, anger, fear, and confusion about everything happening. The tension was crushing, and she had nowhere for her frustration to go. Her bed was still neatly made, her pillows sitting up, looking back at her innocently at first and then taunting her. She pulled away one of the cushions, planted it in front of her, and punched it as hard as she could. Then she did it again and again. Over and over. She imagined nothing in particular at first, just the feeling of her muscles making contact was enough. Then the demon, Doctor Pavi, and those stupid journals all got their turn. Tessa had a longer turn than the demon, which she stopped to notice, and took a breath. She gave several more jabs for her mother not listening to her and for all the times she was told to study, be a doctor, and meet a nice boy.

When she had imagined everyone that came to mind, she fell over and screamed into the mattress. With a final double punch to the mattress, she sat up on her bed, slightly out of breath but not feeling much better about it all. It was pointless to fight. Defeated, she got herself dressed, even though she had nowhere to go so early.

In the kitchen, she sat alone in the dark, the only light coming from the appliances, like the green numbers on the stove. Soo slowly stirred her cereal and tried to imagine what the demon would do next if they all said no to the deal. The refrigerator buzzed as she tried to think. She couldn't imagine being continuously tortured by nightmares or scared to swim again. But on the other hand, she also couldn't begin to think what it would be like to be possessed by an actual demon and help it do its bidding.

She was lost in her thoughts when the familiar creak of her father's office interrupted her. *Had he not slept, either?* Soo wondered. But he was already dressed for work, suit and tie, and wide awake. "Hey, Fish. Why are we sitting in the dark?" He said, turning on the lights.

Soo squinted to look at him. "Were you sleeping in your office?" Soo countered back, avoiding the question.

"I had some work to finish early this morning. Hey, you know? I still owe you a jog. How about tonight?"

"I can't tonight, dad, sorry. I have plans with Mila."

"Ok, but sometime this week." He gave a slight nod, grabbing his coffee mug and briefcase.

"Better sooner than later," she mumbled to herself, but her father didn't hear as he walked out the front door.

~ * ~

Her mother dropped her off, as always, at the back entrance close to the pool.

"Study, study," her mother called after her. She said the same thing every day—not, *'I love you'* or *'Have a good day.'* No. *'Study, study,'* was all she ever said before she drove away.

Soo left the car silently and made her way to the side entrance. The chemical smell of chlorine hit her before she even walked inside, and a nauseating wave of shame settled in. The team would be finishing up practice and likely be getting an earful from Coach Riley this close to Counties. Once in the hallway, tears came to her eyes unexpectedly at the thought as she stood just outside the locker room door. She reached out, her hand just above the door handle, but she thought better of it. It would be too hard to take a look, even for a second.

Hoping no teachers would see, Soo ran down the hallway as far away from the pool as she could get—away from the chlorine smell and everything about her old life. She ran through the back halls with the old, green-painted concrete walls and speckled tile floor and all the way up the wooden staircase to her locker on the second floor. Thankfully the traces of pool smell faded away as she ran and was replaced by the smell of freshly polished floors and banisters. The run and the stair climb had even done her good—her heart was pumping for all the right reasons, pushing away the broken feelings that felt like they could crush her. She dared a small smile at the feeling.

The metal door of her locker squeaked as she opened it towards her, and she realized she hadn't escaped anything at all. The sides and door were covered in pictures of her swimming idols—in the water, on podiums. Travel pictures with the clear turquoise water she always thought she would swim in taunted her, and her heart went back to breaking into a million pieces.

Other students were beginning to arrive, so she had to block the thoughts out, or she would be caught crying in front of everyone. Enough gossip was going around about her that she didn't need to give them anything else to tease her with. But it was too late. She never was much of a crier, but with the lack of sleep, she couldn't hold back her emotions, and it all flowed out. She leaned over and hid her face inside her locker walls, trying to close the door on her head as much as possible and not let her body shake.

Everything had changed now, and she couldn't go back. She needed more time—more time to find out who she was and what she could be and do beyond a teenager, beyond high school, beyond what her mother and coaches wanted. Twenty years old was just not enough.

Then, for a moment, her thoughts became horrifically clear. She stopped shaking and sniffed at the disgust of her own thoughts—she knew what she wanted. She wanted to say *yes* to the demon.

A hand on her back made her jump, and then she heard the sweet sound of Faye's voice. She wiped her face as discreetly as she could before she turned around.

"Hey," she answered as cheerfully as she could muster.

"Soo! My god, Hun. What's wrong?" Faye reached out for Soo's arm to try to console her.

As soon as Faye touched her, she just wanted to break down and let it all out. But they were still in the middle of the hallway, and people were all around them. So, she had to hold it together.

"It's been a rough morning, that's all." Soo sniffed.

"Awww, I'm so sorry you're upset. Come here, hun" Faye reached out and hugged Soo tight, making her want to cry even more. Faye hugged her just tight enough that Soo never wanted her to let go. She could smell the chlorine in Faye's hair, but somehow, Soo didn't mind.

When they pulled apart, Faye wiped Soo's cheek with her hand. Soo smiled as Faye's gray-blue eyes looked right back at her like a doting kitten who just wanted to be there for her. She didn't look at Soo with pity or expectations, just care, concern… or something more maybe.

"Thanks," Soo said with a small smile, though she felt like she might cry again. She desperately had to change the subject. "How was practice today?" she asked but regretted it as soon as she did. Knowing how everything was going on without her wasn't going to help her feel better.

"Pretty average. Tessa's ruling the pool as usual, but I'm working on my form and doing well enough to get into Counties, too, I think."

"Your freestyle has gotten really strong this year. So you could do really well there," Soo said matter-of-factly, trying to get her voice to stop shaking as she wiped her face dry.

"I don't know," Faye said, biting the side of her bottom lip. "I didn't think anyone noticed. Coach Riley sure doesn't say much to me. I think I'm pretty much invisible."

Soo wanted to say something to Faye to make her feel better like she had just done for her. She hoped she could get the words out without stuttering nervously or bursting into tears again. But her hesitation made her remember she didn't have a lot of time to waste on worrying anymore—she had to say what she thought.

"You're not invisible to me."

ROBIN

"Mila!" Robin called from across the lawn in front of Blackrock High.

Mila saw Robin immediately since her head was, for once, not buried in a book. When she turned, Robin almost stopped dead in her tracks. Mila wasn't wearing her glasses, her hair was in smooth, wide curls, and her makeup was overly done, maybe even some contour on her cheeks.

"New contacts?" Robin asked.

"Ya, I thought I'd try them for a change. What do you think?" Mila asked, throwing her hair over her shoulder.

"You look awesome," Robin said, trying not to sound skeptical about what brought all this on. She just hoped makeovers weren't part of the demon sacrifice she had missed. But Mila only gave an overly cheerful 'Thank you' and continued walking.

"I'll meet you in the library at lunch, right?" Robin asked.

"I'll be there," Mila answered, already walking off. Robin felt like she was really reaching out by offering to go to the library of all places on her lunch break, but Mila seemed miles away, as if she was completely disinterested in the whole demon issue for the moment and only wanted to play dress-up. Robin stood back and watched her go into the crowd, some people even turning their heads to notice Mila's new look.

When she got to class, Robin threw her bag on the saw dusty floor next to her unfinished entrance table. She was excited to finish the project, but she was too distracted by their demon deadline.

Still, she had to carve the details into the wood if she wanted to get a good grade on this project—just in case there was life after demons. An unexpected chuckle left her lips as she thought about using 'demon possession' as an excuse for not getting her work done on time.

Robin really needed concentration to get this right, and a small, twisted piece of her wished the demon from music class would show up and help her out. She lined up her dowels but then hesitated. Her street mural that was giving her problems flashed in her mind, taunting her. Strangely, her mind went to the image of the summoning circle on Doctor Pavi's floor and how well she had executed it. She tried to focus on how good she felt when Doctor Pavi praised her, but the memory brought back all of the thoughts related to the demon, and her anxiety about it all pushed any good feelings away. Robin sat back in defeat and stared at the table with a dispirited frown on her dark red lips.

"Cold feet, Rodriguez?" Lester Mead called over from his station. Other guys joined in and laughed, too, guys she actually liked. Of course, she knew they were teasing, probably just trying to wake her from her slump. Their stupid jokes about her black clothes and looking like a vampire or witch would cheer her up. And usually, she'd be able to snap back with something witty, like, *'Oh yeah? Well, I wouldn't touch your micro-penis if it was the last one on earth.'* And they'd all laugh together. But now, all Robin could muster was a small smirk at their efforts.

"Maybe you could summon a demon to do your project for you," Lester teased once again to get more laughs.

Robin froze. She was too shocked to even move while the other guys kept laughing. When she didn't laugh along, they all stopped too and looked at her confused.

"Oh, c'mon, Rodriguez, it's just a joke."

Robin managed to fake a smile and a laugh, but inside, she was screaming. Was it really a joke, or was the demon speaking through them? The demon called her 'Rodriguez.' Was this a warning about how it could take over anyone around her? Or was it really just the regular wood shop guys and their regular banter?

Officially freaked out by her thoughts, she threw her dowels back in the drawer and put her files and chisels away, hoping she could keep herself looking busy on some outlines for other projects until class was over. Thankfully, Lester and the others turned away and left her alone. One more period before she would meet up with Mila. But it felt like a lifetime.

~ * ~

It figured Mila would be late on a day Robin was having a mental breakdown and needed her the most.

"Sorry. I was talking to some guy named Gary," Mila's voice rose at the end like a question, wondering if Robin knew who he was.

"Gary? Gary Barns? Big 'goofy grin' Gary?" Robin said, scrunching her face at the thought of her music partner swindling her for the timpani.

"Oh, I don't know. He's kind of nice. He's in my English class."

"I'm surprised he can even read, Mila," Robin scoffed, sticking her tongue.

"Hey, don't make fun of people who can't read," she said with a sly raised eyebrow that meant they were actually talking about the demon. Mila tossed her hair back and began pulling her notebooks from her backpack. Robin even thought she saw her smiling.

"Are you okay?" Robin whispered.

Mila smiled back, a twinkle in her eye, "Of course," she whispered back. "I mean, *no*, none of this is okay. But we're doing everything we can, right?"

"Right… but I have to ask—what's with the hair, makeup, no glasses? You seem like you're in a good mood or something—like you're ready to embark on the all-inclusive demon-possession cruise of a lifetime."

"Don't be stupid. But I am in a good mood, actually," Mila assured her. "I know I shouldn't be, but I can't help it." Mila sat and leaned in closer to Robin to tell her more. "I mean, I feel like I'm liberated now. I know I'm going to die soon, so what does anything matter? And if nothing matters, then why not try some new things and screw what other people think, y'know?"

Robin made a duck face and nodded. She couldn't argue with Mila's reasoning. Robin had always more or less lived by that logic, but it was strange to see the same color on Mila.

Mila left Robin to check the stacks to see if there were any other sources, or even other Summoners, hiding among the high school's collection. Robin got comfortable at the large library table and started to re-read Mila's notes, being a second pair of eyes to see if she could make sense of anything. Her black nails furiously traced the scribbled Latin and Greek to get to something familiar, but she was starting to think she wouldn't be much help.

Mila walked around, searching, and Robin continued skimming the lists of notes, now mostly in Latin. Robin let her eyes glaze over until she stumbled upon a word she actually recognized. She sat up straight and looked for Mila, seeing if she could catch her eye across the library, but she knew how Mila was around books. Robin scurried towards her and grabbed her by the hand.

Mila gave a small yelp but followed Robin back to the table. The librarian looked over her glasses as a warning not to run.

"What is it? Did you find something?" Mila whispered as they slowed to walk past the front desk.

When they reached the table, Mila plopped down into Robin's chair, and Robin stood beside her, pointing to the page. "I'm not sure, but right here, you have a list in Latin, right? I know some of these words because they're just like Spanish," Robin said, remembering to keep her voice low.

"They're names of herbs, mostly," Mila added.

"Right. Except for this one," Robin underlined the suspicious word. "This is a crystal. My great-aunt used to have a big one at her house. It's like a huge blue rock she brought with her from Mexico, and I remember it because it's really beautiful. And I remember this word carved into the base, *caerulum*. In Spanish, we call it *azurita*. My *tia* used to say it was very important for strengthening her psychic abilities."

"Your aunt is psychic?" Mila asked quickly.

"Of course not, don't be stupid," Robin said automatically but then paused. "Well, I never thought so, but I guess anything is possible now."

Now that she had seen a demon summoned before her eyes, Robin knew she would have to change her mind about a lot of things, especially when it came to her very religious and supernatural-believing family. And even now, she would have to embrace the fact that they would have to fight back in ways she never thought existed. But what she was about to propose was so foreign that the words stumbled awkwardly from her mouth. "I think these are ingredients, and with the crystal, we can do a spell to see into the future. To see what is really going to happen to us."

"So we can really know if the demon is telling the truth." The sparkle of Mila's eyeshadow twinkled around her eyes as she stared at the page, enlivened.

Robin couldn't match Mila's optimism and hopefulness—she had to stay as much in reality as she could. She looked Mila in the eyes, scrutinizing her excitement. "Ya, great. Then we can see how we're going to die for ourselves."

MILA

After school, Mila hurried to pick up Gemma and get her settled at home. Their mom would be home in the afternoon so she could go 'shopping' with her friends. Mila was a little proud of her white lie. Technically, she would be shopping, but not for clothes or shoes like her mom thought. Instead, this was a trip for herbs and spices that would be the ingredients for a demonic spell to see the future—that kind of shopping.

"I dint know it was you wiffout yow gwasses, Miwa."

"I'm just trying something new today." Mila had said the same thing to Robin, but this time, looking at Gemma and thinking about missing out on a lot of things in life was getting her choked up. She took Gemma's clammy little hand in hers and wondered how big she would get to see Gemma grow to be. She wondered how Gemma would feel once she was gone. Would she remember these moments? Would she remember her for long after she died and was grown and living her life? Would she stay safe from demons when she went to high school? *I hope she'll be a fool. That's the best thing in the world a girl can be. A beautiful fool.* Zelda Fitzgerald's words turned over in Mila's mind like a prayer as she swung Gemma's hand all the way home.

Walking into the house, Gemma broke away and ran for her toys while Mila caught a glimpse of herself in the hallway mirror. Without her glasses, her green eyes looked even greener and brighter than usual. The attention she had gotten was fun for the day, but now she was done. She didn't want to be noticed so much all the time. It was just nice to know it was possible with a little makeup and contact lenses. Overall, though, her experiment had failed. Taking off her glasses and leaving her hair down didn't eliminate the headache. She had really been hoping that it was all part of the demon's hold. But now that they were given a reprieve, it was clear she'd have to go through the normal channels of her mom and doctor. Defeated, Mila sighed and slowly climbed the stairs to switch her contacts for her glasses and throw her hair in a ponytail for the bike ride downtown with the other girls.

With perfect timing, Robin and Soo pulled up to Mila's house on their bicycles just as Mila's mom pulled into the driveway. Mila clumsily led her mom's bicycle to the end of the driveway, wordlessly and awkwardly mounted it, and began pedaling. Soo and Robin exchanged looks but followed suit. Mila's mom waved with excessive happiness and excitement, blowing Mila kisses too. Mila put her head down and winced, which made Robin giggle, likely assuming Mila was acting embarrassed. But the truth was Mila's temples had been throbbing continuously for the past two days, and her eyes were so sore that she thought if she ripped them out, it might be an improvement.

~ * ~

The breeze on the bike was a small relief, but if it wasn't her glasses causing her headaches and it wasn't the demon, what was it? The demon said they'd all somehow die before twenty. It hadn't said anything about whether that meant when they reached twenty or any time before. So, maybe her headaches were a sign she was destined to go sooner rather than later. *Maybe it was a sign of disease, a tumor, the C word…?*

Mila didn't want to worry the others with her thoughts yet, so she tried to focus on getting the ingredients for the spell, and maybe she would feel better once she knew the demon was lying. Maybe it would ease her stress, and all the headaches were—stress—just like Doctor Pavi had said before.

The grocery store had most of what they needed—more cinnamon sticks, thyme, and sea salt. But, they'd have to go to the greenhouse, just outside of town, to get the fresh sage. Soo and Robin didn't even think about the distance—Soo was used to jogging and swimming, and Robin was accustomed to hurrying away from store owners in back alleys where she did her murals. Exercise for Mila, on the other hand, was something she mostly ignored or avoided. She'd even had to borrow her mom's bike, which was too big and heavy for her. But she'd also been having those nagging thoughts about how she looked, so she agreed to go with them, thinking she might be able to shed a few pounds.

Before she moved to Blackrock, she felt okay with the body she had gotten from being a homebody. She loved to curl up with her novel of the week, say 'no' to parties, and 'definitely no' to after-school sports. It had never bothered her or occurred to her that she could be anything else but a chubby nerd. She had never been very good at sports or exercise, and she was sure she never would be. Some vague memories lingered of her father teaching her how to throw and catch a baseball, but she never quite got the hang of it. For a long time, she actually wondered if that's why he left—because he didn't want girls—especially the kind of girls that weren't any good at sports.

~ * ~

Outside the grocery store, Mila turned from the wind to let her long ponytail blow forward around her face and tickle her cheeks. The big red bicycle was balanced awkwardly between her legs, and she took a breath before they had to start out again. Robin pointed to where they were headed, and Mila struggled to lift and turn around the front wheel. By the time Mila got herself oriented, Robin and Soo were far ahead. Mila looked around to see if anyone else noticed how much she was lagging and struggling. Across the street were the specialty stores she had noticed on her first day here with Soo. She squinted at first to be sure, and it was... Vivian. She had a brand new phone in her perfectly manicured hands, walking with a gorgeously tall woman in a violet poncho, a wide-brimmed hat, and a clean beige bandage that stood out on her otherwise dark skin.

Vivian turned sharply when she noticed Mila. Neither of them waved, but neither of them turned away. Locked in a stare, Mila was sure they were both thinking they should be talking to each other but couldn't. What would they say? How would Vivian explain to the woman, likely her mother, that a pale frump like Mila was her new friend? It wouldn't make sense. Mila decided to slightly raise her hands from the handlebars. It was the smallest gesture she could think of, but Vivian quickly looked away, just like Mila knew she would.

The bike frame tilted and quivered as Mila stood on the pedals to push it forward to catch up to Robin and Soo, who had stopped to wait. After several rest stops, which Mila herself requested, the girls were at the greenhouse. Most of the pretty summer flowers were gone, and only mums and tulip bulbs were on display out front of the plastic dome greenhouse, practically in the middle of nowhere. The girls parked their bikes in front, not needing to lock them up, and went inside.

They needed to find sage plants, and when Robin called earlier, the greenhouse employee said they had a few still in stock that were pretty much dead, but they could have them for free. None of them had been to a greenhouse before, so Mila had no idea how hot and humid it would be. She was already sweaty from the bike ride, and the heavy, moist air wasn't helping. She grabbed a weekly flier at the front to fan her face, making her own breeze as they walked through the greenhouse door.

"I still think we should tell Doctor Pavi about what we're doing," said Soo, looking back at the straggling Mila.

"No, we can't. What if we do this, and she gets possessed again?" Robin whispered. "Plus, she has her clients today anyway. We're fine to do this on our own at my place as soon as my mom goes to her second job."

"Can we please slow down?" Mila stammered and huffed between words, but Soo and Robin kept walking. They were chatting and enjoying the greenhouse with its bright windows and colorful rows of plants and pots and didn't hear Mila's weak plea. The smell of clean water and fertilizer hung over them like a fake summer. To Mila, it was what she imagined hot yoga would feel like—having to move and sweat through thick heat in a weird-smelling, crowded room. She did her best to keep walking but desperately needed a break. Between overheating, her pounding headache, and being unable to catch her breath since she got on the bicycle, she was feeling faint. Robin and Soo walked ahead as Mila found a decorative bench in the home decor area. Around her, the flowing water features teased with their trickle and flow. She stared longingly into the ponds, wishing she could dive into them to cool off and then drink them up. But instead, she settled for batting the sweat off her forehead with the back of her hand. *How do skinny girls do this?*

She hadn't eaten all day, but she had no idea it would feel like this. She'd read that fasting could even help heal headaches, so it sounded exactly like what she needed. But resting her starved body on a hard bench in a hot greenhouse wasn't making her feel better. Instead, she felt more like a total loser for not being able to keep up with Soo and Robin on their bikes, and now she even had the image of Vivian and her gorgeous mother taunting her even more. From the bench, she could faintly see the cashier area where her two friends were gathering the plants. Mila sighed in relief to know they'd be leaving soon.

Robin and Soo began to walk her way, each holding a large potted plant as they giggled at how they didn't plan on how they would get them home on their bikes. After some searching, they found Mila lying on the bench with her eyes closed.

"Doesn't this whole place make you want to pee?" Robin called out to Mila as she walked closer.

Mila didn't answer.

"Guess she really was tired after the bike ride," Soo said sympathetically.

"Mila?" Robin said again, trying to shake her awake.

"Mila!" Soo and Robin were shouting and shaking together, and then Soo recognized what was happening, *"Someone call an ambulance!"*

10

DOCTOR PAVI

Mila was easily the most sensitive and vulnerable of all of the girls, but Doctor Pavi wasn't expecting to have something happen to her so soon. From the start, Mila had been motivated to know everything about demons and how they make deals. So when the demon said they would have to make a choice, Mila did everything to research all of the possibilities and options, even with her ongoing headaches, which only Doctor Pavi knew about. There was a difference between when Mila was struggling with words and reading and when Mila was just plain struggling, and Doctor Pavi could see it. Stress could still be a big part of what was going on, but it was probably just a culmination of it all. Mila had been through a lot—a new town, new school, new friends, and becoming newly exposed to the world of demons and spell casting—definitely more than average teenager growing pains.

But Doctor Pavi never could have guessed it would lead to Mila lying unconscious in the hospital. The doctors were saying it was heat stroke, but there were more tests to be done. *What were the girls thinking, taking her out there? Mila can't—*Doctor Pavi didn't want to make assumptions, but she had never seen Mila do anything active.

Now she lay still in a hospital bed while a nurse took blood and fluids. Soo and Robin were waiting impatiently in the hallway and rushed to hug Doctor Pavi as she turned the corner.

"We're so sorry," Soo said, her voice muffled in Doctor Pavi's coat.

When they broke away, Doctor Pavi moved to peek into Mila's room. Mila's mom was in the chair by the bed, her face tight and pained. Two raggedy sage plants sat in the hospital room's window, and Doctor Pavi was beginning to get the picture. She slowly closed the door and gestured that the three of them go over to a lounge area where the girls could explain what really happened.

"I don't think it was demonic at all," Soo started. "She wasn't feeling good on the ride to the greenhouse, but we thought it was normal—just a little, y'know, difficult because of her… size."

"We left her to rest, but when we found her…" Robin was fighting against the sides of her mouth turning down, but her voice gave out on the last few words. Doctor Pavi had only started to get to know Robin, but she already could see the girl cared deeply for Mila, who was probably the first true friend Robin had ever had.

"But what were you all doing at a greenhouse in the first place?" Doctor Pavi asked, resisting the urge to cross her arms. She was trying hard not to sound like anyone who was going to discipline them for what had happened. They'd already been through so much.

Soo turned away, looking mortified, while Robin confidently looked straight into Doctor Pavi's eyes and announced, "We were going to do a spell."

Doctor Pavi crossed her arms. "What kind of spell?"

"A spell to see if the demon was lying about us all dying soon," Soo whispered.

"Well, I guess we don't need a spell now to tell us something's wrong, do we?" Doctor Pavi said, leaning back in her chair and looking down the hallway toward Mila's room.

"Nope," Robin said, popping the final 'p'. "But we do need to talk to that demon again."

VIVIAN

In the car, Vivian did her best to be discreet as she watched Mila stop looking her way and turn the giant, junky bicycle around. She wondered what she and the other girls were up to. But before she could imagine any scenarios, her mother got into the backseat beside her. Vivian sat up straight. Her mother immediately pulled out a mirror from her purse and started fixing the brown, cake-like concealer powder on her bandage, trying to make it less noticeable. The driver faced straight ahead, surely pretending not to notice the obvious 'procedure' her mother had recently done in California.

"Be grateful you don't have my chin, Viv," her mother said, snapping the compact closed and tucking it in her purse.

Vivian stayed quiet. She wasn't feeling too talkative lately, which was ironic because when she couldn't talk, she would have given anything to talk about anything, even her chin. But she also had her phone again, so she could ignore her mother's feeble attempts at bonding and silently check in with her friends. She hadn't been back at school since her bout in the hospital over the weekend, but strangely, she didn't really want to talk to those friends anyway. She knew Jacee and Celeste weren't taking her collapse seriously—they still thought she was just ridiculously drunk at the party. Cameron had been great, but he was acting like she was a freak—like she was fragile, and he seemed to be avoiding her. So she sent out a few casual texts from her new number and waited.

The sunny autumn day was hard to enjoy. The jack-o-lanterns on the curbs reminded her of Halloween and her party. Since that night, she hadn't cared about the same things in the same way. Wasn't it strange that she didn't actually care too much either way if any of her friends responded back? Why was she more interested in what Mila and the other girls were doing? She rested her chin in her palm, leaning on the door and looking out of the window the whole way home like a sad dog that couldn't stick its head out.

Vivian's father also had returned from his trip, and as they walked in, she heard him on the phone behind the closed doors of his office. Vivian's mother went directly to her bedroom to rest, and Vivian was alone again, as usual, standing in the foyer with her hands in her coat pockets. The house was so big and so empty. She started thinking about when her brother James was living at home. At least there was a little noise and energy in the house back then. Now it was just quiet to the point of unbearable. She needed to talk to someone, anyone, but no one had responded to her yet. She put her hands deeper into her pockets and felt around for the paper with Doctor Pavi's number. She had no idea what she would say or how she would explain why she was calling, but she dialed anyway.

"Doctor Pavi? Hi, it's Vivian.

I just—

What?

What kind of accident?

I'll be right there."

~ * ~

Vivian found Soo in the hallway, and it was clear that Vivian's visit was a surprise.

"Vivian, hi! What are you doing here?" Soo asked quietly from her chair.

Vivian took a seat next to her, folding her gloves in her lap. "Doctor Pavi said something happened to Mila, and we should all be together, so… I'm here." Vivian waved her arms out to the side in a large shrug with both arms, almost hitting a nurse passing by until Soo pulled her in.

She didn't know why she felt so awkward. It was like she was the loser in the group and suddenly had no idea how to act like the most popular girl in school. Soo, Mila and especially Robin certainly didn't concern themselves with social status, so it was like she had no reputation at all, and it felt like she had no foundation or ground beneath her feet. Around Jacee and Celeste, she never had to think about what to say. But then, she knew they basically worshiped her. At school, it was the same. Everyone knew her as the wealthiest and most popular girl at Blackrock High, and everyone wanted to be like her.

But with Soo, Mila, and Robin, she had no idea where she stood. It was unfamiliar and fun in some ways but difficult and terrifying in others. Robin definitely hated her; that was clear. But, on the other hand, Soo seemed like she tolerated her after her apology for calling her a freak and kicking her out of her house, and Mila… maybe Mila would be glad she had come.

"They're doing a bunch of tests now," Soo whispered. "They said we could go home, actually, but Robin won't leave until she's awake. She's in there now with Mila's mom and Doctor Pavi."

Soo's eyes were red, and her head drooped forward in her seat. She figured they all were probably just as exhausted.

"Why don't we get them something from the cafeteria? Sounds like it might be a while."

Soo got up slowly and yawned in agreement as she followed.

~ * ~

They loaded a tray with several coffees, cream, sugar, and some snacks like giant muffins, overflowing fruit cups, and chocolate-covered granola bars. It was quite a selection for a hospital cafeteria. Vivian wondered if Cameron had been here too on Saturday night. She knew exactly what he would have picked: a granola bar and chocolate milk. Her face warmed at the thought of him. Then she shrugged off the feeling, and the warm feeling was gone as soon as she remembered he hadn't texted her back yet. It wasn't rational, but she hastily grabbed all the granola bars off their tray and put them back on the shelf.

While they waited to pay, Vivian got out her phone and handed it to Soo.

"Here, can you put your number in? It's new."

"Nice," Soo said as she looked the phone over.

"It's nice to feel connected again. It was *hell* not having a phone."

Soo snorted, and Vivian realized it wasn't the best word choice. They paid for the food quickly before they both burst out laughing as they made their way back upstairs.

Vivian wordlessly handed Robin a coffee, and Robin didn't balk or bother to insult her—she even let a glimmer of appreciation slip onto her face. Vivian meant to smile back, but she had caught sight of Mila on the hospital bed, and for the second time that night, she was instantly drained of hope. A wave of memories overcame her as she looked at Mila in the same place she had been only two days earlier. But unlike her, Mila had multiple tubes coming out of her mouth and a tangled web of wires attached to her arms. Her face was so pale that the blue veins showed on her cheeks as she lay there, unconscious. Vivian thought back to seeing Mila downtown. *Why didn't I wave back?*

Robin said they had her heavily sedated because they found a clot in her heart that could suddenly explode if she moved around too much. Robin was putting her own spin on the diagnosis, but Vivian wasn't about to argue—Robin's nails were already down to the nubs.

Mila's mom was sipping her hot coffee with Mila's latest Fitzgerald novel open on her lap, and as Vivian stirred her coffee, she realized how much she admired Mila. Besides Cameron dropping her off, no one else came to visit her in the hospital. If she was about to die like the demon promised, would anyone be there? Would her parents be too busy or out of the country again? Cameron had been there for her, but he was becoming more and more distant. Jacee and Celeste hadn't even called since she had been out of the hospital. How had her life become so different so quickly?

~ * ~

When Mila's doctor came in with some news, they all went into the hallway. Robin began pacing the hall with her nails in her mouth, and Vivian sat with Soo and Doctor Pavi in the lounge. There were other people waiting on their own loved ones, so they couldn't speak freely about their next step with the demon.

"This isn't the… *you-know-what*, is it?" Vivian asked, hoping she was discreet enough. Doctor Pavi shook her head slightly with her eyes closed.

Robin sat down but wasn't still. Her leg shook, and she kept a nail in her mouth as she spoke. "How is this happening already? It said we have until twenty."

"It never said 'until' twenty, only '*before*' twenty," Doctor Pavi pointed out. "That could mean any time between now and three years from now."

Vivian froze. She hadn't realized that. She'd been thinking like Robin—that she still had three good years, and then on her twentieth birthday, something would just 'happen', and it would all be over. But Doctor Pavi was right—the demon had only said, 'before twenty'. Vivian instantly caught up to Robin's panic.

When the doctor came out, Doctor Pavi got up to peek into the room first before they all went back in. But after sticking her head in, she stepped back slowly and softly closed the door again. Then, with a tight mouth and closed eyes, she shook her head at the girls. Vivian took a deep breath to hold back her emotions, but Robin dove into Soo's arms. Doctor Pavi stood with her hands on her hips, taking a deep breath and looking like, for once, she might not have all the answers. Vivian searched her mind for something comforting to say, but nothing came to her. She turned her head down, thinking of Mila, and one tear snuck down her cheek. She brushed it away before anyone could see. They'd probably think the same as her: *you just met these girls… why do you care so much?* But looking at Soo holding onto a sobbing Robin, she realized that these could have been the first real friendships she'd ever had, and it was all about to be over before they even started.

Soo

"We have to give it an answer. How are we supposed to answer without Mila?" Soo raged, overly loud with flailing arms. She paced Doctor Pavi's office, full of pent-up energy. Even in all her confusion, she could only lay into the demon—let out all her rage and pound out the answers to all the questions plaguing her for days and keeping her awake at night. *Why Mila? Why so soon?*

"What do we do, Doctor Pavi? Can we do this without Mila?" Vivian's voice from the sofa was calm and would have been soothing if her question didn't grate on Soo's nerves.

"I'm sure it would come without Mila, and it probably knows what happened to her," Doctor Pavi said.

"Or it's responsible, more like," snarled Robin, her black boots dangling over Doctor Pavi's armchair as usual.

Soo stepped closer to everyone who was near the center of the room. "No way. We can't give Mila's answer without her consent. This involves her too. Her body, anyway."

"But it also said it would keep us alive. If Mila's bonded, it would save her," Robin argued.

"We can't answer 'yes' for Mila," Soo said, swallowing hard and gritting her teeth against tears. "She wouldn't want that. We've been fighting so this doesn't happen. She's been fighting…"

"She could die, Soo!" Robin stood up. "She could die before we figure out something else. We can't wait for her to just die!" Robin was spitting her words between sobs.

Again the room stood still and silent as they all considered the options. But it appeared there was only one.

"So what are we supposed to do? Summon the demon to the hospital?" Soo's words hung in the air. No one wanted to answer before Doctor Pavi. She was the adult, after all, and the one who knew the most about summoning. She came from behind the desk, walking slowly, deep in thought.

"We have to get Mila's mom out of the room while keeping everything hidden from the patient in the next bed." Doctor Pavi's eyes were darting as her thoughts continued to form the plan. "I might be able to convince Mila's mom to take a break and go home for the night."

"And what about the roommate?" Soo added quickly, still circling the room to attempt to dull her anxiety.

"Vivian, can't you use your rich daddy to pull some strings and get Mila a private room?" Robin asked in the sassy tone she reserved for Vivian alone.

Soo stopped her pacing to look between Robin and Vivian's tension-filled atmosphere to make sure they didn't kill each other on the spot.

"It doesn't work like that," Vivian replied back, not giving in to Robin's sass. "My father has power and money, not me. And if I used my credit card, my dad would see the charge and ask questions."

Robin turned on her heel and faced Soo, her jaw clenched in frustration. They had to do something to distract the old lady sharing Mila's room.

"What if we give her something so we're sure she's knocked out?" Robin suggested.

"*Are you insane?*" Soo screeched, looking back and shaking her head. She knew they were desperate, but they weren't about to give a sick person anything else that could harm them, especially an already sick old lady.

"I'm just throwing out ideas here," Robin said, slapping her hands on the leather chair's arms. "Anybody else have any other ideas?"

"I might," Doctor Pavi piped up. "But I was hoping we wouldn't have to do it this way." She stood with her head down and took a moment to lay out her idea on them. She sighed, then looked up and paused. "I'll stay out of the room no matter what," she said suggestively. Robin and Vivian were nodding in agreement, but Soo was confused, her nerves clouding her thinking.

"But then, who will the demon possess?" The last words dropped out of Soo's mouth slowly, like her mouth was full of sticky molasses. She suddenly knew the answer before the sentence ended. If Doctor Pavi wasn't there, the demon would use the only other body—Mila's roommate.

"I don't know," Vivian said with a shaking unease in her voice. "I don't know if we should do any of this without you there."

"I'll be close by, just not in the room. I think it's the only way to get some answers. For Mila." Doctor Pavi assured, looking around at each of them.

"For Mila," all three girls said at once. The chorus sound of Mila's name gave Soo a rush of determination. All of her nerves and anxiety were instantly replaced by anger and readiness to fight for her friend. She was ready to face the demon once again and even more ready to have her friend back. The fact that she, too, could die at any time was far from her mind, but she had already made her decision about that anyway. She would say yes to the demon and let it bond with her. If the only way the demon would be able to help Mila was by possessing her, then Soo wasn't going to let her do it alone.

Soo moved closer to join Doctor Pavi, who was leaning on the front of her desk. Soo was careful not to touch any of the demonic papers or books that still cluttered the doctor's desk. She cleared her throat to ask the question she had wanted to know. "Doctor P.? What was it like?"

"What was *what* like?" Doctor Pavi turned to look at her innocently.

"Being… possessed by… *it..?*"

Doctor Pavi's face drooped at the question, and Soo already knew the answer wouldn't be good. Being trapped inside your own mind while a demon ran your body couldn't have been a great time.

"It was… scary. And very frustrating," Doctor Pavi's words were slow and measured like she was being careful not to give too many details. "But only because it had happened so fast, and I didn't know what was going on at first. I didn't know where I was. One minute I was with you girls, holding onto Vivian, and the next was like being in the dark—down a deep, never-ending hole, and I couldn't get out. I could hear the demon speaking to you girls, but it seemed like forever before I understood what it was saying. Then, I tried to shout to you, scream out what you should do, but no one could hear me. I only recognized what was happening pretty close to when the demon must have let me go. The next thing I remember was you girls helping me up off the floor."

"But did it hurt?" Vivian asked from across the room. Soo turned, surprised to know that anyone else was listening.

"Nothing physical. But it was a very specific kind of pain and frustration to be in there without any control," Doctor Pavi said softly.

"And we're going to let this happen to the innocent old lady in Mila's room?" Vivian asked no one in particular.

Robin abruptly clapped her hands, clearly not wanting to go down the path of this topic. "Okay then, I guess we'd better get to work then."

Soo was actually grateful for Robin's interruption because as much as she wanted answers from Doctor Pavi, she also didn't really want to think any more of what it would be like inside the demon's mind—to be bonded—especially now that it seemed they all had no choice.

Concentrating on the plan was a good way to stay distracted from her darker thoughts, and they only had the night to get everything done. To start with, they'd need a way of drawing the summoning symbols on the hospital floor. Robin had an idea to paint everything on a bedsheet so they could roll it up when they were done. Doctor Pavi had bedsheets upstairs in the house and went to find something suitable.

They'd also need candles, the Summoner books, and more cinnamon. Vivian helped Soo pack everything into a small suitcase. When Doctor Pavi returned, she held the bedsheet almost a little too long, then smirked before handing it to Robin to wreck. All of her personal things were taking quite a beating with all of their demon work and symbol painting, Soo noted. But Robin took the sheet from the doctor's hands and got to work with a permanent marker straight away, mapping out the symbols from memory.

Doctor Pavi sighed as she sat in her high-backed chair, looking off into space while the girls worked. Soo knew she must be thinking of what she would say to Mila's mom. Or maybe how they could first get into the hospital after visiting hours, quickly reach the elevators, get up to the sixth floor, past the nurses' station, and into Mila's room—not to mention back out again.

Her thoughts came to a halt when Doctor Pavi stood up just as Robin crumpled the sheet into a small ball to be stuffed into the luggage.

"Wait—" Doctor Pavi called from across the room. "Robin, will it fit under your shirt?"

Robin grabbed the balled-up sheet without a second thought. She struggled at first but managed to get all of it completely tucked under her black t-shirt. Then, with her hands on her big soft belly, her head slowly tilted to the side. Her narrowed eyes met Doctor Pavi's, catching on to the plan. *"Seriously?"*

11

ROBIN

Great, Robin thought. *I get to play the young Latina teenager that gets knocked up. Typical.* But just when she thought she had a complete, stereotypical look, Doctor Pavi made her swap shoes with Vivian. "No pregnant woman would be walking in those heavy high-heeled boots."

Robin made several audible groans as she changed into Vivian's white tennis shoes.

"This is humiliating." Robin slid her heel inside the soft white leather.

"How do you think *I* feel?" Vivian said, exaggerating the struggle of lifting Robin's black boots. Robin couldn't help but smile at seeing Vivian in her dirty old clunkers. But her smile faded as she looked down at her own feet, seeing them in Vivian's pristine white canvas flats. They were hideous and *really* comfortable. But she wasn't about to admit that to anyone.

Driving over to the hospital, Robin sat quietly in the passenger's seat with her hands on her belly, letting her mind wander into strange and dark places. If all the demon had said was true, this might be the closest she would ever come to ever being a mom. Even if the demon gets them past twenty years old, how could she have kids knowing she might have to leave them at some point, not knowing when, and then put them through the same pain she felt when her father died? Plus, bringing kids into a world where demons were real? No way would she do that to a kid. *Maybe that's why God—* She stopped there.

Turning towards the dark window, she hid her face from the others as she puzzled over it. She hadn't thought about God since she was little—that was her *abuela*'s department. When she and her father were alive, they'd all go to church together. Her *abuela* made sure they were there every Sunday. Robin never liked going because she had to be still and quiet. The only thing she liked was sitting beside her dad, who would sometimes sneak her some Holy wafer even before she'd had her First Communion.

But after her dad died, Robin's mom stopped going—*abuela* or not. Robin's mom blamed God and the church for taking her dad and leaving her behind with three kids. *Abuela* kept saying it doesn't work like that, and God doesn't take people away as punishment. But Robin was only thirteen, and the twins were just babies at the time. It wasn't fair.

Robin never questioned why her mom stopped going. She, too, had stopped being able to concentrate on what the priest was saying when all she could see was the same day over and over, where her father's coffin was in the middle of the aisle, her uncles cried like sad little boys as they carried it out of the church.

But here in the car, her belly puffed out by a light blue sheet covered in demon-summoning spells, she thought about God. She thought about 'a grand plan' and how she was, at the very least, given the opportunity to help raise Esther and Enrique since she would likely not have children of her own before she was killed by whatever was killing Mila.

Robin ran her fingers through her greasy hair and rubbed her eyes of any moisture as they arrived at the emergency ward. The plan was very simple. Doctor Pavi would drop the girls in the emergency room to check on Robin's fake contractions that were still far apart—she had some real convincing to do. It would probably be a while before they called her name, so in the meantime, Robin would sneak off to the bathroom and into the main hospital. Soo and Vivian would act as if they were looking for her if anyone asked.

At the same time, Doctor Pavi would enter the hospital confidently as a familiar face, perhaps finishing up some extra work and then retrieving her forgotten cell phone from a patient's room.

The tricky part was getting to Mila's floor and past the nurses, who would definitely stop them from seeing anyone after visiting hours. Doctor Pavi was the only one who had a chance to get past them, but the others were going to have to create a distraction and then make a run for it. This was where it could all fall apart.

In the emergency room, Robin gave her fake name to the nurse—Mary Jagger—and began filling out a clipboard with even more bogus information. When the nurses weren't paying attention, Robin snuck away as planned, and Vivian went with her. They made it to the bathroom, where Robin thought she would take the sheet out, but Vivian stopped her. "What are you doing?"

"Taking this thing out. It's too bulky, and I can't run," Robin complained.

"But we need you to stay pregnant if anyone asks why we're here," Vivian urged.

Robin gave a dramatic sigh, then re-shoved the sheet up her shirt and started breathing harder, like she was having a baby.

"*Heeheehoooooo*," she breathed while giving Vivian an evil stare. The door opened, and both girls jumped, but it was only Soo.

"Here," Soo said, throwing a patient gown at Robin and a face mask at Vivian.

"Where'd you find this stuff?" Robin asked, happily getting into the garb.

"There was an open closet, so I made my move. This will give us a better chance."

Robin changed into the robe. It was almost impossible to hold the sheet in there without her t-shirt holding it in.

"Just hold your belly like the baby's coming out the bottom—no one will think anything of it," Soo suggested, seeing Robin struggle.

"We hope," Robin said, looking at Soo and Vivian in their masks—her support team. She shook her head at the ridiculousness of what they were doing and waddled past them out into the hallway.

ᗞOCTOR ᑭAVI

Doctor Pavi grabbed the suitcase with everything they needed and jogged to the side entrance. She hated that she couldn't stay with the girls to help them figure everything out, but once she was inside, she felt a little better that they were all in the same place. She couldn't hear any sounds of alarm or panic around, so hopefully, the girls were in the clear. Inside the hospital, she wheeled the small suitcase through the quiet hallways, and it whirred along the Formica tile. One patient who was watching television in the main waiting area gave her an annoyed look, but otherwise, it was a quiet night. She was almost at the elevators when a nurse she knew turned the corner and walked towards her. Doctor Pavi kept her head down.

"Hey, Andra. What are you doing here?" The nurse asked lightly as she approached.

Damn, she thought and hoped her disappointment didn't show. "Oh, just forgot my phone in a patient's room on sixth." With everything she had, she tried to sound casual and not stutter.

"Isn't that a cell phone there?" The nurse laughed, pointing to the phone in Doctor Pavi's hand.

"Oh, ya," Doctor Pavi said, laughing nervously. "Um, no. This is my personal one, but... I left my... my work phone up there," she replied, bopping her finger toward the ceiling and giving a dorky chuckle.

Luckily, the nurse laughed with her and didn't seem suspicious. "Well, good luck. They're pretty strict on the critical care floor," the nurse said, walking on with a raised eyebrow.

"Right. Thanks," Doctor Pavi replied. Then, when the nurse

was out of sight, she scurried again towards the elevators.

Doctor Pavi: WHERE ARE YOU NOW?

Vivian: 6TH FLOOR WAITING IN HALLWAY FOR A CHANCE

Doctor Pavi: YOU NEED TO TRY SOMETHING

Vivian: LIKE WHAT?

The door to the sixth floor opened, and Doctor Pavi got out, trying to look as regular and confident as possible. She needed to get to the nurses' station and hope they'd let her go to Mila's room alone to leave the bag of supplies as well as stick around somewhere on the sixth floor to be a lookout for the girls.

"I'm sorry, Doctor, I wish I could let you in, but it's hospital policy," the nurse said with a sympathetic smile.

"I understand, really. Just had to ask. Thanks." Doctor Pavi's heart dropped. She knew it was a long shot, but she wasn't sure how everything would go from here. She turned around slowly from the nurses' desk to see if she could see or guess where the girls were hiding. She didn't want to linger disobediently, but she was becoming panicked at not seeing any trace of them. There was an unsettling quiet everywhere except for the occasional low beep of monitors from inside the rooms. Doctor Pavi continued to walk slowly and take discrete looks around corners, acting like she was turned around or lost so the nurses didn't get suspicious. Wherever the girls were hiding, they must have been seeing too that there was no way around the nurses' station, especially for a girl in fake labor with her entourage on the critical care floor.

A patient moaning in their sleep broke the quiet. Doctor Pavi turned sharply towards the sound. It started low, like someone having a bad dream, but soon became louder and more frantic. When one of the nurses got up to check, Doctor Pavi skirted to the other side of the hall, hoping to see the girls make a move. Then, on the other side of the floor, another patient started screaming. The nurses at the station exchanged exhausted looks that said it wasn't going to be an easy night, and they all left the main desk. Slowly, more screams and moaning began in an orchestra from all over the floor. It wasn't long before every nurse at the station was occupied, running in and out of every room except Mila's.

Doctor Pavi finally saw the girls come out of hiding from around a corner near Mila's room and rush right inside. They had made it pretty far even before the mass hysteria. She skipped lightly to join them, quickly checking to see that no one was watching.

"You guys were amazing!" Doctor Pavi praised as they all caught their breath just inside Mila's door.

"What started the screaming?" Soo asked.

"It wasn't me," Doctor Pavi said. Soo and Robin exchanged confused glances and then quietly got to work. Mila was still sedated and unconscious, but they weren't sure about the woman in the next bed. They had to be quiet as they worked.

They spread out the sheet Robin made on Mila's floor and set out the candles and cinnamon. Doctor Pavi handed the Summoners to Robin though they had practiced the incantation all day, and Robin had it fully memorized. It was time for the doctor to go. She didn't want to leave the girls to do this alone, but it was the only way to be sure Mila's roommate wouldn't disturb them.

"Girls!" Doctor Pavi whispered. "I should go while I have the chance. I won't leave the hospital, but message me as soon as you can."

Soo was the closest to the doctor and hugged her tight before she left, surprising her a little. Doctor Pavi put her arms around Soo and patted her back. Then she took a quick look outside Mila's door before scurrying across the hall and disappearing into a dark area where the nurses prepared the food. There'd be no one in there tonight since most of them were occupied with a floor of unsettled patients. Letting out an anxious sigh in the dark, she sat down to hide and wait.

ROBIN

Robin was trying not to look at Mila's unconscious body, drooping face and mouth full of tubes. Instead, she turned to check out the view from the window at night. It wasn't a great view during the day—just a lot of angles jutting out from the lower floors of the hospital's east wing. But at night, Robin could see the dark sky if she got up close and looked straight up. No moon but a few stars. It was her favorite time of day when she would usually be painting in some downtown back alley. Her mom would be home, and Enrique and Esther would be in bed. But tonight, she was here, summoning a demon to save her friend's life and maybe her own.

"Robin," Vivian whispered, stunning Robin out of her second deeply emotional reflection of the evening. "Help me with this."

Vivian opened the bag on the chair in the room and handed Robin a couple of candles to set up. When Doctor Pavi left, butterflies fluttered in Robin's stomach once more. Each step got them closer to talking to the demon again and saying 'yes' so that it could possess Mila, and she would wake up.

They had yet to really talk about what they would do once the demon showed. Robin knew her own answer, but what about Soo and Vivian? What were they planning to say? She didn't know what they were thinking about all of this. They hadn't had time to discuss a strategy besides saving Mila's life. And what about Mila? They were about to give an answer for her. Sure, it would keep her alive, but at what cost?

It was crunch time, and they knew it. Soo took Robin's hand and folded the other into Mila's. Robin reached out to Vivian, who was on Mila's other side. They were in this together now. Robin even managed a slight smile through the dark room, realizing Vivian had actually been really cool with all of this, which couldn't have been easy. *Wow, pregnancy made me really empathetic*, she thought. Then she focused more seriously on saying the Summoner spell correctly and getting everything started.

Robin spoke the words perfectly, but nothing happened right

away, just like the first time. They could all hear the moaning in the hallway and some howls of wind from outside Mila's window. Without a moon, only artificial light came in that bounced an orange tinge off the beige walls. Then, the soft, bluish glow began to rise in the center of the summoning blanket on the floor—the light of the four daemons. The glow turned into fog, and the daemons formed in front of each girl with an outstretched hand. Their cherub-like smiles were wide as they uncurled their unexpectedly long fingers, and a stream flowed from each of the girls. Robin looked to the daemon that stood over Mila in her bed. She wanted to scream and pull it away from her, to not take anything from her when she was so weak and vulnerable, but she had to hold still and keep going.

Robin's own daemon faced her—childlike, yet strong and determined. She imagined how even smaller it would seem without its horns. It was merely an outline of features and wrinkles that showcased its impish grin. It faced her with its empty eye sockets as it began, unblinking, tugging away a piece of her soul. It stared at her deeply as it commanded something from her, and she could feel the tug from deep in her heart. It left her body as white light in the same continuous stream flowed out of her friends.

It wasn't long before the daemons had what they wanted, and they moved back, smiling even wider, in satisfaction perhaps, to again become one puff of blue smoke in the middle of the circle. The wind howled louder again from outside the window, and a breeze seemed to blow around them. Then, a stirring, like leaves rustling or… someone in the next bed… moving. In the dimly lit room, Robin could see movement from Mila's roommate's bed. It had worked. *It* was awake.

12

Soo

The old woman sat up sharply and cocked her head to the side. "Are you sure you want me in this old hag?"

The old lady's body swung around nimbly to hop from the bed, but the cracking bones were audible. The demon adjusted, and more bones cracked and snapped into place. Then, as if on a track, it shifted to the center of the circle while the four daemons continued to evaporate into the middle of the bedsheet.

It was clear the demon was struggling to use the old woman's useless mouth as it drooled. The body seemed to be making it difficult as it shuffled its feet stiffly to the center of the summoning circle without sound—like a mute button had been pressed over everything or like the room needed a minute to adjust to the weight of the supernatural being among them.

The girls hadn't had a good look at Mila's roommate before, so they couldn't be sure what the old woman really looked like, but this was worse than they expected. Her wrinkled skin was paper-thin over her legs and bruised arms. It was clear that she probably hadn't stood for a while on her own legs. They shook so hard that they nearly rattled, even with the demon holding her up. Looking at her face, her jowls hung free without teeth, leaving her long cheeks shapeless and swinging. Drool fell from her gums over cracked lips, and she stood uncomfortably but staring forward through thin strands of gray hair with the demon's cold, dead eyes.

"You helped us get in here, didn't you?" Soo said to break the tension.

The demon stood still in the center of the circle, its elbows up and stiff, hips bent. "Oooh, I don't like that word. Let's just say I… 'orchestrated' a few things out there. You weren't doing so well on your ownsies, were you? So I may have helped things along by keeping the nurses busy. But let's not dwell on the *how*. Let's talk business—are we doing this or what? You all desperately needed to bring me here much earlier than we agreed, so I'm guessing it's good news?" The demon's voice was its own, a man's southern drawl coming through.

"We have a few questions first. About Mila," Robin charged.

"Always the questions. This isn't Larry King, you know. Are you in or out?" It hissed.

"Are you doing this to her?" Robin went on. "Are you making Mila sick to fool us?"

Soo had the same question and let out a short 'Mm' in agreement.

The demon shrugged and tried to curl the old woman's lips around the words, "No, she's ill, Rodriguez. You're all dying, like I told you. And, yes, demons lie, but I'm not lying about this."

Soo looked past the demon to Mila. All her fears about summoning the demon and speaking to it directly were nothing compared to how much she cared for her new friend. She hated seeing her lay there so innocently while she couldn't do anything to help her besides summoning this treacherous beast to stop everything. And she or one of the others was next. It could just have easily been her lying there. It wasn't right. It wasn't fair.

"So she's going to die, and you can't help her," Soo confirmed with the demon, trying to make it a sentence rather than a question that might piss it off.

"I can't heal her. I told you, that's not how we demons roll. But I can keep her alive for a while. If I use her body, it will be…

preserved… bonded to me… and she won't die… yet."

"But Mila can't even give her answer," Vivian added, recalling her own experience the last time.

"Hmmm, that is true. But, you know, I don't need her to answer, really. I was just being polite. Being asleep, she'll be nice and quiet… The demon stroked the old lady's hairy chin and gave a gummy smile in Mila's direction. Then it turned again, more deliberately, to the others. "Though I'd rather have the whole set." The demon slightly swiveled the body, seeming to gain more agility in the woman's bones and looking at each of the girls expectantly.

Robin was in tears, trying to wipe her cheeks with her shoulders as she continued to hold hands in the circle. Then, finally, she turned from Soo's gaze and straight at the old lady.

"I'm in," she announced without any hesitation.

"*Robin, what are you doing?*" Soo whispered angrily.

"I'm not letting Mila be alone in this," Robin said through tears and a wet face.

"I'm in too," said Vivian, though her voice shook as she spoke.

Soo turned to her other side, shocked by Vivian's answer. Now it was only her, and the demon had her in its sight. "What about you, Kim? Care to make it a foursome? You do like it with other girls, don't you?"

Soo stuck out a clenched jaw and narrowed her eyes to shield her thoughts as they turned to Faye. Would she be safe when the demon was with Soo? How could she bring a demon around Faye or anyone in her family for that matter?

"I— I'm not sure…"

"*Soo! What are you doing? This is for Mila!*" Robin grunted as loud as she could without actually speaking in more than a whisper.

When Soo came to the hospital tonight, sure, she was planning to say yes because of Mila. She had planned to do all she could to help. But looking at the demon again and seeing everything they were doing, she couldn't help but wonder if there was another way.

She kept thinking of what Doctor Pavi had said and how she had felt so alone inside the demon, and no one could hear her cries. What kind of life would that be?

The demon licked its dry and wrinkled lips. "Ms. Kim, let me make this plain: I want all four of you as my own—I mean," the demon started and then cleared the old woman's throat. "*I'd like* to have you all for my own… project. In return, I will keep you and your friends alive beyond your twenty years. If we work together, I can give you life into a regular old age. But if you aren't on board, I will be back to play more tricks—in the water, at home, with Daddy, and, yes, with *Ms. Faye Gilbert* until I have you."

"Don't you touch them!" Soo spat, forgetting they were trying to keep quiet in the hospital. She couldn't stand to hear the demon talk about her family—the way it said their names set her on fire. But Robin and Vivian were both looking at her with pleading faces, and she remembered the demon was just manipulating her to make her angry, playing its tricks. She did her best to compose herself as the demon glared and licked the old woman's dry, shriveled lips and panted impatiently, watching her contemplate.

"Please don't make me do this..." Soo closed her eyes as she thought about her family and Faye. She knew what the demon meant about playing tricks with them, and she didn't even want to imagine that any of them could be hurt because of her. But she couldn't take the chance. So even though she cried through her answer, she agreed. "*Okay!* I'm in too."

The demon clapped its hands and spun around in an unnatural twirl, getting a complete hold of the old woman's body.

Robin called out to stop it from moving. "Okay! But first things first—you do your bonding thing with Mila, and you make sure she doesn't die." Robin had a finger pointed at the old woman. The demon stopped dead, faced Robin, and squared the old woman's dead eyes to hers.

"You got it."

VIVIAN

The girls remained still except for letting go of their hands as the old woman walked from the circle and back into bed. All at once, Vivian knew what was coming next and rushed to first pick up the sheet on the floor and then hide the candles and cinnamon in the carry-on bag. Mila was about to wake up, and they were definitely not going to tell her, first thing, that they all just agreed to let the demon possess her. She had already been through too much, and they didn't have time to explain everything to her. They also had to figure out a plan to leave and get out of the hospital as quickly as possible before anyone saw them there.

"What are we going to tell her we're doing here?" Soo whispered.

"We won't have to say anything if we hurry," Vivian said, zipping up the bag.

"No way, I'm not leaving until I see her awake," said Robin stubbornly.

Vivian stiffened as a small voice rang out and crawled up her back.

"Oh, that's still quite far off, I'm afraid, Rodriguez," a deep voice bellowed from the bed.

The three girls stopped mid-step and turned to the bed to see Mila sitting straight and aggressively ripping off and pulling out all the wires and tubes attached to her. She stared at them through the room with dead eyes and a vicious grin. Vivian stared back, unable to control how wide her own eyes opened. Seeing the demon in the two adults was one thing, but she could never have predicted how it would feel to look at it inside a friend her own age. She was starting to feel different about the whole thing, and her stomach churned. She was *disgusted* with what they had done. She was *disgusted* by what vile things the demon would do with Mila, with her, with all of them. She couldn't stand to stay in the room anymore with it.

"We have to go," Vivian said as she grabbed the bag and the blue sheet, her hands shaking at the sight of Mila not being Mila.

She had to get out of there.

"Come on, Robin. We'll come back tomorrow," Soo said, agreeing with Vivian, and hooked Robin around her arm, pulling her out, whether she liked it or not.

"Oh, please visit me. I can't wait to do this again, guys," the demon sang as it waved girlishly after them in its best Mila impersonation.

Out in the hallway, the nurses were still busy with moaning and screaming patients— the chaos hadn't let up the entire time. Vivian handed the bag to Soo and the sheet to Robin while she took out her phone.

"Why am I always stuck with the sheet?" Robin complained as they walked casually now to the elevator.

Vivian: IT'S OVER... *Or 'begun' might be a better way to say it,* she thought.

Doctor Pavi: ARE YOU ALL OK?

Vivian: SO FAR, YES

Doctor Pavi: I'LL MEET YOU AT THE CAR

In the parking lot, Doctor Pavi came at them with her arms open for a group hug. Vivian was shaking so hard, desperate to be in the vehicle to see if it was her nerves or the cold making her shake. She appreciated the warmth of the hug for a few seconds, and then Doctor Pavi called for them to get in to go home. Before they got in, Soo stopped Vivian and held her between her shoulders.

"Hey, you were amazing in there. You knew exactly what to do. It was awesome!" Soo put her hand up for a high five, but Vivian could hardly lift her clammy hand away from her shivering body. Soo smirked and gave Vivian's fingers a tap before jumping into the backseat. Vivian crawled in after her, ready to be in the warmth and put more distance between her and the demon inside Mila.

Robin pouted in the front seat. They all knew she wanted to stay with Mila, but what good would it do? It wasn't Mila, it was the demon—at least for now, and they had no idea how long it would stay in her or how long it would be until they'd have Mila back.

"I can't believe we pulled it off. I was out of my mind, wondering what was happening there." Doctor Pavi kept talking as she drove, but Vivian barely listened in. She couldn't stop going over what was happening and that they were really doing this. They were really leaving Mila until the morning. Vivian's thoughts went back to being in the hospital alone only a few days before, confused and lonely. Even though she was repulsed by the thought, she was almost grateful the demon was staying with Mila to keep her safe, or at least unaware of everything that was going on for just a little longer. A bit of stomach acid bubbled up in Vivian's stomach at the thought of leaving Mila alone with the demon. She focused on the fact that they'd have to return as soon as visiting hours were on again in the morning. But they didn't know what or who they'd find there. Would Mila be herself again, or would they be greeted by her shell and the demon taunting them from the inside?

Vivian's breath quickened, and her stomach was churning in waves. She still hadn't stopped shaking, even in the warm car. It was as if her body, as well as her mind, were reacting and rejecting everything they were doing. Soo noticed her shivering and opened her arms for Vivian to sit closer to her to warm up. Vivian smiled at her gratefully and was about to unbuckle her seatbelt to move over when she leaned forward and shouted, "Stop the car!"

Doctor Pavi pulled over without question and darted her eyes to the backseat through the rear-view mirror. Vivian threw the car door open just in time to violently throw up all over the side of the road, then coughing and retching to get it all out. As horrible as it was, she had this feeling before. She recognized her frazzled nerves as they spattered from her anxious gut and all over the pavement. She retched out the anxiety and the sight of the demon inside Mila, the old woman, and Doctor Pavi. She retched until she heaved, and nothing was left. Clear bile dripped from her chin, and she used her shirt sleeve to wipe her mouth. Her teeth chattered as she tasted the vomit.

Doctor Pavi grabbed a bottle of water out of her trunk. "Vivian, what's going on?"

The same thing happened whenever Vivian had to give a speech in front of a class and also once a day for over three months when her father found out she had been taking birth control pills and stopped talking to her.

She took a sip of water but coughed part of it out.

"I just— I can't believe what we've done. I don't—I don't even know what we've all agreed to." Vivian was gasping for air between her words. She put out a hand to lean on the car for support.

"Deep breaths and then drink," Doctor Pavi instructed, coming to Vivian's side.

"None of us do, Vivian," Soo said softly.

"But we did it for Mila," Robin added, getting out of the front seat to look at her accusingly and without sympathy for the fact that Vivian's guts were all over the side of the road.

Vivian had caught her breath, but she was still shaking as she spoke. "I barely even know Mila. I mean, I barely know any of you, and yet here we are talking about her being possessed by a demon. We're actually possessed by a demon now, too, and we have no idea what that means!" She felt a twist in her stomach again and tried to relax and keep down anything that still wanted to come up.

They were all silent on the dark road. A few cars whizzed by as Vivian's words hung in the air. There was a lot at stake, and they really didn't have any idea what was coming next. They acted blindly for Mila because it could have been any one of them.

"Well, there's nothing we can do now from here," Doctor Pavi said matter of factly. "Vivian, let's get you home and cleaned up. You and I can have a longer chat together in the morning, okay?"

Vivian took a last sip of water and spat it out on the road to rinse away the coating of bile. She took a deep breath before she got back into the car. Her stomach seemed to have settled for the moment, but she wished her nerves would calm. But a quick glance at the night sky showed there were no stars for her to wish on.

Soo

Mila was sitting up straight and perky in her bed when they arrived. "Oh good, you're all early! But my mom is here. She'll only be gone a minute to get coffee."

"Mila?" Vivian asked suspiciously, tiptoeing into the room first. The curtains of Mila's roommate were eerily closed, and Soo shuddered as she remembered what they had done.

"Umm, ya? Who were you expecting?" Mila giggled and pushed up her glasses with a balled fist.

Robin pushed everyone aside and ran to fall on top of Mila in a crushing hug that she probably should have thought better of.

"Ugh, hi Robin," Mila groaned from underneath.

"Oh my God—did I hurt you? Can hugs kill you?"

Mila caught her breath and laughed, sounding like her usual self. "No, you can't kill me with a hug, even though you gave it a pretty good try," Mila smirked over at Soo. It was definitely Mila. Soo could see the emerald shine had returned to her eyes.

"Hi, Soo," she said, greeting her with a smile.

"Hey." Soo leaned over and gently squeezed Mila's hand.

"You look so much better," Vivian said as she waved from the foot of the bed. She wasn't sure if they were friends who could hug yet.

"I know, right? I just woke up this morning feeling ready. I guess somehow my body knew I had to be ready for this morning so we could have our sixty-sixth-hour appointment. I even pulled my own tubes out somehow."

Mila's mom walked in at that moment. "Girls, so nice to see all of you here, but shouldn't you be in school? It's almost a quarter to eight," she asked as she turned her wristwatch to show them the time.

"We're only missing homeroom, and the principal knows Mila's in the hospital," Soo answered on behalf of everyone.

Mila's mom smirked but stayed quiet, and an awkward hush fell between them.

"And I don't have to be there today anyway—my parents think I need to take it easy because of this weekend," Vivian added.

"What happened on the weekend?" Mila's mom looked to Mila for an answer while Robin rolled her eyes at Vivian for her overshare.

"Oh, nothing. Just a false alarm." Robin jumped in. "Appendix, y'know. Sometimes it gets confused with just regular gas."

Vivian chuckled quietly and shook her head at Robin, who was smiling widely.

"Well, I hope nothing serious. And if it is, I hope you're as tough as this one here. She's bounced back so perfectly. Gave us all a scare, though, huh?" She said with a smile that beamed with relief.

"Sorry for ruining our shopping trip, guys," Mila said shyly and apologized with her eyes for her mom's gushing over her.

Soo heard Mila talking but was far from listening. She was busy trying to see any signs of the demon in Mila. When they left last night, she could see and even feel the demon there. The spark in Mila's eyes went out, and a devious, arrogant grin replaced Mila's usual shy smile. But now, nothing. Mila was Mila. A little cheerier than usual, actually. But that left a question—Where was the demon? And why didn't Mila remember anything about the demon possessing her?

"Vivian, can I talk to you for a minute?" Soo said at the side of her mouth, taking the opportunity of Robin and Mila talking about the new turquoise laces Robin got for her boots.

Vivian gave Soo a confused look but hooked on to Soo's elbow to walk to the hallway.

As soon as they were out the door, Soo spun on her heels, "What the hell, right?"

"Relax, Soo, or she'll suspect something," Vivian almost hissed. "And stop looking at her like she's got two heads. You have to act cool.”

“We have to tell her what's going on,” Soo pleaded.

“Have you gone insane? In front of her mom? And when she just came out of a coma?” Vivian was making all good points, but there was still the problem of continuing to lie to their friend.

“She thinks we still have to summon the demon this morning. What are we going to tell her?” Soo gritted the words through her teeth. It was near impossible to whisper when all she wanted to do was scream.

“I don't know. I don't care right now. I'm so happy right now that she's alive. Maybe we could say the demon won't come if her mom is there, and it'll wait until later.”

“She's too smart for that,” Soo snapped.

“Okay…” Vivian was trying to look at Soo in her wandering eyes, trying to get her to see she was overreacting, but Soo wouldn't have it. She hated lying to Mila and didn't want Vivian to try to calm her down unless she had a plan. Every time Vivian tried to calm her down, it was like a swarm of bees started buzzing in her body, and she couldn't keep still. She wanted to run a marathon or punch something.

Robin opened the door from Mila's room and joined them in the hallway with a smug look on her face.

“Did you guys think of something to tell her?” Robin smiled and crossed her arms. “Well, I did.”

“Oh my God, Robin. *No,*” Soo said desperately. “What did you say?” Soo ran her fingers through her hair, feeling the tears start forming in her eyes out of frustration.

“Relax, Soo,” Robin said. “She thought we were all here to summon the demon today, but I told her we already did. We told it 'no way in hell,' and the demon moved on.”

Vivian took the bitten thumbnail from her mouth to speak. “She bought that?”

Robin smiled proudly. “Yup. Her mom went to the can, and I had an idea, so I went with it. I told her we convinced the demon that it had no grounds to make a deal because Mila had already become sick. So, I said we convinced it to find another group of girls to pick on. She seems ok with that. She's ready to live life to the fullest while she can. She's in there reading her stupid novel right now. Livin' it up!" Robin popped a stale cracker into her mouth she had stolen from Mila's food tray. Soo thought about it for a moment. It did seem believable. The only problem was if Mila thought the demon was gone, what would she think when she found out the truth?

MILA

"They'll be here in about five minutes to do your last scan, Mila. Do you want to put the book down?" Her mom asked.

"No, not really," Mila said with more attitude than she actually meant, but she couldn't help it. She loved her mom for being there, but all she wanted to do was catch up on reading. With everything going on, she needed some time to escape from doctors, tests, scans, and her mom mispronouncing the words as she read to her. She needed Fitzgerald to take her into his world of glamor, nightclubs, and mystery. And the old lady in the next bed had finally stopped snoring so she could read in peace.

"Well, can you put it down and talk to me anyway for just a minute?"

Mila let the book fall in front of her to listen to what her mom was going to say, trying very hard not to pout. Any time her mom said she wanted to talk to her, it basically meant that her mom would talk, and Mila would listen. Of course, Mila appreciated that her mom had stayed with her the whole time—taking time off work and making arrangements for Gemma. But as soon as her mom started talking, Mila zoned out to think about how embarrassed she felt about everything. She knew it wasn't her fault for having a pneumonic embolism, but she was still the center of attention in front of everyone in the hospital, looking like a fat slob who couldn't even ride a bike. On the upside, she had lost two pounds while on fluids for the past day. And there was a silver lining to all of the demon drama—she had friends—three friends that took care of her, visited her in the hospital, and fought for her while she was sick. Three friends she was going to die with.

"So I want you to know I'm doing my best, that's all. And I love you very much, okay?" Her mom bent over and kissed her forehead as the nurse came to take Mila downstairs for one last scan.

"Okay, mom," Mila said as the nurse came in to take her.

After the scan, Mila was left alone in a holding room with her book. In peace. She was feeling good again and could get used to this life. Sitting in bed, reading by a big window while people brought her food and drinks. Her book was getting really good too. She was in Fitzgerald's world of carefree beauty, where young people partied like it was their last days. "What a coincidence," she said out loud.

~ * ~

Mila: I'M OUT OF THE HOSPITAL

Robin: HOW DO YOU FEEL?

Soo: YA, HOW ARE YOU FEELING?

Vivian: ARE YOU ALLOWED TO GO OUT?

Mila: OMG, GUYS, I'M OKAY. I CAN GO OUT IF IT'S ONLY FOR A BIT.

Soo: MAYBE WE SHOULD ALL MEET UP AND HANG OUT?

Robin: I'M IN. MILA'S BOOK STORE?

Mila: YAAAAASSS!

Vivian: WHERE'S THAT?

Mila's mom wasn't sure she should be out walking around and

180

going to bookstores with friends yet, but Mila promised to only go to the bookstore and call when she wanted to be picked up. Even though the blood thinners made her a little queasy and dizzy, Mila would have snuck out anyway—she was dying to know how exactly everything went with the demon. Robin had a tendency to embellish some things while skipping important details.

Her mom dropped her off right up in front of the bookstore, so Mila barely had to take two steps to the bright blue wooden door. The car stayed parked where it was until Mila opened the door and waved her on.

The door creaked open, and bells chimed just before she was hit with the mixing aromas of coffee, cinnamon baked goods, and her favorite smell of all—books. Robin, Soo, and Vivian were hunched around a small round table close to the cafe window. Behind them were tall wooden bookshelves that showed off trinkets like kitchen tools and knick-knacks with sayings like, 'Santa stop here!' and 'It's wine o'clock.'

Vivian and Robin were actually chatting and giggling while Soo drank her coffee. What exactly had she missed? As Mila approached, they all smiled like people do when an old person is wearing makeup or a baby points to what it wants for the first time.

"Heyyyyyy!" Soo was first to get up and hug her. Then Robin walked up and squeezed her, whispering in her ear, "Please don't scare us like that again."

Mila was about to sit down when Vivian stood to hug her. She came from around the table, "I want one too," she said, wrapping her thin arms awkwardly around Mila in her puffy coat. Mila appreciated the gesture and how good Vivian smelled—like a roasted vanilla cookie—but they were all acting really weird.

"I'm going to get something, okay?" Mila told them, draping her coat on the wooden chair and taking her purse to the counter. She hoped it would give them time to start acting normal. For some reason, her own nerves were acting up, and she couldn't shake the feeling something was happening that she had missed out on. The three girls were all huddled in close now at the table. Mila tried not to think they were whispering about her—she was sick of being out of the loop and still the center of attention. Her purse strap fell, and she picked it up further on her shoulder before sneaking another glance at them. Robin winked back, and Mila smiled. If they were talking about demons, they'd have to lean in and speak quietly, she told herself. If anyone in the café overheard, they'd call someone to lock them all up.

Mila turned back to the chalkboard menu full of choices. Out of habit, she clenched her fists, fearing that the letters might move around, but nothing. Everything besides her nervous stomach was amazingly back to normal. While waiting in line, it occurred to her that they might have bested a true blue demon. But still, something didn't seem right, like it was too easy. Her stomach churned, but she smiled it away and got her tea.

With her cup and ceramic teapot of chamomile tea, she reached the table, and everyone stopped talking.

"What's up, guys," Mila said slowly, hoping everyone was ready to be honest.

"What do you mean?" Robin said, shifting in her seat, avoiding eye contact.

"You're all acting weird," Mila said, pouring tea from the pot into the cup.

"We are?" Vivian said, sipping her coffee with two hands on her mug, letting the bottom eclipse her eyes.

"Well, how do you feel?" Soo asked.

"You've asked me that a hundred times," Mila said, stirring her tea and beginning to get annoyed. She set her spoon on the table and looked at them all with her best, most serious 'cut the crap' face. "I'm fine, ok? Now can you please tell me what really happened with the demon?"

"We already told you," Robin said, still avoiding Mila's gaze.

"I know that's the summarized version you gave me because I was in the hospital." Mila deliberately looked each of them in the eye. "I want specifics now. *What* happened?"

ROBIN

Robin could see Mila wasn't going to let them off the hook. She stared at them intensely, her eyes a deeper green than usual and her auburn hair almost on fire in the sunlight from the big café window. Robin really didn't want to lie to Mila. She was too smart anyway and would likely find out one day and then hate them all for keeping everything from her. Robin hoped her father was right—that it was always better to tell the truth.

"Ok, Mi. But not here," Robin said, standing up from the table.

Soo and Vivian both turned to Robin as if to say, *what are you doing? That wasn't the plan!* But she didn't care. Planning to hide something is different than looking someone in the face and lying—especially when it has to do with that person's life. Robin couldn't live with lying to Mila's face.

Soo grabbed to-go cups for all their drinks, and they walked out of the store. It was a cold, windy day—not really great weather to be sitting around outside to have a chat about demons, but Robin was sure it was the right thing to do. Robin took the lead and stomped across the street to the gazebo in the park. Mila and Vivian stayed huddled close for warmth. Soo hopped up on the railing. Robin paced in the center of the gazebo and searched for the right words to say.

"Before I say anything, let me say this: you were dying and looked like crap. You had a million tubes in you and couldn't move. The doctors said you had an embolism and weren't sure you would come out of your coma because the clot could burst at any moment." Robin paced some more to gather her thoughts.

Mila was nodding along, unfazed, blowing steam from the top of her cup.

"So we had to summon the demon to the hospital to see what was going on—if you were really dying or if it was the demon playing tricks."

Mila sat up straight. "You summoned it there? While I was unconscious? *How?*"

Robin gave Mila the details of how they snuck in, and Mila even laughed at the image Robin painted of herself as a wayward pregnant teen. She got to the part where the demon seemed to distract the nurses in the hallways, and they all got quiet and serious once again, remembering the sounds of people screaming and moaning. But Robin was stalling, and she could see Mila wanted her to get to the juicy stuff—the part where they summoned the demon and talked to it again.

"It said it wasn't hurting you. It said you were dying on your own, and we had to make a decision fast. It said it could bond to you so you wouldn't die." Robin hoped she had made everything clear enough. Now she just had to wait for Mila to respond.

Mila's eyes searched the floor like she was taking it all in. "So you told it to… no. You wouldn't… did you?" Mila looked up at Robin with tears in her eyes. "Is it… in there… now?" Mila pointed to her stomach, nearly unable to get the words out.

"Ya. We think it's in you still," Soo said.

Mila was sure she didn't hide her disgust.

"But we aren't sure," Vivian added quickly. "We haven't seen it since we left you at the hospital that night. The next day you were fine."

"What about you guys?" Mila asked, looking at each of them individually. Then the look of recognition covered her face, her green eyes turning glossy. "You all said… yes… for me?"

Everyone wiped their cheeks of tears, and Soo hopped down off the railing towards Mila. "We're so sorry we spoke for you," Soo said.

"We just couldn't lose you or see you suffer anymore," Vivian added quietly over Mila's shoulder.

Robin tried to imagine what Mila must be thinking. Was she impressed by what they had all risked? Was she angry or feeling betrayed because they'd acted without her? Or would she appreciate that they had done everything they could and were all in this dangerous and appalling situation together? When Mila looked up, it was directly at Robin. The glossy gaze hit Robin right in her stomach, and she readied herself for the worst.

"So it's here to stay," Mila said as a statement more than a question.

Everyone was quiet again, reflecting on what that really meant. Robin felt for the first time like everything was hitting her—now that Mila knew everything, it felt real. The demon could appear at any time, in any of them, for whatever it wanted.

"I think I need to see Doctor Pavi," Mila said.

"Why? You've read all the books. Trust us," Robin said, half-whining because she didn't want to have to help with any more demon homework.

"No, I think I'm going to need therapy," Mila chuckled.

Before she knew it, Robin and everyone else was laughing, and she realized it had been a while since they'd all really laughed.

13

Soo

Back home, Soo knew her father would be hounding her for a jog. She hoped to finish her homework and return to her room before he came home. Dealing with demons and keeping secrets from friends were her priorities right now, and they were tiring her out. There was no way she could lie and keep a smile on her face as they ran.

It was a slow trudge to push through her homework when she kept thinking about the swim team and how far away that life seemed now—she didn't feel like the same person anymore. Before any of this, she was in a routine. Every day was the same, and she never questioned it. She might have even taken it for granted. Of course, she was devastated that the demon came and took so much away from her, but she was also starting to appreciate the wake-up call. Life could no longer pass her by without noticing and taking in what was important. Everything had changed.

With so much to think about, Soo gave up on all hopes of doing homework. There were so many more important things to worry about than English essays and extra credit right now. She piled her books neatly so her mother wouldn't be suspicious before going to her bedroom and flopping onto her bed like a boneless skin sack. Medals, pictures of the swim team, and pictures of her swimming heroes all confronted her from every angle. She closed her eyes and moved her face away from it all, but it was no use. She hugged her pillow, and it wasn't long before her chest heaved in pain with a tearless cry. Everything in her room and her whole life made her feel like a fraud and like she'd been wasting her life. Why did she even care about trophies or praise anyway? Why did it matter? It seemed impossible for these things that at one time seemed so important to her were now so trivial. Supernatural beings, spell books, and demons were her life now. She might as well replace her heroes with posters of Satan himself. But instead of continuing to feel defeated, a surge of adrenaline started pumping through her. She sat up, wiped her face, and turned to her trophy shelf with a clenched jaw. An old duffle bag sticking out of the closet gave her an idea, and she shot up, grabbed the bag, and was back at her desk chair, eagerly sweeping it all into the bag. Medals with numerous counties engraved on them, all colors, but mostly silver and gold, were easy to gather together by the ribbons and stuff deep down in the bag. The trophies, in all sizes, had featureless figures from the torso up, clumsily attached to their base. Soo crammed them in, every way they'd fit, like mismatched puzzle pieces.

When it was all out of sight, she kicked the duffle far into the back of her closet and shut the door. Once the lights were off, the posters and trophies away, she lay on her bed panting, knowing she'd still be unable to sleep. She thought of Mila and wondered if she would really be okay. She wondered when the demon would come for the others, for her. She wondered how Faye was doing with her training for Counties. She wondered what Tessa must still be saying about her not coming back to practice. She wondered if she would get her homework done if the demon would let her complete the assignments she had on the go and if Faye would go to the Winter Formal with her.

Soo was exhausted from all the wondering, but her mind still wouldn't let her sleep, which made her think of something she had never done before. Her mother was downstairs in the kitchen and was sure her father was in his study. She wouldn't have a lot of time to sneak over to their room and into their bathroom medicine cabinet, but she had to get some sleep.

Quietly tiptoeing down the hall, she inched towards her

parents' bedroom. The door was beside the railing, which opened to the downstairs so she could be caught with no excuse— she hadn't been in her parents' room in years. She opened the door quietly and snuck in, being as light on her feet as she could. In the ensuite, she knew her mother's side of the cabinet and opened the drawer slowly, pushing out any imaginings of the punishment if she were caught. She quickly found the silver package she'd seen her mother pick up from the pharmacy, and a few were already missing. Hopefully, her mother wouldn't miss a couple more. She grabbed one of the pills from the package and carefully placed the packet back in the drawer.

Before she left the bathroom, she glanced back at her father's side of the cabinet and paused. It was completely clean—nothing on the counter at all. She opened the drawer on his side. Empty. Under his cabinet, completely bare. She had no idea what this meant right now and could only focus on getting out of there and back to her own room. A quick but focused check of everything she touched, and she was back to stealthily making her way across the room to the hall and to the safety of her bedroom.

"Hey, Fish," Her father called from halfway up the stairs. Soo was just at her door. She could have been coming from the bathroom. "You're quiet tonight. Everything okay?"

"Just a lot on my mind." Soo did her best to sound calm over the pounding of her racing heart, full of adrenaline.

"Well, I'm here if you need me."

"I know," Soo said and nodded to him as she hurried into her room, letting out a deep breath of relief on the other side of the door. Then, with a gulp from her Blackrock High Swim Team water bottle, she took the sleeping pills and crashed on her bed.

~ * ~

In the morning, Soo expected to feel refreshed and energetic after getting almost ten hours of sleep, but she was wrong. The lingering sleeping drugs meant she was greeted with a monstrous headache and major fog-brain. She probably could have slept another ten hours.

In the car, on her way to school, Soo smacked her lips together, slowly attempting to gather saliva before speaking. "Mama, can you please drop me at the front entrance from now on?"

"Why? What's wrong with the side like always?"

"It's… it's near the pool," Soo said, more honestly than she usually did with her mother. In fact, she never talked about her feelings with her mother, and she certainly never asked her for special favors. Her mother sighed as they stopped at a red light. Soo didn't know if it meant she was annoyed, upset, or worried about her.

"Next therapy is tomorrow."

"Yes, Mama. Tomorrow."

"Okay. I'll take you to the front."

Soo bowed deeply as she shut the car door and walked to the front entrance of Blackrock High. Slowly climbing the granite and oblivian-speckled stairs, she started to regret her decision. A pep squad of people was flanked on either side, shoving flyers into everyone's hands and squawking about getting Winter Formal tickets. Asking Faye to the Formal was one more thing on her list of worries. Soo was pretty sure she would say 'yes,' but couldn't be a hundred percent sure. She didn't know if she could take the rejection right now on top of everything else. So, she put a flier in her pocket and decided to wait until she was out of the sleeping pill fog before making any big decisions.

How does Mama take these things? It was like she could hear her own blood in her veins and her heart pounding as she walked down the hall. She was barely hearing people's voices over her own internal sounds—the pounding head, the flow of blood, the thumping heart. Her combination lock thankfully twirled and set out of sheer muscle memory—she could barely think. Then her eyes opened wide at what she saw inside. There, on the bottom shelf, was a tablet screen with a sticky note on the top that said, 'Play Me.' Her mind had been so dark lately that it made her wonder if she should report it to the school as a bomb threat or terrorist attack. But that sounded like a lot of work, so she picked up the little screen and took her chances. When she pulled the tablet out and turned it on, a video was already queued up with a purple screen—all she had to do was unpause it.

The purple faded to show Faye sitting in front of a fireplace, talking into the camera.

"I'm too chicken to do this in person, so please forgive me for being so cheesy and breaking into your locker with help from the janitor. But I have to ask you… Soo Na Kim, will you go to the Winter Formal with me?

You can text me your answer.

And if you don't want to, I understand. We'll still be friends.

But if it's 'yes' I… Well, I hope you're as excited as I am.

Talk soon?"

She waved and blew a kiss to the camera before it faded out to the lavender background once again. The headache and brain fog lifted all at once as she took out her phone and replied: **OF COURSE, YES!**

VIVIAN

Vivian was sick of being around her big empty house doing nothing besides driving herself crazy. She would probably have to go back to school after the weekend, but for the moment, her house was eerily quiet with her father at work and her mother still resting in her bedroom after her chin surgery.

Vivian: WINTER FORMAL STUFF HAPPENING YET?

Jacee: TIX ON SALE

Vivian: SWEET. HAVE TO BUY ONE ON MONDAY. I'LL BE COMING BACK

Jacee: OH, COOL. GOING TO CHEM LAB. TTYL

Vivian: K.

She tried Cameron next.

Vivian: WINTER FORMAL STUFF HAPPENING YET?

Cameron: ...

She knew she should have started with Mila.

Vivian: YOU GOING BACK TO SCHOOL ON MONDAY?

Mila: I FEEL OK, SO PROBABLY. HOW ABOUT YOU?

Vivian: I HAVE TO GET OUT OF HERE! CABIN FEVER IS REAL

Mila: LOL. I KNOW, RIGHT?

Vivian: ANY WORD ON ANYBODY FEELING THE... YOU-KNOW-WHAT?

Mila: NOT THAT I KNOW OF

Vivian: I'M SO FREAKED ABOUT IT SHOWING UP

Mila: ME TOO... YOU WANNA COME OVER?

Vivian: TOTALLY!

Vivian pulled onto Mila's street and stopped her Mercedes a few houses down. She was so relieved to get out of the house that she hadn't, until this moment, realized that she and Mila had never hung out alone before. All of a sudden, she was nervous about the awkwardness they might have between them and considered turning around, claiming to have a family emergency. But knew she would be going back home to be bored and worried about the demon showing up while alone, so she kept going and parked in Mila's driveway.

Mila came to the door, a little paler than usual but cute for being in track pants and a sweatshirt. Her dark red hair was pulled back in her usual bouncy ponytail. Vivian promptly felt silly for taking so long to get ready, fitting into her tight, creamy-white jeans and finding a royal blue sweater that set off the caramel tones in her skin. She had taken half an hour to straighten her hair and do her makeup, too, just as she would if she were hanging out with Jacee or Celeste.

Mila giggled as Vivian walked in, "Wow, Vivian. You look amazing."

"Oh, thanks. Phew, it's getting cold out there." *The weather? Really, Vivian?*

"Oh, I guess. This is nothing for me," Mila said, smiling as she shut the door after Vivian. "This is warm compared to back home. But I guess it must be chilly for you guys."

The girls snickered and exchanged awkward glances as Vivian glanced around. The house was silent. "Is anybody else here?" Vivian asked.

"No, my mom's at work, and my sister's at daycare."

"So, what have you been doing?" Vivian asked as she followed Mila farther into the house. It was cozy and clean, with some toys piled in a wicker basket to the side of the entrance, and a few pairs of small shoes were lined up neatly in the hall. Glancing quickly through to the kitchen, Vivian caught a glimpse of a fridge full of crayoned pictures and assignments with big, red 'A's on them. Sunlight poured in from the window over the sink onto the colorful plastic cups that sat on the drying rack. It was a happy house, filled with people who spent time together like a real family.

"Reading mostly," Mila said as she led Vivian to the living room, where a gas fireplace was giving off a warm glow and welcome heat.

"That's kind of your thing, isn't it?" Vivian said slyly.

"Ya, I guess so. Even the demon knew that, so it took it away from me," Mila said, crawling onto her corner of the living room sofa.

Vivian gave a short gasp at how smoothly Mila mentioned the demon. She didn't expect the topic to be brought up so quickly, but it truly was the only thing they had in common. On the other end of the sofa, Vivian sat upright. Her jeans were a little too tight to be as comfortable as Mila's.

"So what's your thing, then? You lost your voice, right?" Mila said, ready with a notebook and pen in hand.

"And got electrocuted about a dozen times," Vivian added, shaking off a chill. The thought brought her back to the microwave in home economics class, breaking her own phone, then Cameron's phone, and then frying a keyboard in typing class.

"That's so weird," Mila said, taking notes. "Are you like a technology freak or something?"

Vivian paused to think. It made sense why Mila was asking—the other three girls had their passions attacked. But Vivian wasn't passionate about electronics, computers, or really anything anymore.

"Not really. I help my parents with their phones, but nothing special." Vivian shrugged shyly, a little embarrassed she hadn't considered before why the demon attacked her the way it did.

"Hmm," Mila tapped her lips with her pen. Then, quickly pushed herself up and off the couch and ran out of the room.

Vivian listened to Mila's footsteps stomp upstairs and then over the top of her. But before she could wonder what Mila might be doing, Mila was running back down with more books.

The books spilled forward from Mila's arms as she dropped them onto the empty cushion between them. Then, moving several away, she uncovered the one she really wanted—the largest one with a fabric bookmark sticking out. The spine gave out a squeaky cry as it opened, and the fragile spine shifted when she handed the book over to Vivian. "Look at this."

Vivian didn't know what she was looking at. It was like an ancient diagram of some kind, just like the hundreds of other diagrams they had seen in these creepy old books throughout their research at Doctor Pavi's place. This one happened to look like an animal's cage with a basic figure of a goat inside.

"It's a goat," Vivian said dryly.

"No, it's not. I mean, yes, it's a goat, but *look*. What does it look like to you?"

Vivian stared back at Mila, her bottom lip pouting out.

"Besides a goat," Mila laughed.

"Ugh, a cage?" Vivian opened her big brown eyes wide and expectant of the answer.

"Exactly!" Mila cried out, swooshing her pen in the air like a magic wand. "Now read the description," she said, tapping the page with her pen.

Vivian read aloud back to Mila: "*The Knole Cage is forged by four walls: Language, Energy, Art, Passion, opposites of demonic spirit that lack these elements outside of overtaking a human host.*

Demon can not read.

Demon is dark energy, dull.

Demon lacks creativity for is either logical or enslaved.

Demon is unfamiliar and confused by the heat of passion.

Presented with these at once, and the demon in spirit form is kept."

Vivian really didn't get it. It sounded a lot like all of the other confusing books Mila had brought out before. She didn't want to be rude, but she couldn't help but stare at Mila blankly, still waiting for an explanation.

"Oh, right!" Mila grabbed the book back from Vivian and held it up to point at the picture again.

"So… I think we're the four walls!" Mila was beaming as she shared her theory, pointing excitedly between her and Vivian. "I think we're being used as a cage."

MILA

"A cage for what?" Vivian asked, still with a dumbfounded lip jutting out.

"For a demon, maybe?" Mila assumed, squinting and pushing her glasses up her nose.

"But the demon right now is still free to come and go as it pleases. That's not any kind of cage I've heard of. And why would that same demon make a cage by bringing us together and then voluntarily get in… it?" Vivian winced at the idea as she said it.

Mila bit her lip and thought. She had also been stuck on that part for the last couple of days. Why would the demon bring the four of them together just to trap itself? She was kind of hoping either Vivian would figure it out or the act of showing her might jiggle something loose in Mila's brain. But no luck. She wasn't even sure if what she was suggesting made sense. Did the four of them really represent the four walls of the cage in the book, or was she reaching too far to find answers?

Demon is dull energy, like Vivian not being able to touch electricity.

Demon can not read—herself.

Demon is not creative, like Robin's problems with her art.

Demon is confused by heat and passion, like Soo in the boiling water of the shower and pool.

It was a stretch, but maybe it didn't have to be exact. Maybe demon magic was imperfect and meant to be confusing.

"Does it say there's a way to break the cage?" Vivian asked.

Mila shook her head and faced Vivian with worried eyes. That's what she had been searching for since she came across this book, but nothing she had seen talks about any spell or demon trap being able to be broken, especially when it was bonded to the hosts.

"I don't think so," Mila said finally. "I think when we all summoned together and answered the demon, we became an unbreakable bond."

Vivian reached out and touched Mila's cheek, "That's right, we did."

Mila froze and was too confused to move at first, but Vivian's dead eyes made her jump back as far into the corner of the couch as she could. Then Vivian moved quickly forward and grabbed Mila by the throat, pinning her down. Mila's eyes were wide and bulging from the pressure on her neck, looking into Vivian's fierce face for any sign of her, but only seeing the demon. Its flat, cold eyes moved closer to her face as it choked her tighter and tighter.

"And remember, Mila, what happens if you try and break us all apart? Won't your mommy and everyone be very, very sad?" The demon used Vivian's best mocking tones and cackled wildly.

Mila couldn't answer, but she got the message. She squeezed her eyes tight and kept trying to move Vivian's hands from her throat to inch some breath to her lungs. In her struggle, she gagged a weak "OK," and the demon seemed satisfied. The demon released her throat, and Mila gasped for air. But before leaving completely, the demon grabbed her by surprise once again. It picked Mila up by her sweatshirt collar and lifted her over its head and above the couch. Mila barely knew what was happening as the floor got further away.

"OK," the demon said.

It dropped Mila heavily onto the floor, missing the couch completely. Mila's back felt shattered, and her lungs were left winded. After gathering her breath, she slowly turned her neck to where Vivian lay on the floor beside her, unconscious. Mila rolled around in pain, slowly coughing and trying to catch her breath and bring herself back to reality. When she thought she could crawl, she moved toward Vivian.

"Vivian?" Mila croaked. She weakly reached over and tapped Vivian's hand, but she didn't move. Mila was in a lot of pain as she moved but knew she had to somehow wake Vivian or call for help. So she shuffled next to Vivian and rolled completely on top of her, shaking her shoulders and gently slapping her face.

Vivian soon opened her eyes and began slapping Mila back. "Why… Why are you slapping me? And why are we on the floor?"

"It was here," Mila grunted as she rolled herself off to the side.

"What? What do you mean? I didn't see anything," Vivian said, looking around.

"It was in… *you* this time."

"In me? No, I was here talking to you, and then Cameron called, so I took my call outside." Vivian gestured with her thumb at the front door while helping Mila up.

Mila shook her head and looked around for evidence—evidence of not only what the demon did but how it was making Vivian forget.

"Vivian, no," Mila had her square by her shoulders. "Cameron didn't call you at all. Look! Your phone is still at the door."

Vivian looked over and saw her phone stuffed inside her sneaker. She looked back at Mila with teary eyes and a quivering lip. "But… it felt so real… Cameron called." Vivian sniffed. "He said… he said he missed me and wanted to go to Winter Formal and forget everything that happened."

"And here, in the real world, we were talking about breaking the cage that bonds us all together with the demon. Then you choked me and Gorilla-pressed me before throwing me hard onto the ground."

Vivian wiped her tear-soaked face and mouth with her sleeve. "Gorilla-press?"

"It's a wrestling move my dad used to do with me when he was putting me to bed," Mila said softly.

"So it's a… nice thing?" Vivian's voice was hopeful.

"Not this time…" Mila winced and rubbed her shoulder.

"Sorry."

"It wasn't you. I don't think on your best day you could lift me," Mila gestured to each of them, pointing out their difference in size.

"I'm pretty strong, actually," Vivian said, trying to make a joke by flexing her skinny arm under her bulky blue sweater. They both giggled together for a moment, but it soon turned into a real urge to cry when they took in what this all meant. They hugged to comfort one another and stayed like that for a while, holding each other tight. The demon was always watching them, listening, and there wasn't anything they could do.

ROBIN

Robin could almost hear the entry table project taunting her, sitting there unfinished but singing, *na na na na na, you can't do it, you can't finish me, you're a loser…* She still couldn't get up the courage to carve into the wood for fear of screwing it up somehow, just like her other art pieces lately, and really, like her whole life. She couldn't look at her stupid entrance table for one more minute.

Mr. K. had his back turned, and that's all she needed to make a break for it. She skipped to the hallway and out the exit. Then, she hustled across the parking lot while searching her phone for a number.

"Tia?" Robin whispered into her phone as she ducked out of class.

"Roberta! *Qué pasó?*" A soft but surprised voice greeted her.

"You're psychic, don't you already know?" Robin smiled slyly and took a puff of Blackberry Blues.

"Aahhhh, you are always so funny, like your father. Tell me, Roberta, you've never called me on the phone before in your life. What's happened?"

On the street just past the school, Robin sat on a curb, realizing she should have planned what she was going to say. She didn't want her family to worry and make her go to church or something. But her Tia Marisol might be able to give her some ideas, or maybe… Robin didn't really know what or why she felt like talking with her aunt, but it was the best thing she could think of.

When her father died, Tia Marisol told Robin she had the

strength to be a protector and guardian for her siblings and would carry her father's spirit forward in her family. For some reason, of all the things people said to Robin on the day of her father's funeral, those words stuck with her, and Robin had always taken them very seriously. All she wanted was something like that—some type of message that would tell her she could be strong and everything would be okay.

She carefully told Tia Marisol that she had learned something about her future and was afraid. She blurted out that she didn't think she had much of a future at all and was scared to die. Robin could barely get out the last part of her confession as she started to cry over the phone.

"You come here now. We will see together, Roberta."

~ * ~

Robin wasn't planning on skipping the whole day of school, but as she climbed on the bus to go two towns over, she thought of how ridiculous it would be to try and concentrate on school when she was dealing with a demon connected to her and the threat of her life being cut incredibly short. The bus to her *tia* and *tio's* house was only about thirty minutes on the highway, and as she got closer, she started to feel her guilt rising up from not having visited them more often.

Tia Marisol was her great aunt—her *abuela's* sister. She had come from Mexico when they were young to work as a cook and a maid for a wealthy family somewhere up north, where Marisol met Tio Leo. Robin smiled when she thought about seeing her *tio*. He was so funny and cheerful and always gave her some kind of flower. She wondered what he'd have for her today.

At her stop, Robin jumped off the bus and hurriedly walked the two streets over to their house on the corner—the only one on the street that was trying to grow fruit trees in a temperate climate. Being fall, no flowers were peeking out of the fence surrounding their house, but it was just as Robin remembered. She breathed deeply, and her lungs quivered as she let it out. She still hadn't decided how much she should tell Tia Marisol about everything. Maybe she wouldn't have to. All this time, she thought psychics were a scam and demons were fiction, but she was wrong—wrong about it all. If demons were real, maybe anything was possible, and maybe Tia Marisol was really psychic, and she would know exactly how to help.

Robin felt an unfamiliar pang of excitement as she knocked on the wooden front door. It was a strange feeling to be visiting her *tia* without her parents—so grown up. She wiped her boots on the red mat out front as Tia Marisol called from inside, *"Ya voy*, I'm coming!"

From outside, Robin could hear her shuffling feet coming closer to the door.

"Roberta! *Mi hermosa sobrina!*" She held out her soft, chubby hands to Robin to hug and kiss her, just like her *abuela* used to do. She smiled so big at seeing Robin, showing off her prominent features—her pie-slice eyes and a wide smile with naturally red lips. A frilly green and white apron was over a dark rose dress that she probably had since the seventies. And a plain gold crucifix hung outside the round collar.

Robin followed Tia Marisol's hobble to the kitchen, where something smelled amazing. Next, they passed the living room, where Robin noted the *azurita* crystal in its usual place on the mantel.

In the kitchen, Tia Marisol hobbled up to the oven and groaned as she bent down to check on whatever magic was in there.

"*Pan dulce*—sweet bread. For later," she whispered, winking at Robin and closing the oven door. They sat together at the sunny table as it continued to bake.

"Where's tio?" Robin asked.

"Oh, he's resting now in his room. Maybe you'll see him later before you go," she said and then put both of her hands on Robin's, looking at her intently one moment and then snapping her eyes shut in an instant. Robin stayed completely still, half because she didn't think she should disturb her aunt when her eyes closed like this and half because of shock; she had started her whole psychic thing right away.

"Roberta, it's very dark. I can't see too much because you're, *Como se dice? Encuadernada?* You're locked up very tight by… something… something so dark, *Nena*."

Robin didn't know if her *tia* was truly psychic or if 'dark' was just something you say when someone comes to you, desperate for help after not seeing you in four years. But she said, 'locked up,' like *bound? How could she know that?*

Tia Marisol stayed still with her hands on Robin's and mumbled something to herself. Robin stayed still, trying to understand, but the language wasn't Spanish… something less fluid… She had no idea her *tia* could speak anything but Spanish and English. Could her *abuela* speak it too?

Tia continued to mumble and repeat something over and over. Then, after repeating the phrase several times, Tia Marisol hopped back in her seat and half-opened her eyes. For a moment, she sat quietly, still looking Robin up and down. Then, blinking her eyes fully open, her shoulders settled, and she smiled at Robin.

"Pass me my glasses, *Nena*," she said as she pointed.

Robin passed over the round frames, and Tia Marisol promptly began wiping the lenses with her apron. Nothing was said between them for what felt like a very long minute, and Robin was starting to think that when Tia did speak, she wasn't going to say anything good. How could she? If she really was psychic, then she probably knew what Robin and the girls had done.

Tia Marisol stopped rubbing her glasses but didn't put them on. Instead, she shifted to look out the back window and sighed.

"When I was seventeen, I was in love with Gonzalo. He lived in my city, and his family went to our church. I always liked him because he was polite and always smiling, like your *tio*. He used to smile at everyone, not only me. But when he smiled at me, I felt special. One day he asked me in private if I would like to take a walk with him to the lake. I said 'yes,' of course, and it was a beautiful walk. It was the first time we had ever been alone, and we had so much to talk about. He told me the many plans he had for his life. He wanted to be a doctor for children and have his own hospital. He was very smart, Gonzalo.

Then one day, I was at church, and we heard he had become very ill and was unconscious. Everyone said a demon had taken him. His body was crippled from the inside, and he had become violent and immensely strong. The priest in our village said even if the demon left, Gonzalo would probably die. I was scared and heartbroken, but what could I do?

I knew about a so-called medicine man in the next village and told his mother they should go. I spoke to her one day outside our church, but when I did, she slapped my face in front of everyone standing there. She said I was talking about devil's magic and only God would take care of Gonzalo.

I secretly made a plan to go to the medicine man myself the next day. But before I could, your *abuela* came to me and said we had an offer here to work in a house up north, but we had to go right away. So we left the same night, and I never saw Gonzalo again. It wasn't long after we reached here that I sent a letter to his sister, and she said he had died, tragically and painfully, during an exorcism.

I always regretted not getting him to the medicine man, but maybe it wasn't meant to be. God took care of Gonzalo, I suppose."

Tia Marisol wiped her eyes with her apron. Robin turned to catch her tears before they fell. There was a moment of quiet as they let the story fall between them. Then, Robin took a deep breath and made a sigh of relief. After all, the story was not only beautiful, romantic even, but it assured her she had come to the right person. *She knows about demons*, Robin thought.

"I understand, *Tia*, and I'm so sorry for your Gonzalo," Robin said, sniffling softly. "But what does this mean about my future?"

Tia Marisol took a tissue from her apron, wiped her eyes again, and then under her nose. "It means the same as I once told you before," she said, putting her soft hand around Robin's chin. "You are the protector of your family. That's what I see."

More tears fell to Robin's cheeks, mostly because she knew it was true, and it pained her to see her family or friends in any danger or trouble. In some ways, she hated that she cared so much. That's why she always kept it hidden. But there, in the kitchen with her *tia* and the smell of *pan dulce* filling the room, she felt great relief and comfort that someone could see the love in her like no one else in her life ever had.

Tia Marisol got up to bring the sweet bread from the oven, and Robin took some tissues from the box on the table. Tia Marisol set the pan on top of the stove to let it cool and gestured for Robin to follow. Robin skeptically hopped off of her stool and followed behind her aunt as she hobbled down the hallway that led to the side of the house with the bedrooms and opened a door. Tio Leo was there, asleep. He was breathing heavily, his round belly moving up and down, though it was a much smaller belly than Robin remembered. Tio Leo was always so jolly and vibrant—she had never seen him look so pale and small.

Tia Marisol walked in and sat on the chair next to the bed. She began to stroke his head, but he didn't stir or wake up.

"He's on a lot of medication," she said as she adjusted his blankets with such care. She smiled at him with so much love. Robin wondered if she would ever love anyone as much.

"We met at the house where your *abuela* and I went to work. Your *tio* was the gardener there, and I fell for him as soon as I saw him. I've loved him since I was about your age, Roberta. Can you imagine that?"

Robin only shook her head to show her amazement as she knelt beside the bed. She put her hand on her *tio*'s leg as he slept, and something made her want to say a prayer she knew. *Hail Mary, full of grace*, she thought, but couldn't speak. She reached far down inside her to fight off whatever the block was, but she couldn't reach it. *The Lord is with thee*, she thought—words she had recited more than a thousand times without thinking or caring about what they meant. But here, now, when she *wanted* to pray, she couldn't. She says the words she wanted to say to her *tio*, the last time she would likely see him alive. The demon wouldn't let her. And she knew. *She was… bound.*

Robin kept her face hidden by her hair to prevent Tia Marisol from seeing anything was wrong. She mouthed the words she wanted to say, touched Tio Leo's leg with a small squeeze, and then reached out to hold Tia Marisol's hand as they both cried. Tia Marisol dabbed her own face and nose once more, looking at Robin sympathetically and then taking her chin in her hand once again.

"Death is not the worst thing that can happen to someone, Roberta. It's part of life. You shouldn't worry about your future. It's what happens in the present, with the ones you love, that matters."

They sat together for a while, Robin at Tia Marisol's feet and Tio Leo breathing in the bed. They cried together, and Robin wondered if her *tia* meant that saying 'yes' to the demon was worse than letting Mila die. Maybe it was. But there was nothing she could do anymore. Back in the kitchen, Tia Marisol packed up a big grocery bag of *pan dulces* individually wrapped for Robin to bring home. Robin didn't have the heart to tell her she wouldn't be able to bring a single piece of it to her mother or the twins. How would she explain that she had taken the bus to visit Tia Marisol and Tio Leo on her own when she was supposed to be at school?

At the door, Robin hugged her *tia* as tightly as she could without hurting the old lady. She had so many more questions, but she would leave them for the next time she visited.

"Soon," she promised as she hugged her and breathed in the smell of *pan dulce* and the rosewater scent of her *tia's* hair. She thanked her for everything, told her she loved her, and Tia Marisol waved from the porch with tears in her eyes until Robin was out of sight.

ĐOCTOR PAVI

An uncharacteristic nervousness pulsed in her belly as Doctor Pavi prepared for the girls to come over. She wondered what they each might say, what they each had gone through, and if they were all handling everything as well as they could. Was Mila's condition stable? Was Soo finding outlets for her pent-up energy? Was Robin staying balanced by continuing to do art? How was Vivian doing, and was she ready to go back to school?

Doctor Pavi recognized that her anxiety was, in fact, worry—true, maternal worry for the girls. *Maternal,* she mused. She smiled as she folded a blanket she kept on the sofa. For a moment, she held the blanket close to her chest, and her thoughts landed on Brian. Her heart gave a surprising flutter, but as tears began to form, she blinked them away and threw the blanket down, getting back to readying everything they might need.

As she looked over the demonology books and other journals on the table, she let out a soft chuckle looking at the rug underneath that barely hid the symbols Robin had painted on the floor. Doctor Pavi had clients coming in regularly, and none were the wiser to guess there were demonic symbols underfoot as they discussed their troubles at work, childhood traumas, or failing marriages. Though she took her work as a psychologist and psychiatrist seriously, she did get perverse enjoyment from having met a true demon from hell in the place where she helped her patients with their own so-called 'inner demons'.

Soo was the first to arrive, brought by her mother under the pretense she would be having a therapy session. Vivian, Mila, and Robin came together not long after in Vivian's car. Robin walked in with a giant grocery bag of food and flopped it on the coffee table next to the pile of books and research.

"Sweet bread, guys. From my aunt. Please eat more than one 'cause I can't take them home even if I wanted to."

The girls' eyes lit up at the free pastries, and they all dug in before getting started, laughing and eating. From what Doctor Pavi could see, none of them looked troubled, and the demon didn't seem to be present. But how could she really know? She thought she knew with Brian, but that was wrong. She was wrong then, and it cost her.

"Mila, have you come across anything yet about how this all works? I've really found very little on this type of group possession."

"I think I have, actually," Mila spoke with her mouth full, licking her fingers and looking up at Doctor Pavi. "But it's pretty dark, Doctor P., and I really hope I'm wrong."

"What is it?" Doctor Pavi asked, giving up on correcting her nickname.

Mila went to her bag, pulled out an oversized book, and slowly opened it to the bookmark.

"Vivian and I talked about this… and…" Mila trailed off.

"And?" Soo said a little impatiently, with *pan dulce* crumbling from her mouth.

"And the demon appeared… in Vivian. Apparently, the demon gets upset when we try to know more. I think it doesn't want us to find a way out of this. So… if we start talking about this again, be ready for it to show up."

"You think it will?" Robin asked, looking between Mila and Doctor Pavi.

"It's possible," Mila said, giving a cautious look around the room.

"So maybe we shouldn't, Mila," Vivian said sharply.

But Mila stubbornly turned away and found the page with the goat in the cage and the spell that accompanied it. She pointed as everyone except Vivian peered over her shoulder to see the image.

"It's called a bonding spell, and it's technically a cage that needs four walls. I think we're the four walls," Mila suggested, looking up at Doctor Pavi as if she could give some type of confirmation.

"But we're not walls. We're people." White sugar coated Soo's lips as she made her point.

Mila stayed focused. "From what I've read, it works metaphorically. We were each chosen to represent an opposing aspect of the demonic. This is what holds a demon in place—in the cage."

"Wait," Doctor Pavi said. "Go back to what happened when it showed up in Vivian?"

Vivian and Mila exchanged shameful glances.

Vivian answered. "I choked Mila and threatened to kill her."

Doctor Pavi took a small step back at Vivian's blunt candor.

Robin swallowed and shot Vivian a savage look.

Soo tried to break the tension. "So why's it not showing up now?"

Doctor Pavi looked down at the floor to think. *Maybe...* she thought. She tapped her foot on the floor, and the girls followed her gaze, grasping her meaning. They were sitting in the summoning circle. The demon wouldn't just appear in the circle because that's where the girls had the upper hand.

"So this... cage..." Robin started, "Do we know what goes inside?"

The girls discussed their ideas as Doctor Pavi listened and tried to piece it all together. They were right. The demon they had talked to wouldn't go through all this trouble just so it could trap itself. It was up to something—maybe even working for someone else. At the thought of this, Doctor Pavi felt a sudden heaviness in her chest that she recognized from before. It was a feeling of being up against something greater than she could handle. One demon was one thing. But if it was more than one, a mafia or an army.

She snapped out of her speculations before they went any deeper. "Girls, I think we should stop our guesswork for tonight. We can all think about this and meet again tomorrow if we have any ideas. And Mila? Maybe you should leave that book here for now."

Mila nodded in agreement and happily shoved the heavy book under the sofa, which was carefully placed to touch the edge of the rug where the circle began.

~ * ~

"Vivian, I wondered if you could hang back a second?" Doctor Pavi asked, hoping the other girls wouldn't ask questions and give them some privacy.

"I'll catch up in a minute, guys," Vivian said as she threw her car keys to Soo. It was nice to see that Vivian was feeling more comfortable in the group. She'd definitely had a rocky start, and she worried Vivian wouldn't be accepted because of how Robin originally felt, but it seemed this whole mess had brought them together.

"Is something wrong?" Vivian asked, walking back into the room with Doctor Pavi and towards her desk.

"No, nothing's wrong, exactly. I just wanted to share this with you first before I showed any of the other girls," Doctor Pavi said, bringing one of the Summoners back to where Vivian was standing on the rug.

It was the Summoner from Vivian's father's office. Doctor Pavi opened it up to a specific page and handed it to Vivian to hold. She then took out one of the other Summoner books they had decoded with lemon, opened it to the same place, and held it up for Vivian to compare.

Vivian's head moved back as she saw. A page was not only missing but had clearly been ripped out. Doctor Pavi's expression meant she had no answers either. They had never really talked about the fact that the book was originally found in her father's office. It was possible that he knew even more than they had considered.

"This page, Vivian, is another spell. From what I can gather from the other books, it's a bargaining spell."

"I don't understand." Vivian took a step back.

"It looks like someone is perhaps using this book to bargain with demons." Doctor Pavi was slow and careful with her words.

"My father? No. Never." Vivian gave a short laugh and crossed her arms.

"I'm not saying anything for sure, Vivian, only that we know what the spell is and that it's been taken from your father's book. I wanted you to know first. Maybe you can start to think about any difference you might have noticed lately about your father's behavior."

"I can't think of anything at all right now," Vivian said, looking away.

"I think this could be a connection to the demon we know," Doctor Pavi said. "But there's no reason to wonder more about it just yet. Instead, I think we should just be a little more than curious as to what your father was doing with this book in the first place."

"Right, ya. But he has so many books, y'know? I'm not even sure he knew it was there. And we have a lot of servants too. They're in there cleaning all of the time. So any one of them could have put it there."

Doctor Pavi sympathized with Vivian's attempt to protect her father. It was clear she couldn't press the issue with Vivian, at least not yet.

"Hmm. You might be right," Doctor Pavi said, taking both of the books back from Vivian and walking her toward the door.

"Thanks, Doctor P.," Vivian said as she left.

Alone again, the girls gone, Doctor Pavi found the office eerily quiet. She sat on the couch, wrapped herself in the blanket she placed there earlier, and felt a strangeness in the room—the room where she had been possessed by a demon and the place where she hid demon-summoning symbols under a Persian rug. It was where she had been doing her late-night research on all things demonic and finding out much more than she ever wanted to know. The wind blew outside, and there was a loud rustling as more and more leaves fell to the ground. Every creak and ache in the house made her jump and wonder. Every brush of a branch outside the window made her think the worst.

She moved one foot forward slightly to be just on the inside of the circle. She hated being alone in the house. It made her think of Brian and how safe she used to feel. She missed that feeling desperately now. It was a heavy feeling but also a reminder to keep going. For Brian. No matter what.

14

VIVIAN

Vivian walked quickly over the gray-painted porch and down the steps to where the girls were in her car waiting. What if her father was mixed-up with demons? What if he was making shady deals with them? *Like father, like daughter…* The thought sent a shiver throughout her body, and she wished she was driving home alone with no one to answer. She could hear talking and laughing from outside the car, but they all became quiet as she got closer and opened the door. Vivian sat down heavily in the driver's seat, and the heat whirred from keeping the girls warm. The girls said nothing, and Vivian didn't move to put the car in gear.

Mila cleared her throat. Of course, they all wanted to know what Doctor Pavi had said, but how could Vivian tell them? She really didn't want to remind them that one of the Summoners had come from her father's office. She was lucky that no one had questioned before why he would have a Summoner of his own in the first place. But she also didn't want to lie to her new friends, especially since it seemed like she had finally gained Robin's trust.

Robin cleared her throat now, slower and longer than Mila, to be obvious in letting Vivian know they were trying their hardest to be polite but also wanted answers. Vivian gave a small, stress-relieving laugh as she glanced in the rear-view mirror at Robin's mischievous smile.

"Okay!" Vivian smacked her hands on the steering wheel. "Doctor P. just wanted to talk to me about the Summoner we found in my dad's office. A page is missing from it—torn out, actually." Vivian kept a smile as she talked, hoping no one would think it was a big deal.

They all went quiet again, surely thinking the worst of her father and unsure how to react without accusing him or Vivian of anything.

Mila was the first to say something. "Do we know what the page was?"

"Doctor P. thinks it's a bargaining spell," Vivian answered as she got the car going. She could answer questions about her father potentially summoning demons as she drove. The windshield wipers switched on automatically in the drizzle while Vivian turned the car towards the gate at the end of the driveway and pulled onto the dark, tree-lined road.

The old-fashioned street lights barely lit the wet streets, and the hundred-year-old trees swayed and loomed over them, dropping more and more leaves as the strong autumn wind continued to blow. Vivian did her best to concentrate. According to her license, she wasn't actually supposed to drive after dark or have passengers, for that matter, so she was being extra cautious.

"A bargaining spell," Mila muttered to herself.

Then, just as Vivian got comfortable on the road, she couldn't breathe. Her mind went blank, and she couldn't focus on anything but getting free from whatever held her throat. She tried to focus on something, anything, and she could faintly hear Soo and Mila screaming— so it had to be Robin who had her by the throat.

"Pull over *now!*" it wretched from deep in Robin's throat.

Vivian's instinct had been to stretch back and grab Robin's arms and kick, but it meant losing the place of the steering wheel and pedals, and the car would fly off the road. Mila tried to pull Robin off from behind, but the demon was too strong. Vivian managed to reach the brake pedal, and the car was coming to a screeching stop, but Vivian couldn't see where the car was headed. Soo reached for the steering wheel to try and keep the car on the road and from flying head-on into another car in the opposite lane or one of the iron lamp posts that lined the road. Then she somehow got them pulled over to the side. The car stopped, and Robin flew back and dashed out. Vivian dropped back into her seat and took a moment to lean forward and catch her breath while rubbing her neck and throat.

Soo reached her arm around Vivian. "Are you all right?"

Vivian hesitated to speak, hoping she could answer. "I think so," she managed and swallowed slowly to soothe her throat. But before she could test her vocal cords further, there was a thumping on the roof.

"Let's go, ladies... I'm waiting," Robin's voice called from outside.

The three girls exchanged reluctant glances in the dark car before carefully climbing out to face the demon once again. Robin was stomping rhythmically on the roof of the car. *How had she gotten up there so fast?*

Mila and Soo were already outside beside the car, shivering and holding each other while Vivian stood apart, rubbing her raw throat where the demon had squeezed.

"You all need to stop your games." Robin's voice was replaced with the gruff growl they all knew. "This isn't some Nancy Drew mystery you get to play at and find clues, okay? We have a deal—I hang around, and you stay alive." It emphasized the last words like a threat. "Try to learn more about me or how to get rid of me, and I'll do more than leave you alone—I'll leave you gutted like the little fish you are."

Robin rocked back and forth, her tongue flicked across her lips, and her green-tipped hair swayed as it looked from girl to girl.

"What's the cage?" Vivian's voice cracked in the cold.

Robin's head snapped back to Vivian. "None of your concern," it sneered. Robin's expression was twisted. Her pretty face was being stretched and pulled inward and down, her golden complexion dimming to gray.

The girls struggled to see through the dark up to where the demon stood on Vivian's car, but they could feel it looking back at them directly into each of their souls. They were trying to gauge its movements as it squatted ungracefully when suddenly it pushed up high over the car and sank to the ground, landing hard in Robin's combat boots. Then, without missing a beat, it walked straight up to where all three of them were huddled together and breathed a cloud of Robin's warm breath into their faces. They saw the demon now through Robin's features. It writhed underneath in its own shape. It stared at them up close with its dull, dead eyes before growling lowly, "You've made your choice. Now you let me do my work. I see you trying to hide in your circle at the precious Doctor's house. Don't forget, she's there now... all alone." The demon stood silent for a moment and let the threat dangle in the air between them. Then, with great timing, the headlights of an approaching car broke the silence, and as it passed by, Robin fell like a collapsed rag doll on the ground.

Mila rushed over to do what she did for Vivian—to get her up from her living room floor. She shook Robin's shoulders and gently slapped her face until Robin opened her eyes and sat up. When she did, Mila pulled her to lean against the car's back tire.

"Ugh…" Robin dusted off her hands and looked up at Mila and the other girls. "Why am I on the ground?"

The girls were quiet. No one wanted to say the words or be the ones to tell her. But since Robin already had a poor opinion of her, Vivian volunteered.

"The *you-know-what* was here and inside of you this time." Vivian reached out a hand to help Robin off the ground. Robin grabbed Vivian's hand and stood to lean against the car door.

Robin brushed the dirt off her butt. "But we were in the car, talking and laughing. You were talking about your dad's book, and then Soo told that joke about the pickle farmer and–"

"What?" Soo cut her off. "I don't know any jokes, and especially not about pickle farmers." Soo somehow kept a straight face as she answered. Robin urged again that Soo had told the joke and even retold what she remembered. They all kind of snickered at the punchline, but still, Soo confirmed she definitely hadn't told a joke, and this was the first time they were all hearing it.

"So weird… I swear—," Robin muttered, rubbing her head.

"It's okay," Mila chimed in, seeing that Robin was having trouble rendering it all. "It happened that way when it was in Vivian too."

Robin waved her hands in front of her face. "Okay, okay, enough. Can we please stop saying 'in' us? It's like… too sexual or something. Can we think of a better way to say it, please?"

"Okay, how about… 'possessed'?" Vivian suggested but knew it was definitely worse as soon as she said it.

"Take over?" said Soo.

"No, no," Robin shook her head. "We need something non-scary, non-threatening, maybe? Like…" Robin searched around them. It was almost completely dark where they were standing, except for the one old-fashioned lamp post—a light trapped and held by an iron frame like four walls holding a fire. Robin looked back at everyone.

"Lit up? Does that work?"

Vivian raised her eyebrows, and Mila literally chewed on the idea, biting on her inner cheek. "Like, 'Robin thought Soo told a joke about a pickle farmer when she was lit up'?" Vivian laughed.

"It's like we're jack-o-lanterns," Soo laughed and then snorted.

"Oh, by the way, guys? Last night, I was *so lit*," Vivian said, laughing, and soon they all were giggling at getting lit by the demon.

Robin was the first to stop and get quiet. The girls calmed down, and the smiles fell from their faces as Robin asked, "So what did I say?"

Soo

Soo was the only one in the group that hadn't been *lit* yet, at least, that she could remember. It wasn't that she wished to have a terrible freak-out or to choke one of her friends, but from what they had read, the demon had to light up each of them so the bond would take hold. Soo knew she wasn't exempt from the demon's warning that they would die before they turned twenty, and she wanted some insurance. She decided to be patient for a couple more days, and then, if nothing happened, she would go talk to Doctor Pavi.

For the moment, she had other problems to worry about. Winter Formal was coming up, and she had no idea what to wear. For so long, she had lived in her swim team jacket and a pair of leggings most days because anything more complicated could make her late for practice or late for class after a swim. Lately, though, she'd been rocking the same old pair of jeans and a long, beige overcoat she used to wear to church. The thought of getting dressed up was almost as overwhelming as thinking about the demon. There was definitely nothing appropriate in her closet besides some formal pants she wore to funerals and once to her junior high graduation, but they were about two inches too short at the bottom now. She had no idea where to start.

~ * ~

She waited until her father came home, had dinner, and relaxed in the living room, thinking she might ask him for some extra shopping money and a drive to the mall. But after a quick dinner in front of the television, her father returned to his office to get more work done.

"You're working a lot lately, Dad," Soo called after him as he rinsed his dish in the sink. Soo and her mother weren't even finished eating together at the table.

"Big contracts, y'know? I have to put this food on the table somehow," he said, still rather cheerfully. But Soo could hear the stress under his words.

"Something the matter, Soo Na?" Her mother asked sharply from across the table.

Since when does she ask how I'm feeling? Soo looked up at her mother, unsure if she should say what she really wanted to. Her eyebrows were in a pleading position, hoping she could get what she wanted and not get a smack for asking.

"Could you take me shopping?"

"Shopping for what?" Her mother snapped. Her mother had always bought her clothes, bringing home new leggings and t-shirts as soon as her old ones seemed a little worn. New clothes would just appear on Soo's bed, and Soo never had a say in anything, which, up to that point, had been perfectly fine because she really hated shopping. But this was different. This was a dance… with Faye.

"I… I need something for a dance."

Her mother raised an eyebrow, which Soo read as positive, though she could never be quite sure what her mother was thinking.

"Is your homework finished?"

"Yes, Mumma."

"Ok," her mother nodded and leaned in excitedly. "Let's go."

~ * ~

Soo: I GOT MY STUFF FOR THE DANCE TODAY

Faye: REALLY? I BET YOU'LL LOOK PERFECT

Soo: HOPE SO. DO YOU HAVE YOUR OUTFIT?

Faye: I GOT A NEW DRESS. I HOPE WE MATCH!

Soo: SHOULD I TELL YOU OR KEEP IT A SURPRISE?

Faye: SURPRISE! UGH, I CAN'T WAIT!

Soo: …ARE YOU READY FOR COUNTIES?

Faye: I THINK SO. I MADE GREAT TIME IN PRACTICE TODAY. ARE YOU

COMING?

Soo: OF COURSE! I'M YOUR BIGGEST FAN

~ * ~

Early Saturday morning, Soo answered her door to see Vivian's glowing dark face set against a deep blue parka. The white fur on the hood mixed in with her poof of dark curls like tinsel in a dark pine forest. *How does she always look so good?* Soo threw on her beige overcoat that went down to her ankles and grabbed her BLACKROCK RAMS hat and scarf.

The arena was two counties over. Soo was more than surprised when Vivian volunteered to drive her there until she learned that Vivian was still friends with Cameron's little sister, Julia, and she wanted to support her. But also, and more likely, she would be hoping to catch a glimpse of Cameron too.

Soo was grateful for the ride but didn't count on the fact that she and Vivian still had some awkwardness between them. As they got on their way, the radio kept it from being totally silent, but Soo felt like she should try to make conversation.

"So, what should we talk about?"

Vivian's face relaxed like she appreciated the question and wondered the same thing.

"I'm not sure," Vivian started. "We've never really talked about anything before."

Soo was relieved Vivian had realized that too. The only thing they had in common was that they were both hounded by a demon, had summoned it, and had become possessed by it. Unfortunately, that didn't seem like the best topic to start with on a sunny morning.

"What about the Winter Formal? Are you going with Cameron?"

Vivian was quiet and then took a deep breath, "I'm not sure about that either."

"Oh," Soo said quietly. "Sorry."

"No, no worries. He hasn't said anything for sure. I'm actually kind of hoping he'll be there today, and we'll be able to talk."

"He hasn't talked to you?"

"Not really. Not since the hospital. It's weird because he was so great to me by taking me there and making sure I was okay. But then he kind of ghosted me. He doesn't understand why I've been hanging out with you guys either." Vivian smirked.

"I bet nobody really understands that," Soo said, along with a snort.

The heavy awkwardness in the car started to lift as the girls laughed together.

At the arena, Soo found them seats with the other Rams while Vivian found Cameron. Soo slid into the stands and immediately felt uncomfortable being there alone. There were parents from the team that she knew, including Faye's. They all must have heard about what had happened with her, Faye's rescue, and now her absence from the team. Soo pulled the collar up on her coat, hunched over, and kept her face forward, focusing on the races. Luckily, Vivian soon climbed the stands to join her in watching the freshmen compete. Her light perfume huffed past Soo's nose as she sat down.

"That was fast. Everything okay?" Soo asked.

"Yep. I guess it doesn't take long to break up with someone," Vivian murmured more to herself. She wasn't crying, just staring straight ahead with her jaw locked and full lips pursed.

"Viv, I'm so sorry. Are you okay? Do you want to leave?"

"Nope, I'm good. I just want to watch," she said, giving Soo's arm a reassuring pat. A moment later, she was shouting, *"Go Julia!"* louder than anyone as the first swimmers walked out to take their places on the blocks.

MILA

Mila had all three Summoners at her house among the many other demonology books covering her bedroom floor as she continued to search for answers. Doctor Pavi asked Mila to dig deeper into the missing spell from Vivian's father's book, so she hunkered down with determination and snacks. It was strangely becoming normal for her to be surrounded by the demon lore each night, and, thankfully, her mom had stopped asking about her hyper-focused study regime.

The demon may have wanted them to stop trying to find out more, but what could it really do to her anyway? It sounded like the demon needed them as much as the girls needed it in return. And, really, when it came to research, Mila couldn't help herself. It was Saturday night, and she was writing down the spell ripped out of one copy and cross-referencing some of the more obscure Latin terms while tossing plain popcorn into her mouth amidst sips of Diet Coke when her phone pinged.

Gary: HEY, WHAT ARE YOU UP TO TONIGHT?

Mila thought quickly.

Mila: AT A FRIEND'S HOUSE WATCHING A MOVIE

Gary: COOL ... ... I HAD A QUESTION

Mila: OK?

Gary: ARE YOU GOING TO THE WINTER FORMAL WITH ANYONE YET?

Mila: NO, NOT YET

Gary: ... ... GO TOGETHER?

Mila read the text a couple times to be sure her eyes weren't playing tricks on her again. Had someone just asked her to the dance? Her heart was beating so hard she could almost hear it. She fumbled as she tried to text back, writing and erasing her responses over and over. He'd be waiting for her answer, and she didn't want to be the typical girl that led boys on and played hard to get. But she was struggling to sound cool and casual about it all until she settled on...

Mila: SOUNDS FUN

Mila had never been to any type of dance, even in junior high. She was always content to be home, reading. Not to mention no one had ever asked her before. She figured, *what the hell? I'll probably be dead soon, so maybe I should go.* And Gary was nice. She liked how big and goofy he was when he talked to her. He was a sweet enough guy who would be okay to spend time with for the night and— *Oh no, I have nothing to wear!*

It would be impossible to concentrate on the Summoners any longer now, so she pushed them to the side of her bed and bounced off the floor to probe her closet. But before she could really start looking, she turned on her toes because of a knock at her bedroom door.

Expecting to see her mom or Gemma, Mila opened the door wide, like she was practicing her curtsy for the dance. She started to say 'Do come in,' in a British accent but trailed off on the *in* part when what she saw took her breath away. Her mind went blank, and she lost all control of the muscles in her jaw as she stood staring at the impossible.

"Dad?"

"Hey, kiddo," he said with the bashful smile Mila remembered, though she was barely registering what was happening. Her instincts said to wrap her arms around him after not seeing him for two years… after he disappeared one day without a word. But her brain quickly caught up, and she was back to remembering the nights she spent crying and, more especially, the times she had caught her mom crying and desperate.

"What… what are you doing here?" Mila stammered.

"I wanted to see you—all of you—your mom, Gemma too," he answered, his eyes soft and glossy.

"Does Mom know you're here?"

"Ya, she knows. She said we should all talk, so I offered to come up here to get you."

"Okay, ya. Let's go talk downstairs… Dad." Mila hesitated to call him 'Dad' after he'd been gone for what felt like ages. Out of habit, she pushed her hair behind her ears even though it was in a ponytail and walked past him, heading down the stairs.

"So, are you even going to tell us where you've been this whole time?" She said, landing heavily on each step. Her father didn't respond.

"Are you going to stay this time?"

He still said nothing.

"Oh sure, keep it all a secret and then want to come back, huh?" Mila walked into the kitchen to find her mom and Gemma playing with dolls at the table.

"So let's do this," Mila announced as she walked in.

"Do what, honey? Who were you talking to?" Her mom said, smiling absent-mindedly as she brushed the hair of one of Gemma's dolls with a small comb. Mila gestured to the doorway where her father should have been standing, but it was empty—all the way through to the hallway. No one was there.

"Dad?" Mila called, going back upstairs to check the hall and the stairs. She continued to call, *Dad? Daaad?* But the hallway all the way up to her bedroom was an eerie echo.

Her mom called her from the bottom of the stairs. "Mila! What are you doing?"

"He was here, Mom. Didn't you see him?" Mila's words were frantic and shaking.

"Your *father?* Mila, what are you saying? Come down here, now." Her tone was both angry and pleading. But Mila continued to look around the hallway and then in her room one last time, running in and checking her closet, behind the door, and in every room on the top floor, desperate for an answer to what she had seen. *He was here!*

Her mom waited at the bottom of the stairs until Mila finally looked down into her eyes, her eyebrows triangles and cheeks wet, and Mila realized her mom hadn't seen anything—her dad was never there. She'd imagined it all.

Mila realized what was going on. A possession dream, like Vivian and Robin, had. Everything had been in her head as the demon used her. And now she had acted like a crazy person and probably scared the crap out of her mom.

"I— I'm sorry, mom. I guess I must have been dreaming," Mila said, coming slowly downstairs again. Her mom met her halfway and wrapped her arm around her shoulders before they walked down together. At the bottom, her mom held the sides of her head to give her a long, strong kiss on her forehead and then turned Mila's chin upward to look intently into her eyes.

"I love you so much, you beautiful thing. Everything's okay," she said as she hugged Mila tight and patted down the baby hairs sticking up around her face. "It's probably just all that medication you're still on. We'll ask the doctor this week if sleepwalking is a side effect. And we'll get you some more sessions with Doctor Pavi, okay?"

Her mom took her hand, leading her to the kitchen where Gemma was playing at the table. Mila sat down without a word, still looking around, dumbfounded and confused by how real everything had seemed just minutes before. With her eyes wide and her brain still searching for answers, she grabbed a naked doll, a pink plastic comb, and started brushing.

15

Soo

The last time Soo got dressed up was for her cousin's wedding almost five years ago, and her mother had picked out an awful yellow dress that itched in the back and made her feel like a banana cream puff. She never thought she would feel so good in fancy clothes, but standing in front of her closet mirror, she found herself with a proud grin on her face. Her crisp white shirt with black suspenders and her gray and black plaid pants were perfect. It was simple, comfortable, and, more importantly, no itching. She hoped it was neutral enough to match anything Faye had planned to wear. *Faye.* Her stomach flip-flopped when she thought about her. She wanted so badly to text her a picture of her outfit and to see Faye's dress, but she remembered their pact to leave it a surprise.

She tried the outfit with the jacket and then again without it a few more times, checking every angle in her bedroom mirror. Then she spun, giving herself a sly smile and a wink when her phone buzzed, waking her from her red carpet fantasy.

Mila: HAVE YOU BEEN LIT YET?

Soo: NO, NOT YET. Soo huffed. WHY?

Mila: I WAS… AGAIN!

The flip-flop in her stomach was quickly replaced with a dark pang of frustration and jealousy. But before she could even answer Mila back, she hurled her phone across the room onto her bed before she said something she'd regret.

With her hands in her silk-lined pockets, she began to pace the room. It wasn't Mila's fault, but it wasn't fair. The rest of them were probably getting impatient with her and wondering the same things—Why wasn't the demon coming for her? What was it waiting for? Did it want her to die? Was she even part of this?

As much as she didn't want to, she got out of her new clothes and changed back into something to ride her bike in.

Soo: ARE YOU AROUND? NEED TO TALK

Robin: WANNA COME OVER? BABYSITTING

Soo: K, SYS.

Soo didn't care that Robin's house was on the other side of town. The extra time and exercise might help her burn off some of her rage. Even as the cool wind blew against her, Soo was covered in sweat. She purposefully pedaled slowly, and her mind reeled with her desperation to bond with the demon on the one hand and her real fear of it actually happening on the other. But as she rode, her fears of it actually happening was melting away more and more. Halfway to Robin's house, she was even more torn by her feelings. By the time she arrived, she was delightfully exhausted, sweaty, and less angry but still a big mess of discouragement and confusion.

"You got here fast," Robin said, waving her hand in front of her face. "And *man*, you *smell*."

"Ya, thanks," Soo said without cracking a smile as she walked past Robin into her house. She found the powder room off the hall, where she splashed her face in the sink and took a long, slurping drink from the tap. As she was holding her face in the towel, panting, Robin knocked on the doorframe.

"So, are you gonna tell me what all this is about?"

Soo breathed deeply into the towel, letting out her final knots of frustration. "I'm the only one that hasn't been *lit* yet."

"Awwww, the poor thing feels left out of the demon possession," Robin teased, reaching up to pinch Soo's cheek. Soo pulled back but smiled a little.

"I'm serious, Rob. It means I'm vulnerable, right? Doesn't it mean that I'm not bonded or protected? Mila just got lit again, and here I am–"

"Wait—*what?* Is Mila okay?" Robin's voice raised in panic.

"Oh my god, she's fine!" Soo whined. "The demon gave her another dream thingy. Can we, for once, focus on me, please?"

"Ok, relax." Robin took Soo's hand, leading her around the hall to her bedroom, and made her sit on the bed. Then she went to the closet and began rummaging through junk and a pile of clothes as she explained her idea. "I was thinking, maybe if I'm bonded from being lit, I don't need a Summoner to get in touch with the demon. It certainly knows when we're talking about getting rid of it, so it must be just… around. Maybe I can call it here somehow."

Soo's eyes widened as she peered at each corner of the room. "You think it's around, like, now?"

"I guess? We don't really know how it all works except that it doesn't like it when we go poking around or asking questions." Robin grunted as she continued to search on all fours through her closet.

"Do you really think we should provoke it?"

"I think it would know if we were tricking it. Maybe if we just… ask it?" Robin turned from the closet, pulling out a box from behind her back.

"You're kidding," Soo scoffed. "A Ouija board?"

ROBIN

"Do you know how to play?"

"I think I remember. But, man, my mom would freak out if she knew I was doing this," Soo said, looking over the spade-shaped planchette.

"You think this is the worst thing we've done lately?" Robin asked, sharply raising the peaks of her eyebrows.

"Good point. It's just that my mom always warned me about this stuff, and she specifically didn't want me to play with Ouija boards. I told her once that one of the girls brought one of these to a swim team sleepover, and she banned me from sleepovers for life."

Robin couldn't imagine not being able to go to sleepovers. Not that she had been invited to many over the years, but still.

"You're mom's super strict, eh?"

"And religious," Soo added as she helped unfold the board.

"My family too," Robin said, thinking again about how she kept imagining her *abuela* and her father looking down on her from heaven, shaking their heads at everything she'd been up to lately. "But at least you didn't have to hear about demons growing up," Robin added.

"Are you kidding? We have tons of demons and goblins in Korean culture. My mom and grandma always talked about *dokkaebi.*"

"Doka-wha?" Robin asked, wincing at the sound of the word.

Soo giggled. "It's like a goblin that can play tricks on evil people or even bring diseases. My family is always saying how we need to be careful to be good, so we don't tempt the *dokkaebi.*"

"So I guess all religions and cultures are about the same thing—be perfectly good, or something bad will come for you." Robin snickered as she turned to grab two small candles she had under her bed. She didn't want to say anything out loud, in case Soo wasn't thinking the same thing, but she wondered what they had done to deserve everything bad that was happening to them.

When the candles were lit, and the planchette sat in the middle of the board, Robin nodded at it all, satisfied that she had made a good trade with one of her friends downtown—some paint cans she didn't need anymore in exchange for the board game.

It was just a game anyone could buy at any toy store, but the famous lettering, the plastic planchette made to look like wood, had a definite spooky vibe, especially in the candlelight. Before they got started, Robin felt the urge to check on the twins once more. She snuck to their room and peered through the crack in the door, then squinting into the darkness, she could see they were both sound asleep in the beds that Robin, with Mila's help, had carved with protection symbols.

She breathed a heavy sigh of relief for the twins being safe, but also a slimy residue of anxiety about getting ready to get in touch with the demon again. It was never a fun experience, and they really didn't know what they were doing. Plus, she had never seen the demon on her own before—without Doctor P., Mila, or Vivian. She and Soo were going rogue, which was kind of exciting and adventurous. Soo's weird awkwardness had grown on her. She was really nothing like what Robin had originally thought a jock could be like.

They sat within the circle of candles, the Ouija board between them, and Robin began to feel the heaviness of what they were doing. She closed her eyes to concentrate. Soo was serious, and even though it was completely perverse, Robin felt bad for her for not having been lit by the demon yet. *Normal people don't have thoughts like this. No one has ever wished for their friend to become possessed. How weird is my life?*

"Do you know what question you want to ask?" Robin asked Soo in a whisper.

Soo settled in closer with closed eyes. "Oh, great Ouija…" Soo had put on a low, bellowing voice that made Robin snicker. Soo peeked at Robin to scold her, and Robin grimaced back but made a zip across her mouth so Soo could continue.

"Oh, great, Ouija, is there a demon here?"

The planchette moved swiftly to 'NO'.

"Oh, great, Ouija, is there a spirit here?"

The planchette moved swiftly to 'YES'.

Soo and Robin had both opened their eyes and exchanged

puzzled glances.

"What's your name, spirit?" Robin continued.

The planchette skimmed the board carefully as Soo and Robin looked on.

D - A - D

Robin shot back from the board like lightning bolts of both pain and fear had struck her heart. She moved across the floor as far from the board as she could crab-crawl and caught Soo's eye, shaking her head. Soo got the message and took her hands off the board quickly, putting it to the side and moving forward to comfort Robin.

Robin stammered, "It can't— he can't be a s-s-spirit. He just can't."

"You're right. He can't," Soo said in a deep voice and leaned back coolly against the post of Robin's bed. "It's *me*, actually." The demon flashed a look at Robin that she knew too well—never-ending, dead eyes. "I was just joking around. What the hell are you two doing now?" it asked, bored or even frustrated with the uncooperative girls.

"We need to talk to you." Robin did her best to steady her voice while continuing to push back and away.

"Ya, I got that with the whole talky-talky board thingy. What is it you want?" The demon examined Soo's fingernails but stayed back.

"Well, I guess it doesn't matter now, but we wanted you to come and bond with Soo. We didn't know why you hadn't yet or what you were waiting for."

The demon narrowed its eyes and seemed to be considering its answer carefully for once. Robin was watching all of its tiny expressions as best she could, attempting to foresee any trouble it might be about to cause. She hadn't thought to have a plan in case she was alone with the demon. And even though Robin was looking at Soo's tall and toned physique, she felt very, very alone.

"That ship sailed long ago, Rodriguez. I never needed to

possess each of you for us to be bonded. We did that in the hospital. Plus, I've been using each of you equally every day, as per our agreement. Haven't you noticed? This isn't my first rodeo here." It gestured to Soo's torso.

"But how? We don't even remember when you're here—we just get these confusing dreams."

"Isn't that–" The demon cut off and cleared its throat, "…*kind* of me?" A wide grin grew on its face as it pained to utter such a friendly word.

"But—" Robin started, but the demon held up a hand close to her face.

"There's no need to worry, Rodriguez. Everything is like I said. I use each of you to get what I want, and you all escape death. At least until sometime after you turn twenty or maybe longer. I gave you my word, didn't I?"

Strangely, the demon turned slightly away and continued mumbling in a mocking voice, "Demons love words, don't they? … and contracts and paperwork… and I'm the lucky son of a bitch who gets stuck filing it and going over it all..." It sneered at its own ramblings and then turned back to Robin. "So, we're all good here?" It said, rolling Soo's eyes so far back that Robin only saw the bottom whites of her eyeballs. Then they ghoulishly bounced back into place, squaring its face at Robin, looking dead serious. "And I apologize for the 'D-A-D joke." The expression suddenly left Soo's face, and her body crumpled to the floor—though not for long. Almost instantly, Soo groaned and pushed herself back up to standing, holding her head in her hands.

"Soo, it was here! You were lit!"

"Ya, I know," Soo said groggily. "I was awake."

Soo

"What? What do you mean 'awake'?"

"I saw and heard everything." Soo stretched out her back and rubbed her eyes. "And that whole eye roll trick was no joke. That really hurts."

"Well, I guess that's that—you're official," Robin declared.

"Ya. I guess I got what I asked for… and more," Soo said, continuing to blink her sore eyes.

While the demon spoke to Robin, it showed Soo something else on the inside—how it had come for her the first time she took the sleeping pill. From then on, it had used her on the nights she was sleeping.

"It let me look at you through my own eyes, but I had no control. It kept me back but also calm. It wasn't scary. It actually felt like I was safe like *protected*."

Robin listened with her mouth open like she always did when she was really concentrating. Then, about halfway through Soo's description, Robin scrambled to find a pen and a top off a pizza box. "Sorry—not Mila," Robin apologized as she furiously scratched the cardboard to make the pen work.

Mila, Soo thought. How could she have ever been jealous of Mila for having been lit? She felt so guilty for having thought of any of those things. Mila may not have known it, but to Soo, it felt like they just had their first fight.

Robin and Soo called Mila's phone and put it on speaker to tell her everything—even the part where Soo didn't feel like telling Mila or Vivian what was going on because of her jealousy.

"Hey, I get it, Soo. I think we've all had some messed-up feelings since this all started. I'm just glad you're both okay. A Ouija board, though, Robin? Really?"

Even though Mila was quick to forgive, Soo continued to apologize profusely and then started to read her the pizza box notes about what had happened so she could keep them in the records Mila was keeping about everything.

When both Soo and Robin had told her as much as they could

remember, Mila, changed the subject abruptly. "Are you guys going to Winter Formal? Soo, you said you're going, right?"

"Ya, I'm going with Faye. How about you?"

"Gary just asked me, and I said yes. How about you, Robin?"

"Winter Formal? Ugh, no. Over my dead body."

"Be careful what you wish for," Mila joked. Then Soo and Robin's laughter was cut off when they heard the front door open.

"Mila, my mom's home. I gotta go."

Once her mom had walked through the house to her own bedroom, Robin snuck Soo out the front door. Soo quietly wheeled her bike from the side of the house and jumped on the seat with a small skip. The ride home was much different than how she had come. She was calm and even enjoying the slower pace with the strange feeling of freedom that had come from knowing she was officially bonded to the demon. Knowing she wasn't going to die was a load off of her mind.

When she got to her driveway, she stopped to adjust her eyes to what she was seeing. Her father's car was gone. *Where would he be on a Saturday night at midnight? He never goes anywhere.*

Soo crept to the kitchen to get some juice in the dark. At the fridge, she stood in the light and drank juice straight from the pitcher. Then a voice spoke to interrupt her innocent fun.

"Soo Na! What are you doing drinking from the fridge like that? And where have you been?"

"I told you, mama, I was babysitting with my friend."

"You never told me this. I never would let you go out at night, coming home past midnight on your bicycle on a school night."

"But mama, you said I could go after my homework was finished."

"Enough lies. Don't you try to make me seem crazy. Get to your room."

Walking up the stairs, Soo thought back to her conversation with her mother from earlier in the afternoon. It was too good to be true, and she should have known. She must have been lit even then.

So what had been real in the last two weeks? What had she said to people while the demon took her for a spin? What had she not said to people and thought she had? Then the worst thought came in, and her stomach wretched. But it was too late to call, and she honestly didn't really want to know the answer. What if she had dreamed the whole thing and Faye hadn't asked her to the dance at all?

VIVIAN

The cool silk fanned and fell perfectly as Vivian pulled the dress from her closet. The mermaid green silk was meant to contrast her dark skin like a fresh mint with brown and green swirls, but now she had nowhere to wear it. She and Cameron were finished, and any dreams she had for the dress were gone, replaced with regret. She tilted her head to the side as she admired the lonely dress, letting the heaviness fill her chest before she sighed to try and flush the feelings away.

At least she wasn't angry anymore. She understood why Cameron broke up with her—she was different now. The demon and all she had gone through had changed her. She had new friends that had changed her too, which made her really excited and happy even. But it also meant some other things in her life no longer made sense. Holding up the dress on its hanger, waving the material back and forth, she felt a lump in her throat as she knew the same logic applied to her pretty dress too.

When she eventually rehung the dress and shut the closet doors, a loud clang came from downstairs. At first, Vivian brushed it off as being one of the servants or maybe one of her parents still awake. But she felt strangely compelled to see what it was for sure. Vivian wrapped her robe tightly around her slim waist and descended the grand staircase to the hall. She turned the lights up and headed down the wide, mahogany-encased hallway. There was another noise coming from the kitchen. Vivian stepped lightly, and she didn't know why. Maybe she thought she could surprise whoever or whatever it was. One thought was that it was the demon at her house coming to make trouble. She had no idea how she'd defend herself against it alone, but she had to try—it might come for her family.

Vivian approached the kitchen to find a dark shadow in front of the bright light of the refrigerator, standing comfortably and about to drink straight out of the juice carton. Vivian switched the light on.

"James?"

The person turned, and the fridge rattled as he nearly dropped the carton of juice and bumped one of the shelves.

"Viv! God, you scared the shit out of me," James said, laughing and holding his chest from the shock.

Vivian leaned back in the doorway with a sly, knowing smile, "What are you doing here?"

"Uhhh, I live here?"

"No, you don't, actually. You're supposed to be in your dorm," Vivian said, throwing the attitude right back at him.

"Ya, well, we ran out of food," James bit off a mouthful of a salami sandwich.

"You ran out of food, so you drove over fifty miles to get a midnight snack?"

"Basically, ya," he said as he chewed.

"I call B.S."

"Okay. Think what you want," he said as he strolled past Vivian and headed out of the room. "Hey, is dad out of town again?"

"Not that I know of," Vivian said, furrowing her brow as she tried to remember the last time she saw her father. But she also knew no one had said he'd left to go anywhere.

"His car isn't here," James pointed out.

"Well, where would he be at this time of night?"

~ * ~

In the morning, when Vivian opened her eyes, the first thing she saw was her closet door ajar and her green silk dress shining, looking back at her. She knew exactly what she wanted to do.

Vivian: SO, DO YOU KNOW WHAT YOU'RE GOING TO WEAR?

Mila: WHY ARE YOU AWAKE? AND NO... (sleepy face emoji)

Vivian: GET UP. WE'RE GOING SHOPPING

Being before noon, the morning frost was still wrapping the edges of trees as they drove downtown. Vivian's white mittens hugged the steering wheel as she smiled at Mila in the heated passenger seat, who was trying to curl up and go back to sleep.

"Hey, no sleeping!"

"I'm just resting my eyes," Mila said, yawning.

Vivian scoffed and rolled her eyes but couldn't quit her excited smirk as she drove, her green dress lying across the backseat. She hadn't been to the shops since she bought her phone, so she was thrilled Mila was taking her up on her offer. They were both still technically on bedrest, but Vivian told Mila to tell her mom that shopping is a proven type of therapy too. Vivian was feeling proud of her witty argument even though Mila wasn't too sure it was a good idea at first. But Vivian could see Mila's excitement even behind her heavy eyelids.

"I need to exchange this for a different size."   Vivian hung the dress on the rack next to the peppy salesperson.

"Oh honey, this color is gorgeous for you. But this seems to be a good size, no?" He had no shame in looking Vivian up and down.

"Not for me," Vivian said, moving her eyes toward Mila and then back to the confused clerk.

"Oh! Let me just see what sizes we have available," the clerk said, walking to the back of the shop. The girls were left to browse.

Mila whispered nervously to Vivian, "They're not going to have my size. And everything is so expensive! We should go!"

"Shhh. Just think positive," Vivian said. "Go look around and see what you like. But don't touch anything. They hate that."

Mila turned and tried to look like she belonged, except for her hands crossed awkwardly behind her back. Vivian saw Mila's eyes begin to shoot around the room, catching the shimmer of the sea of sequins and shining silk in the store. Vivian had bought countless gowns here with her mother, but the mermaid dress was by far her favorite of any she had seen over the years.

"I'm sorry, ladies, we don't have any other sizes left of the light green."

Vivian's heart sank—Mila was right. Maybe this was going to be more difficult than she had thought. Vivian had never had anyone Mila's size for a friend before. If she had ever overheard a clerk say anything like that to a customer, her automatic response would be to crack up laughing with Jacee and Celeste and maybe make some fat jokes, just loud enough to shame the customer. She felt so ashamed of who she used to be not that long ago.

"But, I do have this one," the clerk said suddenly, holding up a darker green shimmering gown with a long slit up the leg. Mila's jaw dropped, and Vivian clapped.

16

ROBIN

Robin let out a breathy laugh as she opened her phone to a picture of Mila in a revealing, emerald-green gown.

Robin: HOLY CRAP, YOU LOOK LIKE A SEXY 'POISON IVY'

Mila: THANK YOU!! I LOVE HER

Robin: I'M SURE GARY WILL DROOL

Mila: I'LL GET HIM A BIB — NO WAY IS HE RUINING THIS THING

Robin: WAS IT EXPENSIVE?

Mila: NOT FOR ME, BUT I'M SURE IT WAS FOR VIVIAN. SHE TRADED HER

OLD DRESS FOR IT. ISN'T THAT AMAZING?

Robin: WOW, YA IT IS

As much as she didn't want to admit it, Robin was FEELING a little jealous of Mila—not because of the dress, but because Robin had been at Blackrock High for two years and had never been to a dance—she'd never even been asked. And she definitely never had the most popular girl in school buy her a dress. Mila had just got here, but she had already fitted in better than Robin ever had. As she thought about it more, she realized that in the last few days,

Mila somehow had both Soo and Robin wanting to be in her shoes. But once Robin thought of having to dance with someone like Gary, the envy completely crumbled to dust, and she resumed her crouched-down position on her bedroom floor to draw in her sketchbook.

She reached for her sketch pad that was, of course, on the bottom of a pile. The pile toppled as she pulled the pad out, and everything on it fell to the floor, including the Ouija board. Robin stopped and stared, remembering the trick the demon had played last time. *It wasn't real. It wasn't him,* she told herself. But her imagination reeled at the possibility that her father wasn't in heaven like he should be.

Heaven?

It was true. As much as she tried, she always came back to an image of her father and *abuela* looking down over her from fluffy white clouds, maybe up there dancing to *banda* music at a great ancestral picnic. Logically, she always knew it was a ridiculous picture to have. But now she was starting to think, if there were demons from hell, maybe there really was a heaven too.

She pulled the Ouija board closer but then pulled her fingers back and away at the thought of trying it alone. She told herself she was being stupid but then quickly grabbed the planchette from under the pile and placed it on the board with intention. Like before, she closed her eyes and concentrated. She conjured up an image of her father in heaven and held it there.

"Can you hear me?"

Robin opened only one eye at first to check the room, which was empty. She blinked her eyes open and wondered… the Ouija instructions were very clear—you needed two people, but who would she get? Her four-year-old brother or sister? Definitely not.

Maybe there was a way to strengthen the power, so she could use the board on her own.

She grabbed a red China marker from her wooden art box and turned the board over. She began etching the symbols she remembered from the Summoner—the same ones that were now graffiti on Doctor Pavi's office floor.

When she was done, Robin closed her eyes almost restfully and concentrated again on her father's image in heaven.

"Dad, are you here?"

Nothing. She tried several more times, asking for him and her *abuela* specifically. But nothing. Then Robin had another thought that made her lips go dry. To make sure her dad really wasn't around, the board needed to be tested—to be sure it was working at all.

Robin hesitated to ask but pushed through. "Any other spirits want to chime in here?" She really wanted to wait around for an answer, but as she stood up, ready to hide the board in the closet, the fog crept in. Robin stopped and watched as the familiar blue smoke circled and swayed in the air in front of her over the board before hovering over the middle board. The daemon formed and stood before with childlike innocence, except for the notable horns. With only the outline of a face, similar to so many in Robin's sketchbook, she couldn't detect its exact expression. *Is it good or evil?* The daemon held out its hand and reached toward her; she remembered this part well—where the daemon takes a piece of your soul to keep forever in its vessel.

Robin stayed still as the white glowing stream was pulled from her chest until the daemon seemed satisfied and released her. Then, it wistfully turned back, silent and thankless, into a light blue fog and disappeared.

Robin heard a scratch and looked down at the board. The planchette moved to 'yes' and vibrated in place impatiently.

Robin swallowed the lump in her throat and considered her question carefully. "Are you a spirit?"

The planchette smoothly rode over to 'NO'.

"Are you my demon?"

It remained and vibrated on 'NO'.

"How can I be sure? What's your name?" But as soon as she asked, Robin realized a few things. One, she didn't know if demons had names. Two. She didn't even know the name of the demon they were bonded to. And three. The demon would probably lie.

As the planchette moved on its own, Robin took note of the letters in her sketch pad.

'NO NAMES. NO CONTROL. R U A RAM?'

"I guess?" Robin technically was a Blackrock Ram, but she felt strange admitting the title that was usually reserved for jocks.

'TO THE DANCE'

"No, I'm not going to the dance," Robin said, wondering where this was going.

The planchette hopped up from the board into the air and faced Robin like a floating dagger, the pointed end bobbing between her eyes threateningly. Robin stared back, looking around and under the planchette for trick wires or a ghostly hand. When she blinked, it slammed back down hard onto the board.

'TO THE DANCE'

"No, I'm not going to the dumb dance," she nearly shouted.

'BYE'

The air returned to the room, and the spirit was gone. Robin's mouth hung open and dry as she stood dumbfounded. *What was that? Who was that? Why does it care if I go to the stupid dance?*

She crossed her arms and shivered as she thought about anything else creeping through. She quickly checked the corners of her room, closet, and under the bed. Then, she pushed the Ouija board hard, so it flew under the dresser and hit the wall behind. Robin rushed under her bed sheets, still in her clothes and the lights still on. She pulled the blankets over her head but didn't sleep.

Soo

"It's been a while since we've had a session with just you and me. There's quite a lot to go over, don't you think?" Doctor Pavi said from her chair while looking through her notes.

Soo was only half-listening. Nothing, in particular, was going on outside the window, but she couldn't help but look out. Maybe she didn't feel like focusing on her problems. Or maybe she was trying to avoid the fact that just under the rug where she sat were ancient and very powerful demonic summoning symbols that gave her the creeps.

"Soo? What's on your mind?"

Soo snapped back into reality, surprised at the question. But she didn't know how to answer. "Doctor Pavi, can I ask you something?"

Doctor Pavi raised her eyebrows and waited.

"Why do people get divorced?" Soo wasn't expecting much of Doctor Pavi. There were a million reasons why people got divorced. But she just couldn't bring herself to say any of it out loud. She thought that was what might be happening with her parents.

Doctor Pavi balked slightly at the question but answered just as Soo imagined she would.

"What makes you ask that?"

Soo recounted the night she snuck into her parent's room and saw her father's side of the sink and nightstand completely empty. Doctor Pavi gave a sympathetic smile but again answered as Soo expected.

"Adults have complicated lives, and marriage is a complex and unique relationship between two people. There could be something else your parents are dealing with. Your job is just to respect their privacy for now and not jump to any conclusions."

"That's such a 'parent' answer." Soo looked down and picked at a hangnail.

"What would you like me to say?"

"I don't know. Maybe, like, it's okay to confront my mother and demand answers, and I shouldn't worry about her disowning me for disrespecting her."

Doctor Pavi was silent again, and Soo wasn't surprised—it was what psychiatrists do in therapy when the patient should be talking and interpreting their own feelings. It was all starting to grate on Soo's nerves. Through all of their demonic adventures, she had gotten to know Doctor Pavi, but it was like she had returned to her regular "doctor-patient" relationship like they weren't friends all of a sudden—just when Soo just needed to talk and not be analyzed.

"Is it possible you're connecting some of this to your relationship with Faye?"

Soo flushed at the mention of Faye's name. Maybe she was still a little worried about her and Faye. There was still the possibility that nothing between them had really happened, and it was all a demonic dream. But if it all did turn out to be true, she was worried that if her parents separated, she would seriously question her ability to be a good partner. Faye deserved so much better than that. Plus, Soo worried about the fact that not only had she never danced with anyone before, but she'd also never even been on a real date. Not to mention what was bothering her the most—Faye was her teammate, and she had already seen her naked dozens of times in the locker room, and there were certain images she had in her mind that she wasn't sure how to catalog. Should she forget them or cherish them? Or was she a total pervert for recalling them at all?

"No, not really. We're just going to the dance."

VIVIAN

All the buzz about the Winter Formal made Vivian wish she could have stayed home from school longer. It was cool that Mila and Soo were going, but she felt like strangling anyone else that mentioned it. The cheesy paper snowflakes that hung in every hallway grated on her nerves, and she dreamed of being tall enough to rip them all down. Jacee and Celeste still hadn't spoken to her or texted, and when she saw them in last period, they made some lame excuses about staying around to help a teacher for extra credit. Vivian laughed about it, seeing the blatant lie, but it also made her realize she didn't actually care what they did anymore. They hadn't come to see if she was okay after being in the hospital, they hadn't checked on her since she and Cameron broke up, and they were cutting their conversations shorter and shorter in their text messages. She was over it.

Thankfully, the week went by fast, and it was the Friday of the dance before she knew it, and it would all be over soon. Plus, knowing everyone would be hyper and distracted, teachers weren't going to give any pop quizzes or surprise essays. In English, they watched a movie version of Hamlet, and, for once, Vivian didn't get a pile of math homework for the weekend.

She felt such relief as the bell for her last class rang, and she wasted no time lingering around and headed straight to her car. Keys in hand and ready to press the button on the fob, Vivian caught sight of her car and someone standing next to it—waiting for her. The person wasn't much taller than the car, wearing a dark hoodie, fingerless gloves, tights, and big black boots with turquoise laces, like Robin. But it couldn't be Robin—Robin would never wait for Vivian after school to talk to her voluntarily.

But as Vivian approached, she slowed her pace, and Robin stared back with her usual smug grin.

"Robin Rodriguez…?" Vivian said in disbelief.

"Vivian Voorhees…" Robin threw back, mocking her.

"How can I help you?" Vivian decided to be as polite as possible but also hoped this wasn't part of a secret plot to befriend her and then suddenly beat the crap out of her when they were alone and her guard was down. The last few weeks, Robin had only been tolerating her because they had bigger problems. There was no reason Vivian could think of for Robin actually wanting to talk to her.

Robin leaned near the rear wheel with a black fingernail in her mouth. "You're not doing the Winter Formal thingy, are you?"

"Nope. I gave my dress to Mila, and I'm staying in. Why?"

"I wondered if you wanted to… like… not go… together." Robin looked at the ground as she spoke.

"Like, hang out tonight while everyone's at the dance?" Vivian's tone was still of disbelief and distance, waiting for Robin's punchline or literal punch to her face.

"I mean, maybe we could pick up some of the slack that Mila's been doing with the research or compare notes or something." Robin looked away and went back to chewing her fingernail.

Vivian decided to be the bigger person. "Robin, are you asking me to *not go* to the dance with you?"

Robin still avoided eye contact. "Maybe?"

Vivian paused for a slight moment, just to make Robin sweat. "What did you have in mind?"

Robin turned towards her with a mischievous smile, bouncing her eyebrows.

17

VIVIAN AND ROBIN

When Vivian drove up to meet her, Robin was shivering outside the bookstore, vaping Blueberry Ice in the cold. It was already pitch black outside, and most of the stores had closed.

"So, what are we doing anyway?" Vivian asked as she got out from the driver's side, brushing a bit of snow from her fluffy white mittens.

"Just come here, Spaz." Robin waved for her to follow, and Vivian was thankful to get moving. Robin hurriedly led them off the street and down an alleyway. It was too narrow for a car to pass through or for even the two of them to walk side by side. They had to walk down it single file, and Vivian had to do her best to keep the sleeves of her jacket from touching the walls. Robin looked back, and even in the dark, Vivian could tell Robin was rolling her eyes at her. There were graffiti tags, messages, and random pieces of amateur street art on both sides of the brick walls, some authored by Robin herself. *So this was it,* Vivian thought to herself. *This is where Robin's going to kill me once and for all.*

Then Robin made a turn behind the post office to a small parking lot surrounded by a wall of tall evergreen bushes. Vivian followed Robin's quick pace through the parking lot to another shadowed crevice between the post office and the next building, where it was another tight fit but just enough space for a large, rusted metal plate on the ground.

"Look at this. Do you recognize it?" Robin flashed a light off a keychain towards the ground to show a symbol embossed in the metal.

Vivian squinted and shifted out of the shadow to see the embossed metal clearly. She looked up and shared her look of deep curiosity with Robin. "From the Summoners books?"

"Exactly. But what is it doing here, etched into a sewer grate at the post office?"

The low hum of a slow car came near. Both girls expected to hear it keep going past them, but it slowed and turned into the driveway. Robin pulled Vivian back further into the shadowed alley but still where they could peer out from their hiding spot. But as the men got closer to the building, the security lights showed them both in black suits and ties, carrying black blankets or maybe robes. They walked through the back door of the post office without a word to each other.

The girls didn't have time to come out of hiding to see where they went as more and more cars started coming in steadily, and more men in black suits continued to enter the back door. Then, one man, in particular, caught their eye, but it was too dangerous to speak. Vivian and Robin only turned to one another and tried to communicate their confusion. *Soo's father?* They only saw him a couple of times when he dropped Soo at school, but there was no doubt it was him.

Next, a recognizable sound pulled Vivian's attention—tires on pavement and no engine—an electric car. *It couldn't be...* A uniformed driver walked around the side, and Vivian's father got out. His driver carried a wardrobe bag as he delivered Mr. Voorhees and the bag to the door and then returned, dutifully, to the car.

Again, the girls exchanged looks. Vivian wanted to burst— scream or at least talk, but she kept her lips tightly pursed. Finally, there was a lull in the action—the perfect chance to see if they could get into the post office to see what was happening. But just as they peered out, someone blackened the door window with a sheet and turned off all the outside lights. There was no way in. They walked up to the door anyway, and Robin jostled the locked handles.

Vivian tapped a light fist against the brick in frustration to find out what her and Soo's father were doing there together, but also to get inside to warm up. Her toes were starting to numb.

Robin pointed again at the grate.

"We can't," Vivian used the loudest whisper possible.

"Why not?" Robin only mouthed the words as she lifted the lid that didn't even creak. "C'mon," Robin said quietly. "We can just hide in here to keep warm, and then when everyone comes out, we can follow them."

"I'm not getting in there," Vivian grumbled, turning her nose up.

"Yes, you are, Princess. Don't you want to find out what your dad's doing here—at night in some *mysterioso* club that meets next to a grate with a creepy demon symbol?"

Vivian jumped a little in place as she thought. Robin made all good points. "How do I know this isn't your trap to kill me?"

"Because I'd be more creative than this," Robin said with one eyebrow raised and attitude coming straight from her hip.

Vivian scrunched her face as her best reply and gave one last look around the parking lot for any better ideas. There was a harsh current of wind that kept whistling down the alley where they stood, and she relished the idea of being out of the cold, even if it was down a dark and creepy hole.

She bent down closer to the ground when another car pulled in, flashing its lights just over Vivian's eyes. It parked hastily, giving a screech as it turned. All Robin could see was a tall, athletic form running from a blue BMW. Vivian quickly stepped down several rungs on the ladder and pulled Robin down closer to the ground. Vivian's hand was over her mouth. As the man came closer to the building, Robin saw the resemblance. A handsome dark-skinned boy in a black suit with a leather university jacket over the top. Vivian's wide eyes followed him as he jogged gingerly to the door.

She took her hand from her mouth only to whisper, *"James, my brother.*"

Vivian was even more determined to discover more of what was going on inside. She reluctantly continued down the ladder, making her way further into the dark, where it was hopefully warmer than the alley. Robin followed just above her after she threw her bag between the shaft and the heavy metal door to make sure they had a way out.

They each held and steadied themselves on the cold metal rungs going down, neither of them knowing just how far they'd have to go. They did their best to be quiet, but the cold of their boots was a hard clang on each step.

Then, after no warning, Vivian was out of rungs. She grabbed the rungs in her hands tighter as she stretched her foot towards the ground to check for a solid bottom. In a leap of faith, she hopped off the ladder and slid her phone from her pocket to use the flashlight.

"It's okay, Rob. You can hop down from there."

"How do I know it's not just your trap to kill me?"

Vivian chuckled as she grabbed the back of Robin's coat and pulled her down. Robin gave a small screech but caught her balance easily—she was right up against Vivian, back to back, closer than they'd ever been. Vivian reluctantly removed one of her mittens and reached to touch the freezing-cold walls around them. The entire shaft seemed to be made of iron and had a rough and rusted coating. Aside from the metal ladder rungs, it was a completely round metal tube in the ground, right beside the post office. *What the hell was this used for?* She wondered.

"Hey, Robin?"

"Yes, Vivian," sassing back at the mention of her name, like who else was going to answer her?

"Don't fart, okay?"

Robin snorted a laugh and then coughed from the shock. She never expected Vivian Voorhees to say anything so crude or hilarious.

"You too," Robin whispered, and then she heard Vivian

breathe out a small, nervous laugh.

Robin grabbed Vivian's hand with the flashlight and shone it lower down. It wasn't completely round and smooth around them after all. Instead, there was an impression from an old welding job. Something had been removed and replaced like there used to be a door, just big enough for someone to crawl through. But all that was left was the rectangular scar now.

Robin pushed on the middle of the slab, and the rust slightly cracked and crumbled. As it shifted, there was a creak louder than she expected, and all they could hope was that it wasn't audible from the parking lot. Robin hesitated to push it further in case the entire block fell out, but it shifted like a crusty pastry.

Vivian turned slowly to face the metal split, then put her hand inside it. It was warm, like an opening to a room. Then both girls went still as they began to hear the murmur of voices reverberating in the metal around them. They barely even breathed, knowing that if they could hear *in*, then maybe the voices could hear *out*. Then, the pounding of a gavel brought everyone to order.

The first man to speak wasn't her father or brother though the voice sounded familiar to Vivian. He spoke of ceremonial welcomes and then something in garbled Latin, which the crowd repeated back to him. Most of what was said were incomprehensible to the girls until after the formalities, they quit the Latin, and the words flew through the metal shaft more clearly.

"Demon Benastra," the same voice stated officially. "Can you confirm the heirs have been spared at the sacrifice?"

"In... in... indeed," the next voice was high-pitched and laughed impishly as it spoke. "My bookkeeper, Laustruv, assures me that a Miss Voorhees and Miss Kim are to be spared. Their minds will be purified at a later meeting."

Vivian looked to Robin, whose cheeks were puffed out, holding a scream.

"A pleasure doing business with you folks as always. I am satisfied, Master Keeper."

"Keeper Voorhees, what say you?"

"I am assured my daughter is safe from the sacrifice. I am satisfied," Vivian's father said.

"Keeper Kim?"

"I am satisfied," Soo's father answered.

Robin mouthed, "SACRIFICE" through the darkness. The familiar man's voice continued the ceremony.

"Sixty-six years we, The Keepers, have waited to receive instruction and now await Demon Benastra's return to wipe the slate clean and continue the sworn protection of Blackrock and its people."

"Demon Benastra's work will commence this night, the sacrifice of all who attend the pagan ritual of the celebration of winter. We thank the many for their young souls. May they all rest in peace."

At the last word, Vivian grabbed Robin's forearm and dug in her nails. Robin tried not to scream, but she knew what it meant— *The Winter Formal.*

Vivian shifted around to Robin's side and spoke as quietly as she could manage, her lips grazing Robin's ear in a hot whisper. "We have to get out of here to warn everyone!"

Robin closed her eyes in defeat. *I guess we're going to the dance after all.*

MILA

Boys never make an effort, Mila thought as Gary stood in his too-tight suit that was probably what he was forced to wear to family functions like weddings and funerals. He reached his arm out and down like a stiff parking lot barrier to hand Mila a white corsage in a plastic box.

"Oh my goodness, Gary. It's beautiful," Mila said, genuinely appreciating the gift. She hadn't expected him to be so thoughtful or traditional. Gary didn't say a word. In fact, he hadn't much stopped grinning and staring at Mila in her green dress since she opened the door until Gemma snapped him out of it.

"Hi, Gawy, I'm Gemma," she said as she held out her toddler hand for a shake. Gary and Mila giggled together, taking advantage of the break in the tension. Next, it was Mila's mom's turn to embarrass her. She rushed Gary inside to take pictures in the hallway, nearly closing the door on Gemma on the doorstep before Gary picked her up and held her like he knew what he was doing. He stood beside Mila with Gemma in his arms, and they took a photo of the three of them together.

"Good catch. Thanks," Mila said, keeping her smile up for the camera.

Gary leaned over closer to Mila. "Five siblings, four younger," Gary said as he bounced Gemma in his arms. Mila's mom snapped the last photo and then took Gemma from Gary, giving an annoyingly large wink as she finally left them alone.

Gary took back the plastic box from Mila to open it and put the white carnation on her wrist. "You look so beautiful," he said with a huge smile. His hands shook as he slid the band onto her arm.

"Thanks, Gary. You look nice too." Mila lifted her wrist to her nose to smell the flower.

"Thanks. I got a new shirt, but I spent the rest on your wrist thingy," he said, blushing.

Mila's heart fluttered at the same time her stomach sank. She felt terrible for judging him on how he looked. It's not like she would have looked as good as she did if it wasn't for Vivian.

Gary helped her put on her everyday winter coat over her dress, and they walked out, arm in arm, to Gary's truck, where his older brother was idling at the end of the driveway. Mila blushed and let out a small 'woo' as Gary boosted her bottom into the truck seat and swished her dress up so it didn't get caught in the door. Mila said a quick hello to their driver, who only nodded back, and they were on their way to their first dance ever.

~ * ~

Mila and Gary exchanged excited glances as soon as they could hear the music coming from inside the school, but before they went in, Gary stopped. "Hey, Mila?"

Mila faced him and smiled.

"I just wanted to say again that you look really beautiful, and thank you for saying yes to me."

"Well, thank you for asking me, Gary." Mila beamed her biggest smile as she spoke while Gary looked down at his shoes. It was the perfect opportunity to lean in and kiss him on the cheek. Immediately, his freckled skin went redder than the lipstick mark she'd placed there. Mila took his hand, and whatever tension Gary was feeling seemed to melt away in that instant. He leaned forward, whipped the front door open, and bowed to Mila as she stepped inside. They locked arms as they made their way to the gym, beaming with excitement for whatever the night would bring them.

Going from the regular hallways to the threshold of the decorated gymnasium, there was an otherworldly change in mood. Dreamy lighting from hanging twinkle lights shined everywhere while cobalt spotlights around the ceiling danced back and forth to the pulsing music. A few couples were already holding onto each other as more people were still coming in.

Mila wanted to find Soo and show off her dress before she got it wrinkled from dancing. It wasn't hard to spot her, as Faye and Soo were the only couple locked together in a slow dance to the fast-paced song. Faye was a perfect winter fairy in her white and blue tutu, wearing a silver tiara, and Soo complimented her perfectly in her suit and sparkling suspenders.

As they approached, it was Faye who noticed Mila first. "That dress is gorgeous on you, Mila! I love the color!" Faye spoke without breaking the ring of her arms around Soo's neck.

Then Soo looked up from Faye's shoulder. "Wow! You owe me a dance later, ok?"

Mila's cheeks reddened.

"Looks like I'm here with the most gorgeous girl at the dance," Gary said, beaming and taking Mila's hand to lead her to the dance floor.

Mila felt the biggest smile she'd had in a long time stretch across her face, and everything that had sucked since she moved to Blackrock suddenly disappeared behind the pop music and the hold of Gary's arms.

VIVIAN AND ROBIN

"We have to get Doctor P.," Vivian said, her chin nearly touching the top of her steering wheel. It had just started to snow, and the roads were getting slick, making Vivian even more determined to get where they had to go.

"What? Why?" Robin screeched, confused and terrified by Vivian's sudden urge to live out her *Grand Theft Auto* fantasies.

"What do you mean, *why*? This is way too scary for us to handle, and there are adults involved that we didn't even know about." Vivian was talking almost as fast as she was driving. Robin luckily had time to sneak her seatbelt on but was still holding the handle over the door for dear life.

"But what's she going to do, Psychologize the demon to death? We should just go to the school to get Mila and Soo first." Robin was trying her best to convince Vivian while keeping her eyes closed at the terrifying turns on the road.

"We have to tell her what we heard. Message her and tell her we're coming now!" Vivian made a sharp left, leaving Robin pressing against the door once again as she texted Doctor Pavi.

Robin had never seen this side of Vivian. But as much as she was afraid for her life in the car, she also snuck an admiring glance at this new side of her frenemy.

Vivian skimmed the last corners, slid around other cars on the roads, and sped up the final stretch to Doctor Pavi's place. Doctor Pavi was standing in the driveway when they got there. She was bundled up for winter in a bubbly parka and mittens the size of feet, holding a cloth bag full of demonology books she might need for whatever they were doing. Doctor Pavi took a slight bunny hop back as Vivian skidded in and stopped on a dime with the passenger side door already open. Robin happily climbed through the seats to the back and buckled up tight.

"Put your seatbelt on, Doctor P.!" Vivian shouted.

"Vivian, please don't call me—"

"No time," Vivian cut her off, and she squealed out of the driveway onto the wet road.

"Okay, I got your message but tell me again, what do you think is happening at the school?" Doctor Pavi groaned as she grabbed the handle over the door.

"There's about to be another massacre," Vivian said, her focus unwavering.

"Just like there was sixty-six years ago… by some demon called 'Benastra'. Does it mean anything to you?" Robin leaned up to the front and almost tumbled forwards as Vivian turned left just in time to miss the red light.

Doctor Pavi turned to Vivian sharply with her eyes wider than Robin had ever seen. "Holy crap, yes!" Doctor Pavi exclaimed. "My patient, Joseph. He says that word—that *name*… all the time. I could never figure out what it meant. How do you know it's a demon?" Doctor Pavi was nearly out of breath, taking everything in and also trying to keep herself upright in the passenger seat. Between holding her breath and shouting at Vivian to watch out for other cars and garbage cans, Robin started to tell Doctor Pavi about the gathering at the post office.

"They're some sort of secret society," Robin started.

"Ya, and my dad is part of it." Vivian took a sharp turn, skidding around another corner.

"And Soo's dad, too," Robin added.

"But we think they're planning to save Soo and me." Vivian accelerated faster at the thought of everyone else at the dance.

"So what do Mila and Robin have to do with anything? Why are they part of the bonding?"

Aside from the strain of the engine and the sliding tires, there was a quiet hush inside the car as they each considered. How *were* Mila and Robin connected to all of this? They didn't seem to have any connection to the men at the post office at all. They didn't even have fathers.

Doctor Pavi's shoulders bumped between the door and the dash as she bent down into her bag of books. She strained to pull out the largest one onto her lap. Robin turned on the interior light and hoped it wouldn't make Vivian's driving any worse.

"Remember Mila's theory about the cage? Well, you can't be a cage with only two walls. Are you sure they only mentioned you and Soo?" Doctor Pavi's voice shook over the bumps in the road as she continued to skim the text.

"That's not important right now," Vivian said, putting her foot down on the gas for the last straight stretch to the school. "Right now, we have to get to the school to warn everyone else to get out."

Ignoring the designated roads and paths, Vivian pulled up onto the front lawn of Blackrock High and slammed her car into park. The three of them ran inside the school, having no idea what they were in for.

18

Soo

"I love this song," Faye said, leaning on Soo's chest. Her heart was pounding so loudly that Faye must have been able to feel it bounce against her cheek. Soo kept her feet moving and tried to focus on identifying the scent of hairspray coming from the top of Faye's head instead of how nervous she was. She took shallow breaths, not wanting to disturb Faye from her position, but there was a lot to take in: blue, white, and silver balloons were clustered in all the corners of the gym and in an arch over the stage with twinkle lights intertwined. Sparkly snowflakes hung from the ceiling and bounced the light around even more. The decorating committee had done a really good job, though Soo had nothing to really compare it to, being the first dance she had ever been to. She never thought she would really like going to dances with cheesy themes, dance music, and getting dressed up. Maybe she just liked dancing with Faye.

It was almost impossible to catch Mila's attention, whose round eyes were dreamily fixed on Gary's grinning face, like big green olives on a pizza. But when Mila eventually did look over, she gave a dreamy smile, and then Gary turned her away to spin her around in the magic of shimmering decorations.

Faye was still attached to Soo's chest. The two of them fit perfectly together. Everything was perfect—she was at the dance with Faye, and they were swaying, flirting, and having fun. She was definitely nervous, but only because it was new, and she didn't want to disappoint Faye. But at the same time, she was very comfortable with her arms around Faye's back, feeling like she had to be strong for her, protect her, even though Faye had been the one who'd saved her life. Every time she breathed and saw Faye in her arms, she got butterflies and chills all at once. She settled her temple against Faye's hair and hoped there'd be more moments just like this.

But what about after? The inevitable thoughts crept in. Soo did her best not to stiffen up and scare Faye. But what about when the demon decided to use her body? What if Faye ever found out that Soo did things like summon demons just so that she could swim again, even though it could put everyone around her in danger?

A sudden touch on her arm woke Soo from her musings, and she was startled to see a worried and sweaty Robin. Faye gave some space between them.

"Robin, you came!" Soo went for a hug, but Robin stopped her in her tracks.

"We have a situation, Soo. We have to get everyone out of here."

Before Soo or Faye could react, the loudest rumbling like thunder erupted, and the gym floor began to shake. Soo reached out and held onto Faye. People were losing their footing and stumbling over—mostly the girls who were in heels for the first time. Their dates were busy picking them up and holding them as the music stopped, the lights went even dimmer, and a very familiar alum in a black suit and tie hopped proudly onto the stage.

Vivian

"James, no…" Vivian breathed. She could see the demon inside right away, its flat eyes dull and menacing, its slinking walk overtaking her brother's usual rhythmic gait.

"Benastra," she whispered. It was all she could do as she watched it walk in awkwardly among everyone, and no one was the wiser as it strolled to the stage. The demon faltered, missing a step and nearly stopping its approach. *Had it heard her?* It looked around suspiciously before taking the microphone from the stand. The microphone screeched, and the high voice rang out, not James's voice at all. Instead, it was the shrill drawl she and Robin had heard from inside the iron shaft only earlier that night.

"Thank you all so much for coming," it said, and some of the boys snickered. It turned to spot them and licked its lips, taking in each of their faces. "This is a very special night and, as such, we've got quite a surprise for you all. You're all part of something very special." It continued to lick its dry, cracked lips as it spoke, clearly loving to hear itself talk. "I don't really know how to say this, so I'll just say it: We've locked you all in! Don't try to get out!" It let out a high-pitched cackle and threw its hands up like it was shouting 'surprise' at a party.

There was a short murmur around the crowd. No one was taking anything seriously.

"But I guess… feel free to run? *I like it when you run.*" The demon growled into the mic. Still, the crowd awkwardly remained on the dance floor, many looking around for a cue on how to react.

"Let's get this party started!" The demon cackled, looking out at the confused couples. The low murmur continued to surf through the crowd, but still, no one moved.

Robin was with Faye and Soo, so Vivian pushed through the people to get to Mila. She saw her emerald dress catching the light, facing the stage, and leaning on the tallest guy in the crowd.

The demon continued, "If you have any questions be sure to file them with my trusty secretary—I mean, 'assistant' here," it said, using air quotes and then pointing out to the back of the gymnasium. Vivian followed the demon's gesture to the back corner. A figure stood there in the shadow, one leg cocked over the other, the twinkle lights flashing a slight glow in its eyes—dead eyes, but familiar. She couldn't be sure, but he seemed just as irritated by the show as everyone else. Vivian didn't recognize the rugged face, but she knew at once it was *their* demon—the bookkeeper: '*Laustruv*,' she whispered, remembering the name from The Keeper ceremony. It flinched in the shadows, and in the crowd, it found her and locked its gaze on Vivian. It unraveled its arms and stood up straight.

At the ceremony with her father, the men used the demons' names, but their demon had never once introduced itself to her or the other girls, and she wondered why. Now she knew—she could feel it—there was a tension when she whispered its name. A secret, like an ace in their favor. Vivian stood her ground and glared back at Laustruv, her teeth clenched and chin strong, hoping she could be ready for whatever might be coming next.

There were fewer laughs, and more concern was mounting. The students were looking for an explanation for what James was talking about. Some of them knew James and even tried to catch Vivian's eye for an explanation, but she was turned away and focused on her task.

Where were the chaperones? Vivian heard several people say around her. Only then did she break her stare with Laustruv and join the others—they were right—there were no teachers or chaperones anywhere. Some people looked to Doctor Pavi, who was the only adult in the room, but, at the moment, in her bubbly coat and long mittens, her expression was just as innocent and clueless as everyone else.

While the demon was still babbling into the mic, Vivian turned and made her way to Mila near the front of the stage in the densest crowd of people. Vivian tapped Mila on the shoulder, and Mila turned with glee to see Vivian and wrapped her in a hug. Vivian remained completely limp and struggled away to show Mila the serious look on her face without having to say a word.

Mila's face settled, and she took a step back. Her cheery expression fell into a desperate frown. "What's going on, Vivian?"

Vivian stuck her chin out and pointed to James.

Mila turned to look and then back to Vivian *'DEMON'?* She mouthed.

Vivian nodded.

Mila swiftly grabbed Gary's hand with one hand and Vivian with the other and quickly led them both away from the crowd to the side of the room.

But before they could get very far, the screeching voice called out. "Oh heeeeeyyyyy! Where are you guys going? The fun's about to start." The demon jumped from the stage and into the front part of the crowd. The crowd moved back, still unsure if this was part of a show, a band, or a disgruntled show host going rogue.

"Hey, Voorhees," the demon said to Vivian. "Yes, yes, *your sister*, calm down in there." The demon tugged at its shirt collar and rolled James's eyes all the way back to show their white bottoms. The people up close enough to see let out sounds of shock and disgust.

"What the hell is this?" Someone shouted.

"Ya, put the music back on," someone else called out.

When its eyes rolled back to a muted version of James's natural dark brown, Vivian stood between Mila and Gary in a desperate sweat. She had no plan of what to do, only that she was pretty sure she was protected, either by the ceremony she and Robin had overheard. Or maybe James, who must still be somewhere deep down inside the demon, looking at his only sister.

"Sorry about your friends," the demon raised its hand in a twist, looking at Mila and Gary.

"No! Vivian screamed," putting her hands out to push James away from her friends.

Mila's eyes blazed forward at Vivian's bravery. She didn't move until she felt the dead weight of Gary falling into her. Instinctively, she held out her hands to hold him, but he was much too heavy. Gary toppled on Mila, and they both fell. Vivian wanted to run to help, but she had to stay between them and Benastra. Somehow she had to hold the demon back.

Mila called out, "Vivian!"

Vivian rushed to Mila, who was crushed below him, trying to crawl out.

"Gary, come on, get up!" Mila clawed at Gary's arm as hard as she could to move him even an inch and scurry out from underneath him. Vivian pulled her arm, and Mila was free. She looked back at Gary, so lost about why he was on top of her. She bent down to shake him awake. Mila slapped his still warm cheeks, but his head was impossibly turned and twisted to the side, his eyes open and gawking, and Mila knew.

"Noooooo!" Mila couldn't hold back a scream that filled the room beyond the confused hum of the crowd. Everyone stopped to look over at Mila and where Gary was on the floor, Mila wailing over him and wildly pounding his chest.

BLACKROCK HIGH

Benastra left Mila and Vivian with Gary, twisted and dead, on the floor and continued walking toward the back of the room. Panicked juniors pooled around the locked doors jiggling the handles and pounding the middles for someone to hear.

Celeste and Jacee knew Vivian's brother, James, and wanted the inside scoop on what was going on.

"Hi James, it's me, Celeste, Vivian's best friend?" Celeste smiled, and she and Jacee fell in, walking beside Benastra eagerly. "So what are you doing home from school? Is college a total bore? Isn't it funny how we used to flirt all the time? I had such a big crush—" Celeste's neck snapped in two before she could finish her story and fell face first to hit the hard gymnasium floor, dead before she hit the ground. Jacee screeched out an otherworldly, high-pitched scream just before the demon sent a deep cut through her windpipe, and she toppled over Celeste into a bloody pool.

Benastra continued to make its way to stand under the raised basketball nets and watched the scurrying of teens with evil pride. It turned to Laustruv, "I just love this part," the upper demon cackled in a nasal trill of a voice. Laustruv rolled its eyes, the shadow pulling back over its face while leaning out of the corner to get a better view of its girls. Mila was sobbing over Gary, and Vivian was there to hold people back from the scene, her eyes darting around the room wildly from her friends on the floor to her possessed brother.

Soo and Faye were running, hand in hand, through people charging in all directions. The four girls were almost together. *Four walls.* Waiting for this, Laustruv finally made a move. The lower demon, secretary to Benastra, moved away slowly from its superior, who was busy killing more people at random. Remaining in the shadows of the decorations, where the twinkle lights didn't reach, Laustruv slid around in its human suit, a rather ruggedly handsome man in an expensive beige three-piece, complete with gray snakeskin cowboy boots.

Soo and Faye reached Mila and Robin, who was flushed and wet with tears on the floor next to Gary. Vivian was in front of them, on guard, looking around for Doctor Pavi, who seemed to have disappeared. She then caught sight of something else and froze. Their demon had left the corner and was moving toward them.

Vivian stood as she had before, in front of Gary and Mila, with her fiercest face but also tears in her eyes, knowing she had no idea how to stave off a demon, especially one she was bonded to.

"*No!*" She commanded. "You said we would be protected," she charged.

"And that's my word," Laustruv said, adjusting its sleeves. Vivian wondered if she was hearing its true voice.

It angled its glance around Vivian to view Mila next to Gary's lifeless body and then stood to face Vivian again. It leaned into Vivian's ear. "There's a way to end this."

Vivian remained still, not budging from her spot for anything as she considered what Laustruv had said.

End this? How? Demons can't be trusted, she reminded herself. *Even this one.*

No, really, it answered without voice, but inside Vivian's head. It moved to the side, to a shadow but spoke with Vivian as if it was next to her, in her ear, in her head.

Bond together and be protected,

The walls are safe when you're connected.

The demon pushed all other thoughts out of Vivian's head and took control.

Vivian turned to her friends. "I have an idea. Put out your hands."

"What?" Robin spoke up with her arms tight around Mila and more upset than she ever thought she could be about Gary from Music class.

"Just put out your hands! I think I know how to stop this," Vivian urged them all, holding out her own hands toward them.

Mila moved first, breaking from Robin and wiping her face. She stood dutifully, keeping her legs from shaking and hoping Vivian really did have an idea. Mila helped Robin up from the floor, who held out her hands reluctantly, sure they had no play here against two demons. Soo grimaced at Faye apologetically as she reached past her to hold Mila's hand and Vivian on the other side. Faye looked on curiously from Soo's side.

Amongst all of the chaos, her dead 'almost boyfriend' on the floor, Mila's mind flashed to a memory of her father. He kept a magnet in the garage that collected metal dust. He always used it to clean up when she came into the garage in socked feet. She felt something similar now—the pieces were collecting, and she understood all at once what was at stake. Just behind Vivian, a man was back in the shadows, unmoving but his eyes on them intently. Their four pairs of arms were linked... *four walls...*

Mila called out past Vivian to Laustruv, "Why should we trust anything you say?"

Because I'm your last hope of surviving, it said in Mila's mind.

What about everyone else here? All these people…

There's nothing I can do.

The last thing Mila saw was the demon shrug and smile to one side of its face just as a flash of the brightest fire surrounded them, illuminating their circle and burning everything in the room.

19

BLACKROCK HIGH

Mila didn't want to open her eyes, sure she wouldn't like what she saw when she did. Sitting up, she coughed from the thick smoke heavy in her lungs. One by one, she lifted each eyelid, struggling as her eyes stung against the dust, smoke, and floating ash. One eye was noticeably blurrier than the other, and she worried she had been hurt until she remembered she wasn't wearing glasses— she must have lost a contact lens. The gym was quiet—no other movement, though she could hear a soft crackling and tapping, like footsteps, in the distance.

Soo walked carefully, dipping below where the smoke hung like a low cloud. She moved to where she last remembered standing with Faye, but a pile of debris stopped her search. Her stomach clenched as she bent down to dig. There were big pieces of wood and ceiling tile covered in knots from strung-up paper snowflakes. Something jungled as she shifted the boards. She reached down towards the sound and pulled out a warm piece of metal. She lifted it close to her face to see it through the smoke—a buckle off of Faye's shoe.

Soo's face wrenched, and her mouth opened in a silent cry that dug past her voice until she couldn't breathe. Her heavy chest loosened its clench, only for a second, to let out a long, tortured howl. *"Faye!"*

The other girls heard the call and worked through the clouds to get to Soo. Mila found her first on the floor. Robin came to her other side as she cried. Vivian stood on guard again, still trying to look around, as the smoke settled more and more. *Where was the tapping coming from?*

There were two others still in the gymnasium, staying quiet. One was James, sitting against what was left of one of the walls. The other was the rugged man from the corner, helping James stand.

'*Laustruv,*' Vivian whispered as she had before. It turned to her at the call, just as she thought it would. Robin noticed their eyes lock and moved to join her.

The rugged man spoke to them both in his southern drawl. "I'm not usually the thanking type, but I must thank you."

"Thank us for what?" Robin sneered as she marched next to Vivian.

"For your innocence, naiveté, willingness, and equal parts good-old fashion gumption. Thanks to you four, I'm free. No more paperwork, contracts, or running his little errands. I'll be taking over now. Now that Benastra's locked up nice and tight." The demon tapped a finger against its head to signal what the girls already felt and could already hear.

Mila spoke next to confirm with the girls what she feared she already knew. "Are you just going to keep Benastra… *here*?" She couldn't bring herself to call herself *a cage*.

"For the time being, yes. You don't mind, do you? No, of course, you don't. You're all too ready to have a demon around."

"So we were never sick. We're not dying." Vivian's voice was strong and steady.

"Oh, I can smell the putrid rot of death getting closer every second as you age and lose your sweet youth. And it wasn't a lie— technically, you were in danger. Mila and Rodriguez were never protected by The Keepers. You almost got dragged down with the sacrifice and burned like the rest of your class."

"But what about Mila in the hospital?" Robin charged.

Laustruv grinned in delight and waved a light hand in the air. "Coincidence."

"Coincidence?" Robin started to run, but Vivian caught her and held her back.

"Hmmm. I can see Benastra's in there nice and tight. You four are a pretty sturdy container, four walls bonded in four ways…"

But before any of them could ask what 'four ways' it was talking about, a sound came through the dust—a shuffle in a corner. *Had someone survived?*

'Laustruv,' was the only word Robin and Vivian recognized, but everything else was a stream of chanted Latin ringing out in Doctor Pavi's voice. Laustruv turned and writhed at being called, but still, no one could see Doctor Pavi through the dust.

"No!" Laustruv screamed, and a path of smoke cleared with a wave of its hand to reveal Doctor Pavi walking intently in their direction. She continued her chants from the book in her hands, not missing a beat, and determined to finish the end of the spell.

Again they heard its name, *'Laustruv.'* Doctor Pavi had found a new spell, one to speak to their demon and maybe even cast it away or, better yet, kill it.

The demon was held in place, pleading back, "No, you can't. I'll slit your throat like a *real* doctor and watch the ligaments spring forth your blood. The end of your failure of a life." Laustruv's voice lowered to a growl and lost its drawl.

Doctor Pavi ignored it and pressed on, knowing it was only trying to get into her most vulnerable feelings and thoughts.

"You'll burn in hell with Brian!" Laustruv squealed the word *'hell'* like a giddy child saying 'Disneyland' before the rugged man's body curled forward like it was being pulled by the Doctor's words. Doctor Pavi balked at the mention of Brian's name but continued reading out from the book, just above the hunched-over demon. All rugged handsomeness had left Laustruv's human form. Its skin went gray and slack on the bones. It drooled and contorted at the words.

Doctor Pavi sneered with a force the girls had never heard from her before. "No. You will. *Tu emotae!*"

The rugged man's body fell to the floor, stirring up a cloud of ash. It crumpled and became no more than the rest of the dust and ash that was already around them.

All at once, the lights in the room brightened.

Mila looked around questioningly. "Was that–?"

"An exorcism?" Robin chirped in an accusatory tone.

"Sort of," Doctor Pavi answered, breathing heavily. "It's gone—at least for the time being." Doctor Pavi closed the book and sat down in the soot with Soo. "My poor girl. I'm so sorry."

Soo rolled into Doctor Pavi's arms and let out heart-wrenching cries.

The lights showed what was left around them. Small shards of what might have been bone or cutlery from the dinner tables shot up through the piles of gray and black. Other than that, there were mounds of black ash and debris. Everything was black. Everyone was gone. Benastra had burned it all.

The loud squeak and bang of a door falling from its hinges broke their trance. It caught Vivian's attention specifically, and she ran towards it on the other side of the gymnasium. She had completely forgotten about James, who was trying to get out.

"What the *hell?*" Vivian didn't let up as she ran towards him, turned him around, and pounded on his chest so hard that it pushed him back to fall on the floor.

James held out his hands in front of him to keep her back. "Vivian, let me explain."

"Explain what?" Vivian snapped through her tears, reaching out to push him again, thinking of all the people who had just lost their lives in an instant. "I already know you and Dad are part of some weird cult that uses demons to kill people. But why the hell would you agree to this? You had friends in there too, and you even put me, *your own sister*, at risk." Vivian spat as she screamed, but her words landed clear and strong.

"Relax! I knew you were protected." James stood up but kept

his hands out in front.

"You trusted a demon, and then you let it wear you to our dance!" Vivian, with one last powerful shove, pushed James to the floor again.

"Just go. Go back to school or somewhere where I can't find you because I can never look at you again." Vivian's words were pure venom. She paused for one last look at how pathetic her brother looked on the ground, then turned to rejoin her friends.

"Viv, please. You don't understand," James called.

Vivian paused without turning around, only slightly tilting her face to the side. "You're right. I don't." For a moment, she felt herself feel the loss of her relationship with James, but she'd mourn that later. First, she had to help the people she loved. She wiped both hands over her face, mixing the tears, sweat, makeup, and soot that ran down her cheeks, creating black streaks like the tribal paint of a warrior.

"We can't stay here," Vivian called over, brushing off her hands on her jeans. "Police and fire trucks are on their way, and there's no way we can explain how we survived. We need to get back to Doctor Pavi's to think of a story."

BLACKROCK HIGH

The girls cleaned up one by one, except for Soo. She wanted to stay dirty. She felt like if she cleaned anything off of her, she would wash everything away. She wanted to believe she still had Faye's touch on her hands, face, and lips from when they danced and kissed. The metal buckle from Faye's shoe was still in her hand, though it had now gone cold.

Doctor Pavi was in the main part of the house making tea. Robin paced behind the sofa, slowly, reeling with thoughts and questions, tapping her fingers against her teeth. Mila lay on the sofa still in her green dress, now stained with black ash and dirt. She stared up at the ceiling, her vision completely foggy without her glasses, but she could somehow see the whole scene clearly in her mind. She imagined it over and over, remembering how sweet Gary had been to her and how it all happened so fast. Tears streamed silently and continuously down her face as she went over and over her shock as he fell into her. Mila jerked forward like it was happening again until she realized where she was. She lay back on the sofa again with the ghostly impression of Gary's body on hers.

Vivian stood behind Doctor Pavi's desk, staring out the window to the front gate. She thought about everything that had happened before they got to the school. She drove as fast as possible, but in the end, it didn't matter. They were too late. All those people… and her own brother was part of it. Her memory went all the way back to being in the shaft at the post office. She went over and over everything that had been said, trying to recall especially what she heard in her father's voice.

"Can anybody else hear it?" Robin interrupted everyone's private reflections. Vivian turned from the window.

Mila raised a limp arm, "I hear it."

"Me too," Vivian said.

"Is it going to continue like this?" Robin groaned.

"I think as long as we're "the cage", we'll hear it traipsing around in there," Mila said wearily like she was ready to give up on trying to figure out how everything with demons worked.

Robin, on the other hand, was full of energy.

"Yes, Mila!" Robin shouted and stopped dead with her pacing. "We just have to find a way to *not be* the cage!"

"But then Benastra will get out and be free to kill again, maybe not now, but another junior class in sixty-six years," Vivian said, reminding Robin of what they knew.

Robin went to Doctor Pavi's desk and pounded her fists down as she sat on the top.

Mila sat straight up and listened. The pitter-patter and knocking in their heads was holding still for a brief moment.

"Say it again, Vivian," Mila urged.

"What?" Vivian scrunched her face.

"Benastra," Mila said quickly and then listened intently to the room.

A low, drawn-out groan rang through all of their minds. Forgetting the ladylike moves her dress called for, Mila hopped up on her knees in the middle of the sofa. Her mind was now quiet enough to think—all at once, she saw how everything worked.

"Doctor Pavi said Laustruv's name to control it and banish it." Mila slapped her thigh. "We control the demon if we know its name! We already know its name, so we can do the spell that Doctor Pavi did or maybe something else that will kill it forever. But first, we should get it out of the cage. Out of our heads!"

Robin tilted her head back in recognition. She knew Mila was right. The demon she had spoken with on the Ouija board had said, 'NO NAMES. NO CONTROL.' It made sense. But she wasn't sure if she wanted to share that she had used the Ouija board alone and that the daemon had taken another piece of her soul along with it. She'd save that fun fact for a better time.

Doctor Pavi walked in with the tray of five steaming mugs and a couple packages of cookies, crackers, and a bunch of grapes. Mila grabbed crackers and let them hang from the side of her mouth as she wrote furiously on one of Doctor Pavi's notepads as fast as she could, squinting to see her own writing without glasses. She listed everything they knew, reading out loud as she wrote—how the spell books worked and what she vaguely understood about the cage. Then Robin and Vivian retold everything they overheard in the shaft by the post office, including the fact that they saw Soo's father there.

Soo added something weakly and quietly from Doctor Pavi's chair, and Mila shushed Robin to hear.

Soo cleared her throat since she hadn't spoken in hours. "And we're bonded in four ways. And we don't know what that means."

And at that, Soo sat back in the chair and stared off again, half-listening.

Mila tapped the pen on her lips—she'd actually forgotten that part. "Right… four ways… any ideas, guys?"

"We're the same age…." Vivian stated.

"Same school," Mila mumbled as she wrote.

"Two of us have dads in a cult," Robin added plainly.

"Two of us don't have dads," Soo piped up unapologetically.

"That's two things." Mila smacked the pen on the table. "Do you think we could get some answers from your dad, Vivian?"

As if on cue, the office door creaked open, and two men walked, uninvited, into the room—Mr. Voorhees stood with James behind him.

"Oh, so you have questions for me?" Mr. Voorhees said, letting himself into the office.

"Dad?" Vivian's head shot around. "What are you doing?"

"I don't know how you all were so well prepared for the evening or how you managed to do what you did, but it stops now. Keeping Vivian safe was my only priority, and now we can move on." Mr. Voorhees's voice was deep and purposeful but also pompous. It was clear he was a man who regularly told people what to do and wasn't often told 'no'.

James came from behind and began speaking in a language no one understood, to no one in particular. Robin tried to argue over the top, but James pointed his finger at each girl as they stared forward and froze. Vivian's knees weakened, and the other girls slumped further into their seats, their heads soon nodding forward and each of them relaxing and falling asleep.

~ * ~

"As for you," Mr. Voorhees said as he gestured to Doctor Pavi, who was still holding the tea tray. "You're really getting mixed up in things you surely cannot handle. Let's stop the charade, shall we?"

Mr. Voorhees moved forward and took the tray down on a side table.

"Please," Doctor Pavi pleaded, "I just want the girls safe, like you." As Doctor Pavi spoke, she quickly checked the sleeping girls, ensuring each of their chests was rising and falling.

"Hmm, if that were your only motivation, we could just adjust your memory as well, but I fear you're holding onto something stronger—another incident from long ago, perhaps. Aren't you looking into something to do with a man named Brian?"

"No—I mean, yes, there is, but what does that have to do with any of this?" Doctor Pavi tried to hide her desperation.

"I don't like outsiders poking around in my town." Mr. Voorhees walked to the large window behind Doctor Pavi's desk.

"Your town?" She knew the Voorhees' had money, but she had never even seen Vivian's father before.

"Yes. *My* town, Ms. Pavi."

He certainly wasn't around in *his town* when his own daughter was in the hospital. The thought helped her correct her posture and gain an inch.

"It's *Doctor* Pavi," she corrected.

"Oh, that's right, *Doctor*," he said as his lips curled around the words. "I apologize." Then he signaled to James with a pointed finger.

"Please, I'll do anything you want," Doctor Pavi said, realizing she truly had no footing. If Mr. Voorhees was connected to demons, as the girls suspected, she was in way over her head and needed to play along to protect the girls.

Mr. Voorhees's eyes widened at Doctor Pavi's desperation. "Anything?"

20

VIVIAN

"James, you're home from school!" Vivian ran to her brother and wrapped her arms around him with a loving smile on her face. When they broke, Vivian saw his serious expression as he held her between his arms, his hands on her shoulders.

"Vivian, something's happened at your school. There's been a fire."

"Is everyone okay?" Vivian asked innocently, imagining some contained accident in home economics class.

"Not really," James went on. "A lot of the junior class… well, they were there."

At the same moment, Mr. Voorhees walked in with a clear plastic wardrobe bag. She could just see the outline of the crest in gold embroidery on the pocket of a blazer and the green and gray kilt hanging below. She gasped in recognition.

"What's this?" Vivian made eye contact with her father, even though she knew exactly what it was.

"I know we've had this argument before, Vivian, but now there's really no choice." Mr. Voorhees folded the bag over one arm as he continued. "In the new year, you'll start at Oakwood Academy and continue there for the foreseeable future."

"But—but what about my friends? What about Celeste and

Jacee?"

James lifted his bottom lip in a shy, sympathetic grin. "I'm so sorry, Viv. It was a really big fire."

"Cameron?" Vivian spat out, her voice wavering in a panic, looking between her father and brother. The two men both avoided her glance, waiting for her to fully understand what they were telling her. Cameron was gone? All of her friends? How could this be happening? She couldn't hold back the burning of tears coming through now. A fire. *A real fire.* Her chest heaved as she reached out for the countertop to hold her. Her father placed the Oakwood Academy uniform next to her and left the room.

"I'm sorry, Vivian. I really am," James said. "But there was nothing anyone could do."

MILA

Mila used to be able to come to the library, and no one would notice she was there. Now everyone that passed by would smile or say hello out of pity, then walk away saying things like, *"Poor girl— one of the only juniors left. She has to study senior subjects now. That's rough."*

The one saving grace was that at least she wasn't the new girl anymore. But it was definitely worse to be known as one of the massacre survivors, even though she still didn't remember how or why she was one of only a few who made it out.

Heads turned in her direction every few minutes, but Mila tried to ignore them and do her best to get to work. Playing catch-up wasn't easy, especially since she had just started attending senior classes, and it was halfway through the year. Still, she was generally happy with her decision. She could have gone to the fancy Oakwood Academy prep school for free, but she liked the challenge of staying at Blackrock High and skipping ahead a year to get a head start on going to college—as long as she could catch up with the work, it was a great opportunity.

A group of seniors came into the library, looking in her direction with sympathetic faces. Mila hid her face behind a textbook and got back to studying. Then, from somewhere behind her, she heard a shuffle and knew someone had sat down in the chair beside her.

"Hey," they said with a hand on their chest and with a short bow. "I'm Harris."

"Mila," she replied, slightly angling her face to the side to speak before turning back to her book. She really wasn't in the mood to make another senior 'friend' who wanted to take her under their wing and give her a makeover.

"I heard about your deal. That sucks," Harris said, leaning in with a rough but sweet voice. Mila wasn't really in the mood to talk about what had happened again. Plus, she still didn't know how it all happened for herself, and she desperately wished Harris would just go away. Most of it was a blur after she and Gary got to the gym. And she *really* had no idea how she survived, no matter how many times people asked her to *try and remember.*

"Ya, it sucks," Mila said eventually and did her best to look up and give a small smile of appreciation before turning back to her work.

"Well, anyway. I just wanted to say I really like your new glasses, and I'm sorry for all you went through. I've been through some stuff too, so if you need someone to talk to, just come find me." Harris said, starting to get up from the table.

"Wait," Mila said before she knew why she was saying it. She wanted to be bold and ask Harris to lunch or to study sometime, but she lost her nerve. So instead, she quickly thought of the next best thing. "Let me give you my number."

"Sure," Harris said, handing over their phone. "Y'know, there's a really cool cafe and bookstore downtown that I love. Would you want to hang out there sometime?"

"I know it," Mila said, though she wasn't sure how. She knew she had been to the bookstore to get her last novel, but she couldn't remember how she found out about the store or who she had gone with. She had the strangest feeling she hadn't been alone, but she couldn't quite grasp the whole picture.

"*Sweet.* I'll text you," Harris said, winking a crystal blue eye in Mila's direction before heading over to the table full of seniors.

Soo

Without any other juniors on the team, Soo now had to compete among the seniors. She liked the challenge, and her mother was even happier that she was skipping a semester and fast-tracking her education. College was getting closer by the day.

After her first practice back, she was feeling good about her swim but needed a few more laps to get her rhythm again. Coach Riley had luckily gone easy on her since she had been out for two months dealing with her stress, and now she was alone in dealing with the deaths of her classmates and teammates.

In the locker room, the seniors, sophomores, and freshmen were acting the same as always—laughing, making jokes, and challenging each other for the next practice. She had never noticed before how loud the girls could be. Or maybe it was just all the extra space in the room now that there were no other juniors.

When everyone had left, Soo took her time getting dressed and went to the showers to ring out her suit—there were some perks to being "Sad Soo"—everyone left her alone, including her teachers, even if she was a little late.

She was alone with her thoughts and memories replaying over and over, yet with big parts and details missing. She still couldn't believe she was the only one that survived, except for that other new girl who she didn't know and everyone said was weird.

A guilty smirk ran across her face when she had a random thought about Tessa. She almost cringed to think of it or admit it, but as much as she hated Tessa, she would do anything to have her back right now. She missed the whole team so much. She had always liked Eva and Faye too. Faye especially had always been nice to her.

When her suit was as dry as she could get it, she threw it into a rustling plastic bag. The crackle echoed in the tile locker room. Once she was packed up, the locker room was quiet again except for a faint squeak, like metal on metal, ringing out from near the bathroom stalls. Soo walked towards the sound to see if a pipe was leaking or if someone forgot to turn off one of the showers. But as soon as she approached, it stopped.

She shrugged and went to one of the sinks to quickly throw on some lip gloss.

As she smeared the greasy gloss over her lips with her finger, the squeak started again, louder and closer, as if it were coming from the sink beside her, but there was nothing there, and none of the taps were on. Then, behind her, she flinched at the patter of wet feet running on the wet floor of the shower area.

"Hello?"

No one answered.

Probably a freshman just finishing up.

Figuring the mystery had been solved, she turned to leave the stalls and collect her things. But as she turned, she lost her footing in a small puddle of water and slid on the tile, losing her balance. She fell to the ground with a thud, smashing her head onto the hard shower floor.

When she opened her eyes again, a fuzzy figure loomed over her and was calling her name.

"*Soooo, Sooooo?* Come on, Hun. Get up," the voice said.

Soo tried as hard as she could to focus her eyes, but when she did, she wasn't sure if she was seeing what she thought. There above her and helping her to her feet was Faye.

"Faye? You're alive?"

As Soo stood, Faye smiled and reached her hand up to Soo's cheek. Soo felt like she remembered this moment, somehow. Faye was someone she knew on the team, but they were never that close, so why did it feel comfortable and familiar. More confusing was that she couldn't feel Faye's hand even though she could see Faye in front of her, reaching out and touching her face.

"Faye, how are you here?"

Faye didn't answer as much as Soo tried to ask again, louder and louder.

The next thing she knew, Soo felt wet and cold from the puddled floor seeping through her clothes and onto her skin. She forced her eyes open and found herself lying on the shower room floor with a pounding headache, a bump starting to form on the back of her head.

"You're so clumsy," she said to herself, brushing herself off and standing. She looked back at the puddle. Why had she dreamt about Faye? And why did it feel now like she missed her so much more than anyone else?

ROBIN

After getting the twins to school, Robin was allowed to come back home. She hadn't decided what she wanted to do about school yet. She wasn't feeling great about going back to either Blackrock High or Oakwood Academy—they both sucked. Luckily, her mom had agreed to let her stay home for a few more days until she decided what she wanted to do. She thought about Blackrock High and the teachers she liked there, like Mr. K. But she also thought about her classmates who wouldn't be there. She couldn't really imagine going back and being a pity case.

But did she really belong at the Academy with all the rich snobs? Her mom thought so. Her mom was urging her to consider the opportunity of going to a prestigious private school for free. She said she might be the first Latina in history to go there, and she could do great things. *Such a mom thing to say.*

She couldn't sleep but didn't want to watch television either. She really wanted to make her decision once and for all and be okay with it, then she could stop this back and forth ping pong match in her mind. Her face smooshed against the mattress, off her pillow, and her tired legs splayed out across the bed. Her arm dangled over the side of the mattress, touching the floor and slightly grazing the sharp edges of a shopping bag that was under the bed. She rolled off the bed with a tumble to the floor and pulled the bag out. The bag slid off of a board with strange red symbols on the back.

She flipped it over. *A Ouija board?* She had no idea why she had it. It must have been something she picked up on one of her nightly adventures—she certainly wouldn't pay actual money for such a hoax.

It gave her some satisfaction that her mom wouldn't approve of as she placed the board over her crossed legs, closed her eyes, and gently placed her fingertips on the planchette. She felt stupid but, at the same time, completely desperate for some insight into what she should do about going back to school. Maybe the spirits could *guide* her, as they say.

For a moment, she had second thoughts—she didn't want any of her burned-up classmates coming to visit her—she couldn't handle that. She was doing a good job of avoiding thoughts on how so many people she knew had died instantly and how she just happened to be one of the kids who survived. It wasn't confirmed yet who else had made it, and honestly, she didn't want to know.

After several minutes, the planchette still hadn't moved, and to top it all off, Robin felt like a ridiculous teenage girl that believed in sleepover party games. Or worse, she was going to end up like her Tia Marisol, who thought she had visions and psychic powers.

Robin got up to throw the board to the back of her closet when it suddenly fell straight out of her hand, face up on the floor, with the planchette clearly pointing at NO.

Robin cocked her head like a confused bulldog, wrinkled brow and all, unsure if she really had just seen what she had thought. Warily, she sat back down, gently putting her fingertips on the planchette. Still, it didn't move for her.

"What the hell?" She said out loud but quickly began to feel a hot pressure taking hold of her hands. All at once, the room went dim, and it was as if all sounds were muted. Robin looked for answers, then her focus was directed straight in front of her, where a small stream of white light was leaving her body and collecting into the hand of a small blue spirit. A numbness crept into Robin's feet, but she wasn't afraid. Something told her she was safe and even knew what to do like she had done this before.

When the stream stopped flowing, the light and smoky spirit disappeared, and the planchette vibrated in the middle of the board.

She spoke before she thought of how ridiculous she sounded, "Hello? Is somebody here?"

YES, the planchette answered.

"Are you a ghost?"

NO

"Wat are you?"

FRIEND

"What's your name?" Robin asked, the feeling in her feet only slightly coming back.

BEN. I LIKE TO PLAY

"What should we play, Ben?" Robin asked, shuffling in front of the board.

NEW GAME

"What's it called?"

OPEN THE BOX

"How do we play?"

GET KEY...

Ashe Woodward

ACKNOWLEDGEMENTS

Thanks to my own girls for the good times calling on Bloody Mary, burning love prayers, cursing bullies, watching *The Craft* over and over, and also for that time we had to break a Ouija board in half and ditch it in an alleyway to save our souls.

So much appreciation and adoration for my husband, Tim, who brings me water and keeps my butt from sticking to my chair.

My eternal love to Jake and Bella (not the *Twilight* ones), who were just there the whole time.

Great thanks to both my moms who hate reading horror but support me nonetheless.

To my horror homies: Marco, Mitch, and Sam, you have made me and all my stories better.

Obey, thanks for reading the raw materials.

Gratitude to Editingle Indie House for taking a chance on a rookie who had a nightmare to tell and a dream to fulfill.

About the Author

Ashe Woodward is a longtime lover of words in horror packages. She has an English literature degree from The University of Toronto where she focused on obscure Medieval texts, learned a little Latin and devoured Gothic poetry and children's literature. Nowadays, her hellhound and skinny pig familiars are always by her side while writing her own spooky stories. She is an English teacher in Ontario, Canada where she is doomed to teach Romeo & Juliet, over and over, until she dies. This is her first novel.

See more at ashewoodward.com.

IF YOU LIKE THIS BOOK SUPPORT AUTHOR BY SHARING YOUR VIEWS AND SPREADING THE WORD.

ALSO TRY MORE BOOKS FROM OUR OTHER AUTHORS.
Visit: www.editingleindiehouse.com

THANK YOU!

www.ingramcontent.com/pod-product-compliance
Lightning Source LLC
Chambersburg PA
CBHW020905160726
47993CB00005B/1824